The singing stones

When fire destroyed the windmill on the crest of Kettle Hill, most people, including the young Inspector Tench, assumed that lightning had struck the sails, but that was too simple an explanation to satisfy Lubbock's always suspicious mind.

The ex-Detective Chief Inspector had spent the first six months of his retirement poking around windmills, and lightning was, for him, too facile a solution. It was also illogical. He had his own peculiar ideas about the case: ideas which Tench found hard to accept.

But Lubbock was determined to ferret out the truth. Why had the mill been working at half-past one in the morning? Why had a bell been ringing somewhere inside?

In this intriguing mystery set on the north coast of Norfolk, Brian Cooper carries a stage further the uneasy friendship between Lubbock and Tench developed first of all in *The Cross of San Vincente*.

THE SINGING STONES

Brian Cooper

Constable · London

First published in Great Britain 1993
by Constable & Company Ltd
3 The Lanchesters, 162 Fulham Palace Road
London W6 9ER
Copyright © 1993 by Brian Cooper
The right of Brian Cooper to be
identified as the author of this work
has been asserted by him in accordance
with the Copyright, Designs and Patents Act 1988
ISBN 0 09 472430 X
Set in 10pt Palatino
and printed in Great Britain by
Redwood Books, Trowbridge, Wiltshire

A CIP catalogue record for this book
is available from the British Library

For
Ian and Stephen
and sometime in the future
for
Katy and Jonathan

'Thy head is full of windmills.'

Massinger and Dekker, *The Virgin Martyr*

Author's Note

This tale is set in the north of Norfolk, but, while I have used some family names known there for generations, all the characters, with their foibles and idiosyncracies, are creations of my own wayward imagination. To the best of my knowledge I have never known anyone who has lived in the coastal strip between Weybourne and Wells.

I have also imagined a few changes to the landscape: built a couple of windmills and moved Kettle Hill with its coastal road a mile to the south. I apologize for the roadworks, but not for the mills. A windmill is always a thing of beauty.

My grateful thanks are due first of all to Tony for his faithful reconstruction of Kettle Hill mill, to Bert in Norwich for some swift and efficient detective work, and to Joan and John who first introduced me to the marshes and the mills.

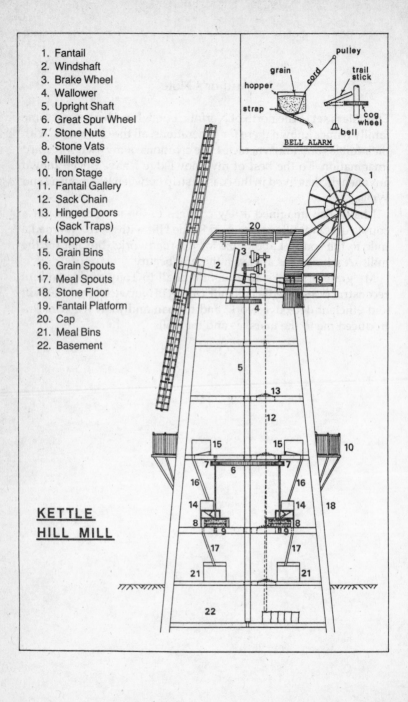

1. Fantail
2. Windshaft
3. Brake Wheel
4. Wallower
5. Upright Shaft
6. Great Spur Wheel
7. Stone Nuts
8. Stone Vats
9. Millstones
10. Iron Stage
11. Fantail Gallery
12. Sack Chain
13. Hinged Doors
   (Sack Traps)
14. Hoppers
15. Grain Bins
16. Grain Spouts
17. Meal Spouts
18. Stone Floor
19. Fantail Platform
20. Cap
21. Meal Bins
22. Basement

**KETTLE
HILL MILL**

BELL ALARM

pulley
grain
hopper
cord
trail stick
strap
cog wheel
bell

PROLOGUE

MONDAY

'There's the wind on the heath, brother...'

Borrow, *Lavengro*

The evening of the night that Simon Pashley died was clear and bright, like most at the end of that long, dry summer of 1947. On that evening ex-Detective Chief Inspector Lubbock was leaning on the gate of Umzinto Cottage in the village of Cley on the north Norfolk coast. He was smoking a pipe and watching the sun go down over Blakeney.

As the light began to fade, he tapped out the pipe on the heel of his shoe and wandered back up the path. Once inside the cottage, he closed the curtains. Then he did what he always did every night; what he'd always done since that winter afternoon six months before, when, for the last time, he'd walked out of his Norwich office and into retirement. He boiled a kettle and brewed a pot of strong Darjeeling tea. Then he poured himself a cup, eased himself into the one armchair he possessed, kicked off his shoes, put his feet up on a stool, stoked up his pipe and began to write up his notes for the day.

Umzinto, named after one of the ships that had traded with Cley when the village was still a port, was a brick and flint cottage, like most of those on that stretch of coast. He'd bought it a few years before the war, when his wife had been alive, partly on her insistence – she'd loved the village and the sea-birds on the marsh – and partly because he'd been as anxious as she to find a retreat from the bustle of Norwich.

When she'd died in the first December of the war, he'd been left on his own and for a while he'd shunned the place – it had seemed so empty – lodging every week from Monday to Friday above his sister Meg's restaurant, the Old Riverside, in the heart of the city. But he'd still come back at weekends, keeping the place in trim; and at last, because he didn't want to trespass too long on her

11

generosity, he'd forced himself once again to face its loneliness. Since then the village had grown around him, enclosed him. He'd come to value its quietness, its isolation on the edge of the marshes a mile from the sea.

Because of the war he'd worked three extra years, and during that time, when the strain of the job had at last begun to tell, the little cottage below the church had proved its worth as a refuge from all the rigours of the day. Driving back of an evening, he'd gradually unwound as his protesting old Morris had rattled its way between the flat Norfolk fields; and when at last he'd seen the sails of the windmill at Cley, twisted through the village and pulled to a halt by the edge of the Green, he'd felt a sense of relief that, cloistered by the walls of the cottage parlour, he could shed all the fret of a long Norwich day, put his feet up and think.

Now, freed from the demands of a job that had claimed him for more than thirty years, he was glad that, in spite of all the pressures to sell, he'd clung to the place. It was home after all, the only home that he had, and he knew he'd never leave it. He'd reached the age when change was hard to endure, and Cley didn't change. It was still the same as when he'd first bought the cottage a dozen years before. It gave him peace to reflect, and that was something he seemed to need more and more as the years went by.

He'd tried to explain it all to young Tench, his detective sergeant; tried to explain, too, just what he was going to do with all the time on his hands. 'I've often thought, you know,' he'd said, 'that there are few sights more pleasant than the sails of a mill turning slowly against the wide Norfolk sky. And they're scattered all over the county, these mills, built to catch the wind that blows straight from the Arctic. Well, laddie, like Don Quixote I'm going to take a tilt at them. Not to slay them. Just to learn. I'm going to make myself rich with a little bit of knowledge. I've armed myself with a notebook and camera, guide books and maps, a sketch pad and a whole variety of pencils. I'm going to track them all down, these mills, one by one: Cley and Burnham Overy, Billingford and Denver, Thurne and Horsey Mere, Sutton, Hunsett and Paston, not to mention a host of others. Don't worry about me. I'll be far too busy for any regrets.'

Well, that was what he'd done all that glorious summer. He'd traded in the old Morris and bought himself a little Morgan three-wheeler. In this he'd scoured the county, searching out its profusion of still-surviving mills, enlisting the friendship of millers and millwrights, admiring the mechanical expertise that had harnessed the winds, leading the power of them down through the stout brick towers by the windshaft, the brake wheel and then the wallower, and down further still, by the upright shaft to the spur wheel and the stones. He'd gossiped amid the flour dust, listened to millers' tales, measured, sketched and photographed, and covered sheet after sheet of his once-pristine notebook with figures and diagrams and detailed descriptions. At night he'd written up his notes and slipped them into his ring-files, where all the mills were listed in alphabetical sequence.

Those files, a full half-dozen of them now, were lodged on the shelves of his glass-fronted bookcase. He drank his tea thoughtfully and poured a second cup. Then he opened the bookcase door, took out one of the binders, picked up his new Waterman fountain pen and turned to the sheet where, six months before, he'd printed the heading 'Kettle Hill Mill'.

He wrote for an hour, then he snapped the file shut, returned it to the bookcase and, tearing up his rough notes, dropped them into a battered wicker basket by his chair. After that he made himself another pot of tea, took it up to bed, read for half an hour till the lines of his book began to run together, and then switched off the light. The air was warm and still, so he left the casement window open on its hook.

He slept soundly, then fitfully, and came awake at last to the sound of wind gusting round the cottage, the rattling of the window, and the knowledge that, as usual, he'd have to get out of bed to relieve himself. That was one of the penalties of growing older. There was rarely a night when he didn't have to totter out of bed to pay a visit. He'd have to stop drinking so many cups of tea.

He groaned, tossed aside the bedclothes and picked his way unsteadily across the room in the dark. Coming back, he closed the window. The weather was turning rough, blowing up for a storm. It was then that he noticed a glow in the sky to the west, somewhere beyond Blakeney; but, still half-asleep, he gave it little thought. It was probably a heath fire. They'd had more than one. The summer had been abnormally dry.

Climbing back into bed, he switched on the lamp and looked at the clock on his bedside table. It showed a quarter past two.

He was still awake, some twenty minutes later, when a savage

13

flash of lightning split the sky above the Green, and a hammer-blow of thunder, directly overhead, shook the walls of the cottage. Then the rain began to fall with a heavy persistence, drumming on the roof.

He lay there listening till at last it died away, leaving nothing but the sound of water dripping from the gutters. Then, as peace resumed, he must have drifted off to sleep.

It wasn't till next morning, when the postman came knocking at the door with a parcel, that he heard what had happened in the night at Kettle Hill.

1

TUESDAY

'In the coldest flint there is hot fire.'
Ray, *Compleat Collection of English Proverbs*

1

Of all the mills that he'd visited, sketched and explored, Kettle Hill was Lubbock's favourite; and, apart from the mill at Cley and a long-abandoned relic close to the church at Blakeney, it was the nearest one to Umzinto Cottage.

Cley mill was a gift to artists, standing as it did between village and marsh, dominating the flat channel-ridden meadows that stretched to the sea; but it was, in a sense, a mockery: little but a shell. It had ground no corn for the past thirty years, its sails were braced forever facing the sea, and its heart had been torn out to convert it into a quaint kind of holiday home.

But Kettle Hill was different. It still throbbed with life.

It was a five-storey tower mill set on the crest of a gently rising slope two miles from the sea, its shuttered sails revolving above a wild stretch of heathland, its nearest neighbour a farm – Morston Bottom Farm – a mile to the north. Apart from Billingford, down near Diss, it was the only mill in Norfolk still grinding corn by wind. It had a small diesel engine, that of course was true – so indeed had Billingford – but young Pashley, the miller, used it only when he had to, and that, on a coast exposed to the North Sea breezes, was infrequently enough.

They were dying out in the county, rapidly it seemed, those mills that relied on the wind to turn their sails. Half a dozen had gone in the past ten years, partly because in wartime damaged parts had been impossible to replace, and partly because most of them were nothing but grist mills, and farmers, more and more, were grinding their own corn for animal feed. But Pashley had never turned over to grist. He ground his corn into flour, supply-ing local shops and bakeries from the fine-grinding burr stones he used in his mill, and he was grimly determined that Kettle Hill

17

would be powered by its four patent sails long after Billingford had gone out of business.

It was this combination of wind power and flour that made Kettle Hill unique, but Lubbock was pragmatic enough to admit that its survival was only a part of its attraction. The other part lay in Simon Pashley himself. Of all the millers he'd met in the course of that summer, he was the one who'd proved the most helpful, the most enthusiastic. As a mere researcher, eager to learn about the complicated machinery that led the power down from the sails to the stones; as a self-confessed student delving into history and the practical problems of managing a mill, Lubbock had found himself not always welcome. Some millers had been uninterested, some – so they claimed – too busy to give him more than a mite of their time, while one at least – Gabriel Jacks at Breckmarsh, five miles along the coast – had been surly and downright uncooperative.

But Pashley had always been willing to talk. He was proud of his mill, only too ready to share Lubbock's enthusiasm, leading him up and down the steep wooden ladders, explaining how the intricate gearing worked, how the chattering damsel fed the grain to the stones, how the power-driven hoist hauled the sacks through the traps, or how the drive from the fantail always kept the sails facing into the wind. Not that he was any less busy than the rest, but he'd always been prepared to talk while he'd worked, to describe what he was doing, why he had to do it and how it was done. Lubbock had learnt more from him than from all the other millers in the county put together. For that he was grateful; and the fact that Pashley had no desperate need to run the mill at a profit, but was fiercely determined nonetheless to make it pay, had aroused his admiration and done nothing at all to diminish his gratitude.

If Kettle Hill was unique, then so was its miller. Simon Pashley was twenty-nine, an only child of elderly parents and a man of distinctly independent means. His father, a gentleman-farmer, had owned Park Lodge, near Wymondham, a compact Elizabethan house with 1500 acres of good grazing land. When he'd died, a widower, in 1944, Simon had been serving with the Royal Engineers in Northern France. He'd survived the Normandy invasion and the drive to the Rhine, but when he'd been demobbed in the spring of '46, he'd had little idea, like many young men of his shattered generation, just what he was going to do with his life.

He'd had no desire to farm, and he'd already half-determined to sell Park Lodge and strike out elsewhere when his father's brother, a wealthy stockbroker in the City and a lifelong bachelor, had succumbed to a heart attack and left him a fortune. Scanning the property that he'd so suddenly and unexpectedly acquired, the young man had been intrigued by a small patch of ground on the north Norfolk coast which included a windmill, with a granary, stables, a cartlodge and a cottage. His uncle, it seemed, had, late in life, developed a passion for windmills. He'd bought this, at Kettle Hill, some fifteen years before, had paid the existing miller to run the place for him, and had spent from time to time considerable sums of money to keep it in repair. He'd fitted a new stock in 1934, renewed the sheers in 1936, and only the year before had replaced two sails that had been damaged in a sudden, violent squall. The mill was in working order, and was still grinding flour from its burr stones installed in 1913.

It had presented to Pashley just the kind of challenge he'd been ready to accept. He'd sold off all the rest of the family property, retired the miller on a generous pension and moved into the cottage, determined to keep the mill running and make it a viable economic proposition. He'd always been possessed of a flair for machinery, and since then he'd managed to work Kettle Hill with considerable success, expanding its trade with local shops and bakeries, driving to the nearby markets to sample the wheat on offer, loading it on his lorry, grinding it at the mill and then delivering it as high-grade flour within a catchment area that he was rapidly extending from month to month.

Now, so it seemed, his brief career as a miller had come to a tragic, unpredictable end.

Survival in this world, Lubbock reflected, as he drove past Blakeney Church and towards Kettle Hill, was a matter of chance. He remembered the shell that had burst in that mudfilled trench near Cambrai more than thirty years before. It had killed everyone else within a range of thirty yards and left him with nothing but a shoulder scar from a flying splinter. And now there was Pashley. The lad had strolled through the fire of the Normandy beaches, dodged the German bullets all the way to the Rhine, and reached the end of the war fitter perhaps than he'd ever been before, only to be struck down in the middle of the night in a quiet Norfolk field.

He parked the Morgan by a kissing-gate, and slowly, reluctantly climbed up the slope to the crest of Kettle Hill. The mill was a smoking ruin, the cap and sails burnt away, the cast-iron wind-shaft, the brake wheel and the gearing to the burnt-out fantail exposed, the window apertures blackened above and around where the flames had pierced the tower and licked along its wall. It was clear at a glance that the wooden floors and ladders must have fallen through the mill in cascades of sparks, progressively consumed as the fire had burnt its way upwards to the cap. Inside there'd be nothing but the metal machinery warped by the heat, and a maze of charred timber choking what had once been the basement store.

Firemen were still damping down the smouldering structure, playing their hoses through the smoke-blackened windows. Lubbock knew one of them.

'What happened?' he asked tersely.

The man handed over his hose to a colleague and lit a cigarette.

'Looks like it was last night's lightning, sir,' he said. 'Probably struck a sail and ran down through the mill. Must have set the place ablaze. By the time we got here it was a rare old bonfire. Couldn't do a thing except douse it with water and hope for the best.'

'What about the miller?'

The man shook his head.

'Seems he didn't get out. Lived in the cottage, did he?'

Lubbock nodded.

'That's right.'

'Reckon he must have wakened up when the lightning struck, and dashed into the mill to try and stop the fire. Always a mistake, sir. Never go back into a building that's alight. We found him on the ground floor, buried in burning timber. Not much of him left. If they need him identified, it'll have to be done by his dentist's records. No other way.'

Lubbock took an instinctive step towards the mill, but a hand on his shoulder stopped him.

'Wouldn't go too close, sir. That tower's still red hot. Lay your hand on the bricks, and they'll peel off the skin like stripping a banana. It'll be hours yet before it's safe to go inside.'

'Try Wymondham.'

'Beg pardon, sir?'

'Wymondham. Dental records,' Lubbock said abruptly. 'That's where he came from.'

Then he turned away with a helpless gesture and began to walk back down the slope to the car.

His long career in the police had inured him to death in most of its forms. He'd looked down at hundreds of murdered men and women, stretched out on beds, on floors or in baths: knifed, shot, poisoned or simply battered out of all recognition. He'd studied them, had them analysed, formed theories about them; but there'd always, in the end, been a motive: a reason why they, out of so many millions, had been pricked out to die. There'd always been a purpose behind their deaths, malevolent and irrational though that purpose might have been. But what was the purpose behind Pashley's death? A bright, eager young man, completely inoffensive, just following a trade that was helpful to many and harmful to none. What rancorous hand had flung that bolt of lightning out of the sky to seek out the tip of a sail at Kettle Hill? What had the lad done that he, like so many murdered men, should have been marked down so unerringly for death? It was all such a waste, pointless, futile, a squandering of talent that the world, in its slow recrudescence from war, so desperately needed.

Less than eighteen hours before he'd sat by the millstones chatting to the boy. He'd shared a sandwich with him, waved him goodbye as he'd started up the car. And now what was left of him? Nothing but charred, solidified flesh.

A stroke of lightning, he'd been told more than once, was an act of God, but he couldn't believe such an outrageous tale. If it were true, then God must be mad. What sane divinity would create a bright talent, wait till it matured and then, at a stroke, blast it out of existence? If God was the well-spring of all creation, could he be the source, at one and the same time, of wanton destruction?

If he could, then it was a strange sort of world he'd created, and a strange sort of God he was, too, into the bargain.

He shrugged and drove on. It was all way beyond him. He'd never understand.

*　　*　　*

21

Back at Umzinto, he scoured out his pipe, refilled it, lit it and blew out clouds of comforting smoke.

Then he opened his bookcase doors, took out a file and turned to the section on Kettle Hill mill.

'Struck by lightning,' he wrote, 'and destroyed by fire, September 1947.'

Then he left a line blank and added a note:

When working:
Tower mill.
5 floors. Height of tower about 53 feet.
Granary, stables, cartlodge and cottage.
4 double-shuttered sails.
Striking by rack and pinion.
Boat-shaped cap.
8-bladed fan.
Wooden gallery.
Iron stage at 3rd floor.
2 pairs of 4 ft stones, French burr, overdrift.

He ruled a line underneath and stared at what he'd written as if the words in themselves were beyond belief.

Then he slowly shook his head, shut the file with a snap and drew hard on his pipe.

It was all that a mere bewildered mortal could do.

2

It was later that morning when he first suspected that something was wrong.

In his experience of such cases, there was usually a catalyst: someone who, by a chance remark, sparked off an abnormal powder-train of thought; and on this occasion, appropriately enough, the catalyst was a soldier: Gunner Robert Ellison of the Royal Artillery.

He knew the boy well enough: fresh-faced, intelligent, doing his National Service; one of the small garrison that still remained at the ack-ack battery down on the marsh. They'd chatted together more than once in the village store. Ellison had ambitions to join the police, and Lubbock had no doubt that he'd make a good recruit. Among sundry dire warnings of the pain and grief that inevitably awaited him, he'd given him one or two tips on how to proceed.

When, about midday, he walked down to the shop for an ounce of his favourite brand of tobacco, Ellison was there. He was deep in conversation with Mrs Brand behind the counter.

Jemima Brand was a gross, cheerful woman whose chief attraction to the villagers of Cley, apart from her well-stocked shop, was her encyclopaedic knowledge of all that occurred, tragic, scandalous or merely absurd, within a range of ten miles. They were talking about the fire.

'Burnt to a cinder,' she said, 'the poor man.'

Lubbock was hardly in any mood to listen. He turned to go out. He had other calls to make and could come back later on. But it was then that Ellison mentioned the bell.

Ten minutes later he'd steered the boy back to Umzinto Cottage, poured him a beer from the small clutch of bottles he kept in the pantry for unexpected visitors, and once again, with great deliberation, was stoking up his pipe.

He tossed a spent match into the old tin ashtray that he'd won years before at a fairground in Yarmouth.

'Now, lad,' he said, 'tell me all about this bell.'

Ellison told him. Somewhat overawed by an ex-DCI, he was only too ready to describe what had happened.

He'd been coming back off leave the night before, he said, and he'd missed his train at Fakenham. It was after eleven o'clock, the last buses had gone, but he'd managed to scrounge a lift on a duty truck that was taking a group of airmen back to their camp on the outskirts of Wells. It had dropped him off at Walsingham and, after waiting there a while, he'd flagged down a van that had taken him to Binham. From there he'd set out to walk the last five miles by the side roads to Cley. It wasn't the first time that he'd had to do it, and he knew the short cuts that led across the fields. There was one in particular that ran past the windmill at Kettle Hill and joined the coast road at Blakeney. He'd used it before.

The sky was clouding over and the wind was getting up. The air smelt of rain and, not wanting to be caught in a sudden downpour, he'd stepped out as fast as he could across the fields. He'd just reached the mill when a bell began to ring.

Lubbock raised a hand and stopped him.

'I'm going to have to ask a few questions, lad,' he said. 'I'm not grilling you, don't think that. It's just that I need to be sure of the facts.'

Ellison nodded.

'Right, sir.'

'Now, what time was this?'

The young soldier thought back. He didn't rush to answer.

'I suppose,' he said slowly, 'it must have been round about half-past one. I wasn't hanging about, and I got back to Cley just after two o'clock.'

'And you're sure this bell wasn't just a phone that was ringing?'

'Certain, sir, yes. It was nothing like that.'

'And it wasn't from the cottage?'

'No, sir. From the mill.'

Lubbock tamped down his pipe.

'What kind of bell was it?'

Ellison pondered.

'Sounded like a shop bell. You know the sort, sir. On a curved steel ribbon. Like down at the stores.'

Lubbock paused for a moment.

'How far from the mill were you when it started to ring?'

'About fifty yards, I'd say.'

'And it went on ringing?'

'Yes, sir, that's right. I didn't take much notice. All I wanted to do was to get back to Cley before the rain came. I walked straight down the hill till I reached the main road. It was still ringing when I stopped to unfasten the gate. I could just about hear it. After that I must have been too far away ... But the mill sails were turning.'

'Didn't that strike you as strange ... in the middle of the night?'

Ellison confessed that he hadn't really given it a great deal of thought.

'I suppose, sir,' he said, 'if I thought anything at all, it was just that the miller was working late to keep up with demand. Maybe someone had lumbered him with a last-minute order.'

24

Lubbock seemed to be counting points off in his mind, checking them one by one.

'Did you see any lights?'

'Not that I remember.'

'The mill was in darkness?'

'It seemed to be, yes.'

'And the cottage?'

'Black as pitch.'

Lubbock dragged on his pipe and blew out clouds of smoke.

'One more thing,' he said. 'When you walked past the mill, can you remember which way the sails were facing?'

Ellison closed his eyes, then opened them again.

'Yes,' he said. 'Towards me. I could see them all quite clearly.'

'They were facing the wind?'

'They must have been, yes. It was blowing from behind me.'

'Strongly?'

'Off and on. Gusting, sir, I'd say. It'd blow pretty hard and then fall away. But a few seconds later, it'd hit you again. You had to brace yourself against it.'

'But the mill was running smoothly?'

'Seemed to be, sir. Can't say I know a deal about the way windmills work.'

'You didn't hear any rasping or grating at all?'

'No, sir, not a thing.'

Lubbock nodded slowly, as if the answer was what he'd expected it to be. He seemed to be brooding.

Ellison leaned forward.

'D'you think there's something fishy about the fire, sir?' he said.

Lubbock raised his eyes.

'Too early to say, lad. All we've got are pointers, fragments of evidence. Might be important, then again they might not. You're jumping to conclusions, and a good detective can't afford to do that.'

'But the bell, sir,' said Ellison. 'You wanted me to tell you all about the bell, so it must mean something.'

Lubbock looked at him solemnly.

'Oh, yes, it does. It means a great deal. It means two and two make five.'

'Five, sir?'

'Five... How's your mathematics, lad?'

25

'Reasonable, sir.'

'You know the old saying that two and two make four?'

'I've heard it, sir, yes.'

'You accept it? It's true? Two and two couldn't possibly add up to five?'

Ellison was clearly baffled by this sudden switch of topic, but, metaphorically at least, he stuck to his guns.

'Not in my book, sir, no.'

'Then suppose that in your book you added two and two, and the answer came to five. What would you think?'

'That I'd made a mistake?'

'Right, lad, first time. So you add up again and it still comes to five. You keep on adding up and it always comes to five. Then, what would you think?'

Ellison shook his head.

'But it couldn't add up to five, sir.'

Lubbock looked grim.

'Oh, yes, it could. And it does. All too often.'

'But it just isn't possible. Two and two can never add up to make five.'

'No, they can't,' said Lubbock, 'can they? That's the problem that every detective has to face. Two and two make four, so how can they make five? Think about it, lad. If you want to be a detective, you'd better think about it hard. It's a problem you'll be facing every day of the week.'

He knocked out his pipe and pushed back his chair.

'Drink up, lad,' he said. 'It's been a useful talk and we've both of us learned something, but you'll need to be getting back and I've a visit to make. I'll drop you off on the way.'

Twenty minutes later he was back at Kettle Hill. The firemen were still there, playing their hoses on the smoke-blackened tower.

He tackled the man that he'd spoken to before.

'Is it safe now?' he asked.

'Safe, sir? Yes. But it'll make you sweat a bit.'

Lubbock stripped off his shirt.

'Then kit me out,' he said. 'I've got to go inside. And can you get that ladder to the top of the mill?'

26

3

Gunner Ellison watched the little three-wheeler reverse and drive off through the village towards Blakeney.

He stood on the edge of the marsh and looked after it, till it turned the corner and disappeared from view.

He was thinking about Lubbock.

Peculiar old chap with his two and two make five. Sometimes it wasn't easy to know what to make of him. He was gruff, dismissive and yet, at the same time, generous with his help. But if he was crossed, you could bet your bottom dollar he'd be an awkward old sod. Unpredictable, too. You'd never be sure just how he'd react. He must have been hell to work under when he was in the force.

Much the same thoughts were running through the mind of Detective Inspector Michael Bruce Tench when, some two hours later, he swung his police car through the Norwich streets and parked it outside the Old Riverside restaurant. He knew Lubbock far better than Ellison did, but there were still odd occasions when the old man seemed determined to leave him groping in the dark.

When, demobbed from the army after a short period of service towards the end of the war, he'd chosen not to go back to Cambridge, but to join the police, he'd been drafted to Fakenham and then, as detective sergeant, to work under Lubbock's guidance in Norwich. That was when Bill McKenzie, his fellow sergeant, already middle-aged and completely unambitious, had offered him a few words of timely advice.

'You want to get on?' he'd said. 'You want to make inspector sooner or later? Well, you could just be lucky. You're with the right man. Watch him and learn. Don't assume that he's past it because his hair's white. The Chief's more than simply a competent copper. He's a legend here in Norwich. Follow him around. Keep your eyes and ears open. He may seem to you to be painfully slow. You'll find yourself saying he's just wasting time. Well, think it but don't say it. He'll drop on you like a ton of bricks if you step out of place. So be careful, watch your step. Learn to duck and weave, and never forget that his conviction record's the best in Norfolk.'

Well, he'd learnt, the hard way; not without the bricks; but he'd kept his head down, taught himself to read the signs: the frown, then the glare and the tightening of the lines around Lubbock's lips that always warned of the scathing comment to come. There'd been months of frustration: months when he'd seemed to act as nothing but a tea-boy, laying on pots of strong Darjeeling tea to quench the old boy's seemingly insatiable thirst. It had been a disconcerting apprenticeship, full of uncertainties, riddled with doubts, but he'd slowly come to realize that Lubbock's methods of training were, like the man himself, unique. He'd been content to let his young assistant trail after him, learning by example to weigh all the evidence, not to move too fast, to think before he jumped to any conclusions. He hadn't spared him the frequent explosions of wrath; had cut the ground from his feet on more than one occasion; but, once he'd felt it was time to let him off the leash, he hadn't been reluctant to trust him with the chance.

If his training had been harsh, it had nonetheless been effective, and he, Mike Tench, had, in course of time, come to see the old man in a different light. He'd marked him down at first as an irascible old devil, difficult to work with, devious in his crab-like approach to a problem, yet intolerant of any step that diverged from his tried and tested procedures; but, almost imperceptibly, he'd come to appreciate that, behind the short temper and apparent illogicality, there was a thoroughness that laid bare the bones of a case, like a surgeon's knife probing the source of an infection. Lubbock, as the Chief Super, Hastings, once said, had a nose for a murder. He seemed to be possessed of a built-in compass that always turned him in the right direction: towards the killer and the motive that had led him to kill. He got the results, and results, as Tench knew, were what counted in the end.

More than that, the old boy had mellowed. Or perhaps that wasn't the whole of the truth. Perhaps he himself, as his confidence increased, had found him easier to work with. What he'd first condemned as faults, he'd come to see later as nothing but foibles; and whereas, in the early days, he'd always watched him with suspicion, that suspicion had gradually melted away, to be replaced by a kind of amused affection.

Since Lubbock's retirement, the bond between them had

strengthened. He'd spent more than one evening in the cottage at Cley, drinking the coffee that Lubbock kept stowed away against such a visit, seeking answers to his own unfamiliar problems, and listening to his old Chief, through clouds of pungent pipe-smoke, rumbling on about his wonderful windmills.

He owed him more than a little. His promotion, for one thing. He'd never have made DI at this early stage – he was pretty sure of that – if it hadn't been for Lubbock's few blunt words in the Chief Super's ear. The old boy had been generous, in that respect at least. He remembered when he'd said so, Kath had been indignant. He hadn't needed any help; that was her tale; he'd have made it on his own. Anyone with only an ounce of discernment must have seen that he was worth promoting. But Kath was his wife, and she'd never reconciled herself to Lubbock's original attitude towards him. It was no way, she said, to train a man of intelligence: getting him to run and fetch cups of tea like a mere office-boy.

He wondered what had prompted Lubbock's telephone call. He'd been, as usual, gruffly non-committal. Something about a fire. No, he didn't want to talk about it over the phone, but he'd like a little chat down at Meg's in an hour. Could he spare the time? Yes, it was important. It might well be urgent, but nowadays he wasn't the one to decide.

That was all he'd said. Just enough to rouse his interest; enough to leave him no choice but to banish all thought of his overflowing in-tray and drive himself down to the Old Riverside.

If he'd taken the call at home, and Kath had been around, he knew what she'd have said: 'Let the old devil wait.'

She'd accepted his job – she'd had to do that – but she resented it taking too much of his time: time she said was hers as much as it was his; and, above all, she resented being robbed of that time by ex-Detective Chief Inspector Lubbock.

Well, fair enough, he could have refused on this occasion, pleaded pressure of work, but if Lubbock said something was important, it was. That was one thing he'd learnt from working with the man. His assessments of a case were always precise.

Perhaps it was a good thing that Kath was away. When he'd dropped her off the night before at her parents' home near Cambridge, he'd felt bereft at the prospect of a whole week without her; but if Lubbock was intent on making his presence felt, it might be all for the best. Her mother's brief sojourn in Addenbrooke's

Hospital could very well prove to be a blessIng in disguise. At least he'd not be torn between loyalty to Lubbock and loyalty to Kath. If the old man was going to make demands on his time, better this week than next.

As he climbed out of the car, he gave a wry smile. It was just like the old days ... Lay on some tea, laddie ... Yes, sir; no, sir; if not three bags full, sir ...

But now there was, as the French might say, just a little difference.

He pushed open the door of the Old Riverside, and the bell on its steel ribbon danced up and down, tinkling into silence as he closed the door behind him. Steering a zigzag course between the crowded tables – Meg did a roaring trade in afternoon teas – he made his way to the little room at the back: the room she'd always set aside as a place where Lubbock could roll his tongue around poached egg and haddock, light up his pipe, consume inordinate quantities of tea, and discuss with his colleagues the ins and outs of their latest case.

Meg – Margaret Dennison as her name appeared on letterheads and bills – was Lubbock's only sister, indeed his only surviving relative. With her husband, a fisherman, she'd run a fish-and-chip shop many years before on the sea-front at Cromer. Then, between them, they'd bought the Riverside, an old disused watermill by the Wensum in Norwich, and converted it into a restaurant; and when he'd been tragically drowned in a storm, she'd continued to manage the place on her own, making it pay, despite all the rigours of wartime rationing, by exploiting her connections with the fisherfolk of Cromer, building up a trade with the local farmers, whispering in the ears of the Norwich grocers, and achieving a reputation as a formidable cook.

When Lubbock's wife had died from a virulent form of 'flu early in the war, she'd presumed it her duty, both to God and the law, to ensure that her brother was adequately fed; and more than one Norfolk murder had found its solution over haddock and egg at Meg's immaculate table. More than one Norfolk murderer had owed his conviction to Lubbock's sense of fulfilment as he pushed back his plate, lounged in Meg's chair and watched the smoke curl away from the bowl of his briar.

Raw-boned and tall, she treated him with a kind of affectionate cynicism, giving him from time to time the rough edge of her tongue – a sisterly privilege – but never complaining when sundry other members of the Norwich police attached themselves to him and spent hour after hour in her little back room, thrashing out their problems.

Tench found her there as usual, hovering over one of her flower-printed cloths, laying out a clutch of fish knives and forks. She looked up at him sharply.

'You eating?' she said.

That was typical Meg. No delighted greeting. Straight to the point.

He'd long since ceased to wonder where all the food came from, or how it came about that, in spite of the meagre quantities still permitted on ration, pot after pot of steaming hot tea and jug after jug of strong black coffee found their way to Lubbock's table.

It was better not to wonder. Better just to accept.

'Must admit I could do with a bite,' he confessed. 'Had to go without lunch. What's on the menu?'

Not that he really needed to ask.

'It'll be haddock and egg,' she said. 'Always is for him.'

'That'll be fine ... Has he been in yet?'

Meg realigned a fork that was an inch out of true.

'Haven't seen him for weeks. What's he been doing?'

'Windmills,' said Tench. 'He's studying windmills.'

'Windmills? He must be mad.' She straightened up, flexed her back. 'What on earth for?'

Tench pulled out a chair.

'Between you and me, Mrs Dennison,' he said, 'I think he's hoping that, sooner or later, I'll have to investigate a murder in a mill. You know, something messy. A body caught up in the mill machinery. Then I'll need his help. He's got ambitions to be something he's never had the chance to be – an expert witness.'

Meg shook her head.

'Can't quit,' she said, 'can he? Still got to poke his nose in. Well, don't you go letting him tell you what to do. He will, you know, if you give him half a chance. He may like to think you're his golden-headed boy, the son he never had, but you're the boss now. So don't forget that.'

Tench grinned.

31

'Don't worry. Little boys grow up, Mrs Dennison. They have to. And once they're grown up, they always seem to like to decide for themselves.'

4

Lubbock pushed aside his plate, poured a third cup of tea and filled up his pipe.

'There's an obvious explanation, laddie,' he said: 'one that's simple and to most people utterly credible.'

'But you don't accept it.'

'It's not that I don't. It's rather that I can't. It's too facile. There's no logic behind it at all. Logic points to the fact that the simple explanation just isn't the right one.'

Tench sipped his coffee.

'You're sure it is logic, sir, and not just instinct? What the Chief Super calls your nose for a murder?'

Lubbock struck a match and, as he usually did, filled the little room with drifting clouds of smoke.

'If he means that murder always stinks to high heaven, then maybe he's right. It doesn't take too keen a nose to detect foul play. But it isn't instinct, laddie. You know me better than that. I've never worked on instinct, and I wouldn't want to lay claim to such a doubtful resource. It's the facts that count. Somewhere at the back of one's mind there has to be some fact that makes one look in a particular direction, and quite often it's a fact that seems to conflict with the popular theory. That's the way it is in this particular case. Such facts as there are refute the obvious explanation. They make me want to look elsewhere for the answer.'

Tench leaned back in his chair.

'All right, sir,' he said, 'let's look at it more closely. The simple explanation is that lightning struck the mill and set it on fire. Don't you believe that happened?'

Lubbock frowned.

'I do and I don't. There isn't any doubt that lightning struck the mill, but to say that it was that that set it ablaze seems to me to be jumping the gun. The facts don't support it.'

'Then we'd better lay out the facts, sir, hadn't we?' said Tench.

'What makes you so sure that the lightning did strike? Did someone see it happen?'

'Not that I know of. The most likely people would have been the Boldings at Morston Bottom Farm – that's a mile to the north – but I didn't need to ask them. There was evidence enough to prove the point inside the mill.'

Tench watched him closely.

'So what was it then, this evidence?'

Lubbock explained.

'When lightning strikes a mill, it normally strikes at the tip of a sail. From there the charge passes along the windshaft to the cap, and then to earth down the sack chain.'

'The sack chain?'

Lubbock nodded.

'Every mill has a sack hoist for raising the grain up through the floors, so that it can feed down to the millstones by gravity. At Kettle Hill it takes the form of an endless chain. This chain runs over a power-driven wheel high in the mill, and hangs down through all the floors. It passes through a series of traps: hinged doors with double flaps that open upwards automatically as the sack rises through them and fall shut behind it. You operate it by pulling on a cord at the bottom. This engages the gearing and so turns the chain wheel, winding up the sacks that are hooked to the chain. Understand, laddie?'

'I think so,' said Tench. 'When lightning strikes a mill, the charge finds the sack chain more often than not and runs down it to earth.'

'That's right.'

'And you think it did in this case?'

'I know it did in this case.'

'What makes you so sure?'

'Something I saw. I may be getting on, but these eyes of mine, laddie, are still keen enough. I got the firemen to kit me out and did a bit of exploring inside the mill. The sack chain was still hanging down from the chain wheel, but the links halfway up were welded together. When I shook it, I could tell. There was a section of it about four feet long that was solid. Wouldn't bend.'

Tench clearly had his doubts.

'But couldn't the fire have done the welding?'

'Hardly,' said Lubbock. 'It would have needed a massive electrical charge to fuse a chain like that, and it's happened often enough

33

before, all over the country. There was a lightning strike at a Sussex mill – St Leonards I think it was – that welded a good three feet of the chain, and another one in Essex – Toothill mill at Ongar. I could quote a dozen more. No, laddie, Kettle Hill's just one in a long succession. The lightning struck it. There's no doubt about that.'

'But it didn't start the fire.'

'No, I don't think it did.'

'Go on then,' said Tench. 'Tell me why not.'

The back room at the Riverside had been built above the wheel-pit of the old watermill. A glass panel, bound in brass, had been set into the parquet blocks of the floor, and through it one could see the wheel turning below and the water frothing in and out of the buckets. Lubbock jerked the stem of his pipe towards it.

'Remember last winter,' he said, 'when that wheel was frozen solid for months on end? We sat here one day and talked about that case up at Elsdon Hall, and I told you I wanted you to play the devil's advocate. I was going to try and fit the pieces of the puzzle together, and it was your job to hack my logic to bits. Mine, after that, was to take the decisions ... Well, now the set-up's different. I'm out of the race. You've got to decide, so you need to be more of a devil's advocate than ever. All I can do is lay out the facts. It's up to you to determine whether they add up to anything or not. Clear, laddie?'

'Clear, sir.' Tench gave a nod.

'Right then. You asked me why I thought that that stroke of lightning didn't start the fire, so let's take a look first at the likelihood that it might have done. It's a common enough occurrence for mills to be struck. I can quote a dozen cases in Norfolk alone in the last fifty years, but out of that dozen there was only one instance when a fire was started that burnt the mill down. That was at Sedgeford in 1910. In all the other cases there was no sign of fire. Damage to the sails, yes, common enough – only four years ago a flash at Horsey mill split the stocks from end to end – but, apart from that, it's amazing just how little harm a stroke of lightning can do. When Hingham mill was blasted in 1861, the charge travelled down the sack chain to the iron tongues that were set in the ground-floor planking, but there was no damage to the mill or any of its machinery, and a man and a boy standing by the tongues were completely unhurt. Fourteen years later, at Sutton mill near Stalham, the same thing happened. The charge came down the sack chain, and when it reached the bottom, cut a hole clean through the boarded floor. The miller's son and six men were standing around within a yard of the hole but, apart from being shocked, none of them was injured. The only damage to the mill was a broken sail and a shattered joist that supported the floor ... So, laddie, if you had to quote the odds on lightning causing a fire in a mill, they'd be heavily against it.'

'But it could still happen.' Tench was duly sceptical.

'Yes, of course it could. I'm not denying it could. All I'm pointing out is that the chance is a slim one.'

'But not slim enough. It's hardly an incontestable piece of evidence, is it?'

'On its own, perhaps, no.'

'So there has to be something else.'

Lubbock relit his pipe.

'More than that, laddie. A number of things. First of all there's the bell...'

5

Mike Tench was well attuned to the ritual of such a meeting with his old Chief Inspector. It had become, for him, all but a routine procedure. Lubbock would unwind the strands of his case with a tantalizing slowness, emphasizing each point, building up the tension like a writer of mysteries deliberately planting a series of clues, while his listener grew progressively more and more impatient. He expected each revelation to be adequately challenged, each scrap of Lubbock logic to be roundly disputed, and yet, at the end of what invariably proved an over-long dissertation, Tench had always found that his argument carried both weight and conviction.

Because of that, across the months, he'd trained himself to listen with ever-increasing patience, to question from time to time, to let the old man proceed at his own measured pace. If the ritual was deliberate and time-consuming, it was usually productive, and he was willing to wait. So, as he poured himself another cup of coffee, he listened with an almost unnatural forbearance as Lubbock, with a meticulous regard for each step, described how Gunner Ellison had missed his connection, tramped across the fields and then, passing the mill, had heard the sound of a bell.

It was only then that he felt it was time to intervene.

'So it wasn't the sound of a phone,' he said, 'and it came from the mill.'

'Right on both counts.'

'And it must be important.'

'Right again, laddie.'

'And I'm right in assuming that it wouldn't mean a thing except to someone who knows about the working of windmills?'

Lubbock gave a shrug.

'I think you could possibly say that, yes.'

Tench seemed amused.

'And of course that someone, sir, happens to be you.'

'Pure coincidence, laddie, nothing more than that. It's simply that I've learnt a lot about mills in the last few months. No skin off your nose. You couldn't be expected to spot its significance. Nor could young Ellison. But I'm pretty sure that what he heard was the sound of an alarm.'

'You mean a fire alarm?'

'Not in the strictest sense, no. A fire alarm only sounds when a fire's already started. This kind, in a mill, gives a warning before the fire actually starts.'

Tench was thoughtful.

'So it warns of some danger, some state of affairs that could well cause a fire.'

'Precisely that, laddie.'

'What state of affairs?'

Lubbock blew out another pungent cloud of smoke.

'One that's never far away. The danger that the stones may run out of grain. If they do, they can touch, and if they touch they throw off sparks: sparks that almost certainly, sooner or later, set the mill on fire. You see, laddie, in a corn mill the grain's ground between stones: a couple of stones set one above the other. The top one's called the runner stone, the lower one the bed stone; but only the runner stone turns. Grain trickles into its eye from a hopper, so there must be some device to warn the miller when the grain in the hopper's running dangerously low. That's the purpose of the bell alarm: to give him that warning ... It's a simple affair really: almost, you could say, a Heath Robinson contraption. There's a

36

leather strap set low down inside the hopper. One end's fixed to the side, the other's fastened to a cord that runs through a hole, and then over a pulley on the floor joist above. The end of the cord's fastened to what's known as a trail stick, and the stick's attached in its turn to the bell. If there's a sufficient amount of grain in the hopper, the weight of it holds the strap down and keeps the cord taut; but when the grain runs low, the combined weight of the trail stick and the bell pulls the strap upwards out of the grain, the trail stick falls against the teeth of a turning cog wheel and, as it vibrates, so it rings the bell.'

'And you think that's what happened? When Ellison passed the mill, the stones were already running out of grain?'

'It's the logical explanation.'

'But surely, in that case, young Pashley would have topped up the grain in the hopper.'

'Yes, of course he would. No miller would ever dare to let his stones run dry.'

'So? What's the answer?'

'The answer is, laddie, that for some reason or other he wasn't able to do it ... And there's another thing, too. This happened at half-past one in the morning, and I've never known Pashley work his mill at night...'

Tench raised a hand.

'Hang on a bit, sir,' he said. 'Let's deal with what we've got before we lose track ... For some reason Pashley didn't fill up the hopper. Is it possible that he may not have heard the bell?'

'Ellison heard it, and he was outside the mill.'

'But if Pashley was in the cottage...'

'He wasn't. His body was found in the mill.'

'But he could have been in the cottage. He could have fallen asleep.'

'No, laddie, it's not on. If the mill was working, that's where Pashley would have been until the moment it stopped ... And it was certainly working. Ellison saw the sails turning, and the bell wouldn't have rung unless the grain in the hopper was beginning to run low.'

'And you say Pashley never worked the mill at night?'

'Never, to my knowledge.'

'But he could have done. He could have had a late order.'

'That's what Ellison thought, but most of yesterday I was at

37

Kettle Hill myself. I left about six, and Pashley had already finished his stint for the day. The mill wasn't working then, and if he'd meant to start it up again I'm sure he'd have told me.'

'Yet at half-past one in the morning the mill was running again and the bell was ringing.'

'That's what Ellison says.'

Tench pondered the problem.

'How d'you know that Pashley didn't fill up the hopper?'

Lubbock reached across the table to one of Meg's ashtrays and knocked out his pipe.

'Two reasons,' he said. 'The bell went on ringing. Ellison could still hear it when he reached the main road; and while I was in the mill this morning I took a look at the stones. They were scarred and blunted. They'd clearly run dry. So the question remains: why didn't Pashley react to the bell?'

'He could have been taken ill. Had a heart attack, perhaps.'

'He could, but he was a young man and fit as a fiddle. He was healthy enough when I left him at six o'clock ... Apart from that, the wind was rising. There was a storm blowing up. Ellison made that clear. But the sails were still turning and facing into the wind.'

'And they shouldn't have been?'

'No.'

'You mean if things had been normal, Pashley would already have taken some action.'

'That's right.'

'So what would he have done?'

Lubbock peered into the teapot.

'He'd have opened the shutters ... As a last resort, he'd have quartered the mill.'

Tench took a deep breath.

'Go on, sir,' he said. 'Tell me all about it. What does a miller do when he quarters a mill, and why on earth does he do it?'

6

Lubbock seemed in no hurry.

He replaced the teapot lid, picked up the pot and pushed through the swing doors into the kitchen. A couple of minutes later

– Tench waited in silent anticipation – he came back with another pot steaming from the spout. He set it down on the table, began to stir its contents with considerable zeal, peered inside it once again and, satisfied that the brew had achieved a sufficiently mellow shade of colour, poured another cup. Then he took out his pouch and began to shred a wedge of tobacco between his fingers.

'When a wind gets up,' he said, 'there's always the danger that a mill may run away. It'll be running so fast that the brake won't hold it. That's when the miller, more often than not, decides to quarter the mill. That means he turns the sails at right angles to the wind.'

Tench watched him intently.

'A difficult job?'

'Yes, it needs a good deal of physical effort, but he wouldn't do it except as a last resort. The first thing he'd do would be to open the shutters on the sails. He'd do that quite simply by hauling on a chain and operating what's known as the striking rod. And there is another safeguard. The striking mechanism's so designed that when the wind reaches a certain strength, the shutters open automatically.'

'So there should really be no reason to quarter the mill.'

'In normal circumstances, no. But if the striking rod jammed, or if, for some reason, he tried to ride out the gale without opening the shutters, there might come a point when he'd have no choice but to quarter the mill. You see, laddie, in these windmills the brake's made of wood, and if the mill's running too fast then the miller daren't keep it applied for too long in case the friction heats it up and sets it on fire. He's then in a position where he can't stop the mill and the only solution is to quarter the sails.'

'And you say it needs some strength?'

'It needs strength and it needs time. A mill like Kettle Hill has what's called a fantail, a small vaned wheel on the back of the cap. It's set at right angles to the sails, and it's connected by gears to a winding mechanism. As the wind direction changes, it begins to spin, and turns the cap and the sails to face the new quarter. In other words, it keeps the sails facing into the wind; so the first thing that a miller has to do, if he's going to quarter the mill, is to disengage the fantail, throw it out of gear. That isn't easy. I couldn't begin to tell you why without taking you up to the top of a mill and showing you the complicated method of gearing; but, once he's done that, he's got to turn the cap by hand. It revolves on a set of rollers – what's known as a live curb – and it's that that requires the physical effort and takes up the time.'

'And what you're saying is that Pashley did none of these things?'

'It seems he didn't, laddie. The sails were still turning and facing the wind. I got the fire brigade to run up a turntable ladder, and climbed up and took a look for myself. It wasn't possible, of course, to tell whether or not the brake had been applied, because the rope and the brake itself had burnt away in the fire; but, from what remained of the sails, it seemed pretty clear that the shutters hadn't been opened and, in addition, the fantail was still in gear. That would have made it impossible to quarter the mill.'

Tench closed his eyes.

'Let me try and work this out,' he said. 'Pashley should have heard the bell and filled up his grain hopper. That he didn't do. He should have opened the shutters on his sails. He didn't do that. He should have disengaged the fantail to quarter the mill, and he didn't do that either.'

'All of them steps that a competent miller like Simon Pashley would have taken without question.'

'So the inference is . . . ?'

'That's for you to decide. I'm merely stating the facts; providing you with data . . . And I've still to provide you with a little bit more. Ellison said it was about half-past one when he walked by the mill and heard the bell ringing. The mill sails were turning and there was no sign of fire. Three-quarters of an hour later, at a quarter past two, I had to get out of bed. Nature demanded it. The wind was gusting round the cottage, and I had to close the window. There was a glow in the sky over Kettle Hill. I put it down to a heath fire, but it seems more than likely now that it wasn't. I didn't see any lightning, didn't hear any thunder. The first flash of lightning didn't break over Cley until twenty minutes later.'

Tench stroked his chin.

'So you think the mill was already on fire at a quarter past two.'

'If what I saw was the mill, it was more than just on fire. It was blazing away.'

'But the lightning could have struck there earlier than at Cley.'

'It could have done, yes. You'd have to check that, find out from the locals; and find out, too, who made the call to the fire brigade at

Holt, and what time they received it. But you see, laddie, don't you? Unless, as you say, Pashley was taken ill or met with some accident, there's a devil of a lot that needs to be explained. At the least, it's a case of suspicious death. Wouldn't you agree?'

Tench nodded slowly.

'Yes, sir,' he said, 'I'm inclined to think I would.'

'And if someone had it in for a decent lad like that; if, in some way, they stopped him from doing what he should have done to stave off a fire, then I wouldn't like to think that they'd get away with it.'

'Don't worry' – Tench was suddenly grim – 'they won't do that. But there are still a good many other possible explanations. He *could* have been taken ill. He could have fallen down one of the ladders in the mill. This striking rod of yours could, as you say, have jammed, or the gearing to the fantail. The lightning might already have struck the mill before you got out of bed. There may have been another fire somewhere nearby. It could have been what you thought it was, a fire on the heath – we've had plenty this summer. You could have seen that...'

Lubbock tamped down the tobacco in his pipe and reached for his matches.

'I'm not denying that any of these things could have happened, and I'm not telling you what to do, but I think it might be worth while to make a few inquiries. And if you're going to do that, you'll need to do one thing right away, without wasting any time.'

'Ledward?'

'That's right.'

Reg Ledward was the police pathologist, a dry man without humour, whose voice always crackled like sheets of parchment. Lubbock had worked with him for years.

'Get him to take a look at what's left of young Pashley, and bring forensics in as well. It'll be difficult for them to glean much from what I've heard, but it's amazing what these scientific johnnies come up with. They might give us a clue, something that'll prove me either right or wrong.'

He struck a match, held it over the bowl of his briar and, half hidden by the smoke that drifted away towards Meg's distempered ceiling, picked up his cup and drained it to the dregs. Then he sat back, breathed deeply and stretched out his legs.

41

'So, if I were you,' he said, 'I'd ring Ledward right away. And the mortuary at Holt. You never know your luck.'

7

At the knock on his office door, Detective Chief Superintendent Hastings looked up from the letters he was signing.

'Come in,' he called; and when Tench appeared, 'Yes, Mike,' he said. 'What can I do for you?'

'Just a few words, sir.'

Hastings laid down his pen.

'Problems?'

'Not really, sir.'

'What then?'

'I had a phone call this lunchtime from Mr Lubbock.'

'John? What did he want?'

'Asked if I could meet him, sir, so I did.'

'And?'

Tench explained.

'It's a case of suspicious death. Might well be murder. And with Chief Inspector Maitland away in Amsterdam on this Nettlefield business...'

Maitland was the DCI who'd taken over from Lubbock. He'd come to them from Ipswich, and the Nettlefield robbery, still unsolved, was a long-running case that had plagued him back in Suffolk. At the personal request of his former Chief and the Amsterdam police, he'd travelled to Holland with one of his old colleagues to follow up fresh evidence.

Hastings nodded slowly.

'You're on your own, aren't you?'

'For the next few days, yes.'

'And you think you ought to follow up Lubbock's line of thought.'

'I think it's worth investigating.'

'It usually is.' The Chief Super had worked with Lubbock for more than ten years, and he was well aware how much his monthly crime statistics had owed to his Chief Inspector's strange intuitions. He looked at Tench quizzically.

'Feeling a bit exposed?'

42

Tench hardly felt exposed, but he chose to be diplomatic.

'Thought I'd better inform you, sir, before I did anything.'

Hastings nodded again.

'Yes, glad you did. Perfectly correct ... Well, you'd best carry on. I've no doubt you can deal with whatever crops up. Just keep me in touch. If you have any problems or need any backing, the door's always open ... What are you going to do? Call in Reg Ledward?'

'First of all, sir, yes. Then put out a few feelers around Kettle Hill.'

'Right.' The Chief Super picked up his pen. 'It's your case, Mike. But you'd better move fast. If I know John Lubbock, he'll be down there already, sniffing round that mill like a grizzled old bloodhound.'

Back in his own office, Tench sat at his desk and stared at the phone. He sat staring at it for fully a minute; then he made up his mind. He rang four different numbers, then he went to the door and called in McKenzie.

'Mac,' he said, 'we've got to do a bit of probing.'

'You mean we, or just me?'

'Both of us. Sit down.'

McKenzie, broad, overweight and heavily moustached, pulled out a swivel-chair and lowered himself into it.

'Right,' he said. 'What's the score?'

'We're going to take a little trip to the seaside. To Cley.'

McKenzie was a man who preferred the bright lights.

'Tell me if I'm wrong,' he said. 'There's only one reason for trailing out to a God-forsaken swamp-hole like Cley, and that's to see the Chief.'

Retired from the fray or not, Lubbock was still to him the Chief and always would be.

'Half wrong,' said Tench. 'It's Lubbock right enough, but I've seen him already. He's down at the Riverside. I've just left him sinking his second pot of tea.'

McKenzie's eyes suddenly flickered with interest.

'So,' he said gently, 'what's he turned up this time?'

'He thinks he's uncovered another of his murders.'

'Does he now?'

'He does.'

43

'But you're doubtful about it.'

Tench was guarded.

'I have to be, haven't I?'

'But you think it's worth a dig.'

'There's just a chance that it might be.'

McKenzie eyed his newly promoted boss with a touch of solicitude.

'Look, Mike – sir,' he said. 'You're still feeling your way, so take a tip from a wily old codger like me who's worked with the Chief for God knows how many years. If he scents murder, you can bet your bottom dollar that that's what it is. He's not often been wrong.'

Tench nodded.

'I know. That's why we're going to take a wander down to Cley.'

He gave McKenzie an outline of events at Kettle Hill and Lubbock's suspicions.

'Since I've been back,' he said, 'I've done a bit of phoning. I've rung up Reg Ledward and the mortuary at Holt. He'll be getting Pashley's body sometime this evening. I've been in touch with the fire brigade, too. They received the first call at 2.31. That's a quarter of an hour after Lubbock got up and saw the glow in the sky, and four or five minutes before he saw the first flash of lightning at Cley. There were no other fires in the area last night, apart from a barn way out near Plumstead. So, if his clock was right and he was wide enough awake to read the time correctly, that seems to confirm at least the first of his suspicions. It looks as if the mill could well have been on fire before the lightning struck.'

'Fair enough,' said McKenzie. 'Who made the call?'

'It came from the Boldings at Morston Bottom Farm, but we need to know precisely what they saw and, as near as possible, when they saw it. I'm going over there. I'll drop you off at the ack-ack battery at Cley. I've spoken to the CO and made arrangements for you to see this lad Ellison. Get his statement in black and white. You know the form. I'll pick you up on the way back.'

Discretion had never been McKenzie's strong point.

'Seems to me,' he said, 'it might pay to let the Chief come in with us on this. He's got the expertise. He's genned up on windmills. Let him nose around and see what he can find.'

Tench gave a grin.

'Don't worry, Mac,' he said. 'He's doing that already. When he left us in March, he told me he didn't intend to spend the rest of his time in the same grisly company he'd shared all his life. But you know the old maxim: once a sleuth, always a sleuth. He'll not let go of this Kettle Hill case till he's ferreted out the truth, so we'd better get cracking before he presents us with all the sordid facts laid out on a platter.'

8

Morston Bottom Farm was on the edge of the marsh: a long, low straggle of buildings, of which the most conspicuous were the brick-and-flint barn with its pantile roof and the square farm cottage that faced a line of cowsheds and a wide cobbled yard.

Tench picked his way gingerly round patches of liquid cow dung, reached the door comparatively free from pollution, and pulled on the bell-toggle.

There was the sound of heavy boots clumping down some kind of stone-flagged passage, then the door was flung open with a rattle that betokened a swollen jamb, and he found himself facing a large, cheerful, ruddy-complexioned man with a day's growth of bristle.

'Evenin',' said the bristle. 'Can't say as we've met, but evenin' jus' the same. You lookin' fer Miss Dixon?'

Tench hurriedly denied any knowledge of the lady and presented his card.

'Detective Inspector Tench,' he said. 'It's nothing to worry about, but I'd like to have a word about the fire at Kettle Hill. You're Mr Bolding?'

The man nodded his head.

'Tha's right. Walter Bolding. Wife's name's Agnes.'

'You rang for the fire brigade.'

'Aye, that we did. Is there somethin' wrong?'

'Just checking on one or two facts,' said Tench.

The farmer stood aside.

'Then you'd best come inside.'

He led the way into a large back room where the whole of one wall was taken up by an ancient blackleaded cooking range. A fire roared up the chimney, a kettle steamed on the hob, there was a sound of sizzling and the smell of roast beef. Though the windows were wide open, it was stiflingly hot.

In the centre of the room was a heavy oak table with a spotless white cloth. Three places were laid for what was clearly intended to be a meal of some magnitude; and, kneeling on the floor with a cloth in her hand, peering into an oven, was a wispy, nondescript woman in an apron.

'Ag,' Bolding said, 'it's the police, about the fire.'

The woman stood up, closed the oven door, wiped her hands on the cloth and smoothed down her apron. Then she cleared a morning paper from what was visibly her husband's armchair, brushed a hillock of cigarette ash from the seat, and gestured towards it.

'Please sit down, Mr ...?'

'Tench, Ag,' said Bolding before Tench himself could answer. 'Tench. Like the fish. Detective Inspector Tench.'

The top of her head could only have reached the line of her husband's shoulder, but she swept him aside as if he were merely a feckless schoolboy. It was easy to see, deduced Tench, which of the two was the driving force at Morston Bottom Farm.

'You haven't much grace, Walter, have you?' she said. 'Fish, flesh or fowl, he's a guest in this house, so offer him a drink.'

Tench raised a hand.

'Not on duty,' he said, 'but thanks all the same.'

'Then you'll stop and take a bite with us,' she said very firmly. 'We always have a meal at this time of day. Walter, set another place.'

Tench was sorely tempted. The smell of roast beef wafted back a reminder of pre-war Sundays when his father had pierced the joint with a carving-fork and, sharpening the knife on a horn-handled steel, had sliced into the middle cut of the round. Since he'd left his parents' Lancashire home, he'd never seen a piece of beef to match those Sunday joints. Wartime rations, which still showed little sign of fading away, had put paid to such luxuries save on farms such as this.

He hadn't any doubt that Mrs Bolding's roast would combine size with succulence. It smelt magnificent. The pity was that he could never do it justice. Meg's haddock and egg had taken the edge off his appetite. Added to which, the twin blasts of heat from the fire and the oven were, second by second, killing any desire that he might have had for food. He could already feel the sweat standing out on his forehead.

'Thank you,' he said, 'but no. I've got other calls to make. Perhaps some other time.'

'He's only come to ask us some questions, Ag,' said Bolding in a plaintive tone of voice.

She ignored him. And, thought Tench, it wasn't the first time she'd done it.

'Young man,' she said, 'you look as if you could do with a good hot meal. Walter, lay that place. We can talk while we eat.'

Tench was tall and slim, and despite Lubbock's assertion that he was wasting away on a diet of nothing but coffee and sandwiches, was well content to be so.

'Oh, I'm healthy enough, Mrs Bolding,' he said. 'I'm what they call the wiry type. Swift and long-lasting.'

'That's as maybe.' She measured him against her husband's spreading paunch with obvious disapproval. 'But if you want to ask questions, you'll have to stay and eat. I'll have no time to think till the meal's on the table, and it's no good asking him.' She jerked her head towards the strangely complacent Walter, who was searching the drawer of a tall Welsh dresser for knife, fork and spoon. 'He'd have slept through it all – thunder and lightning, flames and fire-bells – if I hadn't dragged him out of bed.

'And anyway,' she added, dealing the *coup de grâce*, 'you'll be needing to speak to Miss Dixon about it, and she won't be back for another half-hour.'

Tench remembered Bolding's greeting as he'd stood on the doorstep.

'Who's Miss Dixon?' he asked, taking out a handkerchief and mopping his brow.

Walter roused himself from the table-setting.

'Lodger,' he said. 'Temporary like.'

'She's more than a lodger,' said his wife, 'and well you know it.'

It seemed that poor Walter could do nothing right, but he remained to the end uncomplainingly cheerful.

'You tell him then, Ag.'

She turned back to Tench.

'Miss Dixon's an artist,' she told him with pride. 'She's been painting a picture of Kettle Hill mill.'

47

9

When, an hour and a half later, he started up the car and drove away from Morston Bottom Farm on the coast road to Cley, Mike Tench had not only endured the fiery furnace of the Boldings' spacious parlour and steeled himself to consume sufficient roast beef to meet the demands of social etiquette, he'd also acquired a certain amount of information which he felt might, or possibly might not, be useful.

The Boldings' account of what had happened the night before added little, except as confirmation, to what he already knew. Their bedroom was on the northern side of the farm, overlooking the marsh, the opposite side of the house to Kettle Hill. They'd gone to bed about eleven o'clock and both had slept soundly till Mrs Bolding had been disturbed by the wind rattling a cluster of milking pails that were stacked against the wall of the cobbled yard. She'd lain there a while, had possibly drifted off again to sleep, but the rattling had persisted, waking her again; and she was just about to nudge Walter and urge him to get up and deal with the nuisance, when the room had been lit by a brilliant flash of lightning and then a clap of thunder, right overhead. She'd switched on the light and looked at the clock. It was twenty-five past two. Walter was lying on his back and snoring peacefully as if nothing had happened, so, in sheer exasperation, she'd slapped him on the chest with the flat of her hand and told him to go down and put the pails in the cowshed.

He'd grumbled mildly, but he'd gone. She'd heard him fumble his way downstairs and unlock the front door; then he'd called out to her that the mill was on fire. She'd slipped her arms into a dressing-gown and gone down herself. It was raining heavily by that time, and she'd stayed at the door for a moment, looking at the flames in the sky at Kettle Hill. Then she'd dragged her mackintosh from its hook in the hall, pushed Walter aside and set out across the yard, shouting to him not to be such a load of old squit, but to get on the phone and tell the fire brigade at Holt.

'Tha's right,' Walter said, still as cheerful as ever. 'She call me a load o' squit, so I do as she say.'

48

Tench pondered for a moment, then turned to Mrs Bolding.

'You said you stood at the door, and there were flames from the mill.'

'More ner flames,' Walter said. He seemed determined not to be snuffed out of the conversation. 'Look to me like a bloody big bonfire. Ragin' away it were. Hull mill were like a grate full o' red-hot coals.'

Tench kept his eyes fixed on Mrs Bolding.

'Is that right?'

'Aye,' she said grudgingly, 'that's right enough. The sky was full of sparks, and flames were shooting out of the little slit-windows.'

'So you wouldn't think it was the flash of lightning – the one you saw – that set fire to the mill.'

She shrugged, tight-lipped.

'Could have been, I suppose, but it didn't look that way. Seemed to me it had already been burning for a while.'

Tench shifted his glance to the girl on the opposite side of the table.

'And what do you think, Miss Dixon?' he said.

She'd arrived promptly in time for the meal: a small, trim figure in a white cotton blouse and a printed skirt, and one that Tench had welcomed as a pleasurable contrast to the lumbering Walter and his wisp-like, disillusioned Ag. There was nothing lumbering or disillusioned about Hilary Dixon, nor was she wisp-like in the sense that a breath of wind might have blown her away. Small as she was, she had shapely legs, a slim waist, and, as Mac would have said, plenty up top: so much so that now, as he turned his eyes towards her, he found it difficult to concentrate his gaze on her face. Not that that was unpleasant. It was, on the contrary, as delightful as the rest of her: delicate bones, full lips, a straight nose, bright, intelligent eyes, and dark hair swinging in a pony-tail at the back of her neck. Now, as she turned towards him, it swung again provocatively.

'What do you think, Miss Dixon? You sleep on the side that faces the mill.'

She smiled at him.

'Yes, I do, but I'm afraid I saw nothing at all of the fire. I remember vaguely hearing the sound of thunder, but I simply

49

turned over and went back to sleep. It was only this morning, when Mrs Bolding brought me a cup of tea, that I heard about the mill ... You see,' she added, 'I did a bit of painting and went to bed late.'

'How late was that?'

'When I switched off the light, it was ten to two. I know that was the time, because I always wind my wrist-watch last thing at night. There was no sign of a fire then.'

Tench brushed the back of his hand across his forehead. It came away wet.

'How d'you know that?'

'I went to the window and drew back the curtains. I like to sleep with a window open and I took it off the hook, but the wind was so strong I had to close it again.'

'Tell him about the noise, dear,' Mrs Bolding said.

'Aye,' echoed Walter, 'tell 'im about the noise. Reckon tha' were a bit rum. Could well mean somethin'. Tell 'im about it, gul.'

'Well' – she hesitated – 'it may not be that important. It could have happened before, and I mightn't have heard it, but last night the wind was blowing towards the farm and it carried the sound straight across the fields.'

'What kind of a sound?' asked Tench.

'Difficult to describe,' she said. 'A sort of grating noise. The sound you get if you rub two pieces of sandpaper together. But it must have been loud, because I heard it quite clearly.'

'You didn't hear a bell?'

'No.' She looked puzzled. 'Why? Should I have done?'

'Maybe not,' said Tench. 'You'd be too far away.'

'But the noise. It could have something to do with the fire?'

Tench nodded.

'Yes, it could. It could mean there was something wrong with the mill.'

'There you are,' said Walter. 'I say it do, Ag, an' you say it be nothin'. Not worth mentionin'. Tell 'er what it were, Mr Tench, sir. You tell 'er.'

He leaned forward, half in triumph, half in eager expectation, and swept the knife from his plate. It clattered to the floor.

'Clumsy,' said Ag. 'Really, Mr Tench, he should know better than to ask.' She rounded on Walter. 'You don't think the inspector's going to tell you all his secrets, do you? He just hasn't the time. He's got other calls to make. He told us so, didn't he? Now get the table cleared, then you and I can wash up. Miss Dixon'll see the inspector out to his car.'

She turned back to Tench.

'You enjoyed the roast beef?'

'Excellent, Mrs Bolding. Thank you very much. It was done to a turn.'

'It's the oven,' she said. 'You don't get many ovens like that one, these days. All these new-fangled electrical things. No use at all. Get the meat in, and they cut off the power. Wouldn't have one if you paid me. Not even if one was delivered to the door ... Watch those plates, Walter, or there'll be nothing left to eat off.'

Walter remained still as buoyant as ever. He stacked the plates noisily.

'I'll do that, Ag,' he said. 'I be allus very careful. I ent bruck a plate since this time las' week.'

10

Out in the yard, Tench strove to disentangle the Alice-in-Wonderland world of the Boldings from his normal one of mayhem and what, in this instance, might possibly be murder. He mopped his brow with a handkerchief already far from dry, ran it round inside his collar and then wiped his hands.

'Hot in there,' he said.

'You get used to it.' Miss Dixon closed the farmhouse door.

'Yes, I suppose so.' Tench doubted privately whether, in his case, that would ever be possible. 'They're an oddly assorted couple, the Boldings, aren't they?'

'Lovely people,' she said. 'Walter's a dear, and though Agnes barks a lot, she rarely ever bites. He's a bit uncoordinated is Walter. That might be dangerous if he had to work with machinery, but he's only got the cows. She tells him what to do, and he always does it. When it comes to making hay, she does the cutting; she can swing a pretty scythe; but even so, last June, he drove a pitchfork through his foot.'

Tench needed to know more, and not about the Boldings.

'You're a student?' he said.

51

She nodded.

'Yes. The Slade.'

'On vacation?'

'For the moment. I'm due back in a fortnight.'

'And you've come up here to paint.'

'Water-colours,' she said. 'I wanted to do landscapes, and Norfolk's perfect for that. Wide-open skies and a bright, silver light; shadows, mists and marshes, not to mention the windmills. The light's wonderful here. It tones down harsh colours to limpid shades of pastel. Lends itself to water-colours: thin strokes of the brush and delicate tints. I first thought about coming late in the spring, and a friend of mine in Norwich told me about the Boldings wanting to let a room, so I took it for the summer. I've been up here three months.'

'Painting windmills?'

'Among other things.'

'You've been painting Kettle Hill?'

'Yes, for the last month. Off and on, that is. Luckily, I'd almost finished.' She was suddenly sombre. 'It's a terrible business, isn't it?'

Tench was silent for a moment.

'Did you know Simon Pashley?'

She hesitated.

'Yes and no. I met him, of course, when I first started painting. Told him I'd like to do a picture of the mill. He seemed pleased about that. Said if there was anything he could do to help, he'd be only too glad to do it. Well, there wasn't much he could do. I did most of my work out on the heath, a good distance from the mill, but I dropped in a couple of times for a cup of tea when I'd finished for the day. Once he showed me round. We got on well together. I liked him, yes, but I didn't really know him.'

They stood by the car.

'Sometime,' he said, 'I'd like to see the picture.'

'It's not very good. Water-colour's a particularly difficult technique, and I'm still only learning.'

'Even so, I'd like to see it.'

'OK,' she said. 'I'll show you. If you promise not to laugh.'

'I promise.'

'Then you'll have to come round the back.'

She led the way to the other side of the farm. Parked by one of the windows was an Austin Seven that had seen better days.

'I call it Wallis,' she said. 'It was born in the year of the abdication, but it still coughs its way around, and there aren't many hills in Norfolk to make it breathless.'

She opened one of the doors. On the back seat were a folding stool, a collapsible easel, a drawing-board, a wooden paintbox and a number of sheets of water-colour paper. She pulled one of them out and handed it to him.

'There you are,' she said. 'Don't say I didn't warn you.'

He held it out at arm's length.

'But it's good,' he said.

'Not very.'

As she'd told him, she'd painted the mill from a distance: a reference point amid a wilderness of heathland set against a high, wide, cirrus-drifting sky; and though his knowledge of art was limited, it seemed clear to Tench that she'd managed to capture that delicate silver light that she'd spoken about with such obvious fervour.

'If it were mine,' he said, 'I'd be happy to have it framed and hang it on the wall.'

'Then do that.' She laughed. 'Take it away with you and keep it. It's yours.'

'But surely you don't want to part with it.'

'I'll do a better one soon,' she said. 'Go on. Take it.'

'You'll sign it?'

She laughed again.

'Don't flatter me. I'll maybe begin to think I'm an artist after all.'

'You're far too modest.' He held the picture out again. 'I like the lorry parked at the side of the mill. That's a good touch. It conveys the right impression. Shows that Kettle Hill was a working mill ... I suppose it's Pashley's lorry?'

'No,' she said, 'it isn't.'

There was something in the way she spoke that made him glance at her swiftly.

'Look,' she said suddenly. 'Let's get things straight. You're a detective inspector.'

'Yes.'

'That means you're CID.'

'Right.'

'And CID stands for Criminal Investigation Department.'

'Right again. You're brilliant.'

She frowned.

'Don't make fun of me. This is serious.'

He stared at her for a moment.

'Yes,' he said, 'I can see it is. I'm sorry. What's the trouble?'

She took the picture from him and put it back in the car.

'You can pick that up later. Let's take a little walk. There's a causeway at the back of the farm that runs out across the marsh.'

Double summer time had yielded, as usual, a long sunlit evening, but now the light was fading and, as the sun began to set, it flooded the clouds above the sea with ragged bands of colour. They rose from the dead man's arm of Blakeney Point in streamers of orange, grey and lemon, impenetrable black and crystalline blue that turned the tidal creeks into ribbons of gold.

She said nothing for a while, and Tench was content to wait; then she stopped without warning, curled herself down on the fringe of the causeway, smoothed out her skirt and patted the ground beside her.

'Come and sit down,' she said. 'It's dry enough here.'

He lowered himself on to the grass, his feet dangling over the edge of the marsh.

'Someday,' she said, 'I'll paint one of these sunsets, when I've learnt the trick of blending all the colours together.'

'That's difficult?'

'Yes. You have to overlay them, then grade them so that one blends into another. Clouds are frightfully difficult.'

He nodded.

'Yes, I can imagine they would be.'

She plucked a spear of grass and twisted it round her fingers.

'I've got enough sense', she said, 'to know the police don't send a detective inspector to ask questions about a fire unless there's something suspicious. D'you think that someone started it? Deliberately, I mean.'

Tench was guarded.

'It's possible. I wouldn't go any further than that.'

'But wouldn't that be murder?'

'It would if the intention was to kill young Pashley.'

54

'And was it?'

He shrugged.

'We don't know enough to say. It may all have been an accident. We've no firm evidence to prove that it wasn't.'

'But you are trying to find it.'

'We're just making inquiries.'

There was silence. Tench waited.

'He was a nice boy,' she said. 'I liked him a lot. Who on earth would want to kill him?'

'Your guess is as good as mine.'

She stared at the sky, dissolving now into darkness.

'You never know,' she said. 'Mine might be a little bit nearer the mark ... I think perhaps I'd better tell you about that lorry in the picture.'

11

It was two days before the fire, she said, late in the afternoon. She was packing up her equipment ready to carry it across to the car, when she'd seen the lorry grinding over the crest of the hill. It must have come from the main road, and was following the track that she herself used. When it reached the mill, it pulled to a halt, the door was flung open and a man clambered out. The mill door was ajar, but he didn't bother to knock. He kicked it open with his foot and walked straight in. She heard him shout Pashley's name, but after that there was silence.

She carried her easel to the car and packed it away; then the rest of her gear; and she was just about to get in and start up the engine when she heard a lot more shouting, and the man she'd seen before stumped out of the mill. He seemed to be in a temper, and when he reached the lorry he yelled, 'I'll get you for this, Pashley. See if I don't.' Then he slammed the lorry door shut, and drove off at speed down the track to the road.

'How close to the mill were you?' Tench wanted more facts.

'A couple of hundred yards away. Something like that.'

'So you didn't see the number plate on the lorry?'

She shook her head.

'No.'

'What colour was it?'

'Black, or dark blue. It was difficult to tell. It was covered in dust. Looked as if it hadn't been cleaned for a while. I suppose it might even have been a dark green.'

'You say it looked dusty. Anything else about it? How big was it?'

'Not very big. Just the normal size, I'd say. Low sides and a tailboard.'

'Did it look new?'

'No, it was pretty old. One of the mudguards was loose, and it rattled a lot. Creaked a bit too, as if the springs were wearing out.'

Tench nodded.

'Fair enough. Now what about the man? Was he tall or short?'

'Tall. Very tall. If I had to make a guess, well over six foot and broad with it too. Much bigger than Simon. A rough sort of chap. Dark hair, I think.'

'And how was he dressed?'

'What looked like a pair of blue dungarees. Light blue, but pretty filthy. Looked oil-stained to me.'

'Someone from a garage?'

'Could have been, I suppose.' She looked at him, troubled. 'D'you think you'll be able to find him?' she said.

'Don't see why not.' Tench seemed confident enough. 'Must be a local chap, and there can't be many six-footers with oil-stained dungarees who have connections with Pashley and drive a dusty old lorry with creaking springs and a broken mudguard. I reckon we'll be able to trace him without too much trouble ... He said "Pashley", not "Simon"? You're sure about that?'

'Oh, yes, it was "Pashley".'

'Sounds as if he wasn't very close to him then. More a business acquaintance.'

'He wasn't in any mood to use Christian names.'

'No, maybe not. Did he see you, d'you think?'

'No, I'm pretty sure he didn't. He never looked my way. All his attention was focused on the mill.'

'And you didn't see Pashley?'

She tossed her head again.

'Not a sign of him. He didn't even come to the door.'

'And you didn't call in to see him?'

'No, I didn't somehow think he'd be in the right frame of mind to entertain visitors. I just drove past the mill and straight back to the farm.'

'You didn't see him next day? Didn't speak to him about it?'

'The day before the fire? Yesterday, you mean? No, I didn't do any painting out at Kettle Hill. I needed some more colours, so I drove into Norwich. But even if I'd seen him, I don't think I'd have mentioned it. After all, it wasn't really any of my business. At least, I thought it wasn't. Now, I'm not so sure. If I'd talked to him, he might have told me who the man was.'

'It's not your fault,' he said. 'You mustn't blame yourself for it.'

'Oh, I know it's stupid.' She looked away from him, out across the faded ribbons of water. 'But since I heard about Simon, I haven't been able to get it out of my head. I forced myself to drive down and look at the mill. That was this afternoon. But when I reached the gate at the bottom of the track, I just sat in the car. I knew I didn't want to go any closer, so I drove on to Blakeney and spent a couple of hours sketching boats at the quay. But it didn't do any good. I kept thinking to myself: if only I'd stopped and asked him what the trouble was...'

'... He mightn't have told you anything at all.'

'I suppose not,' she said ruefully, 'but I'm glad you came to the farm. I knew I had to talk to someone, and you're the right person.'

'Because I'm a policeman?'

She turned back towards him.

'You're fishing for compliments, Inspector,' she said; 'but no, not entirely.'

'Then thank you for the vote of confidence.'

'Just find him,' she said softly. 'Find him, for me.'

12

At much the same time as Tench reached for the bell at Morston Bottom Farm, Lubbock parked his three-wheeler at the foot of Kettle Hill where a second track led from the road to the mill.

Here there was a field gate, and swinging it open he began to climb the slope, scanning the ground with some care as he climbed. Once or twice he stopped, squatted down on his haunches and examined the surface a little more closely; then, reaching the top, he ambled slowly round the blackened ruin of the mill till he came to a point where something at his feet seemed to catch his attention. Bending down again, he ran a finger across the ground, and then examined its tip with undisguised satisfaction.

Wiping his finger on the grass, he straightened up and made his way towards the cottage. Adjoining it was a solid brick-and-flint building once used as a cartlodge, where Pashley garaged his lorry and the old Humber Snipe that he'd inherited from his father. Hauling back the double doors, he stepped inside and looked round. Both vehicles were still in place, parked side by side, the lorry half loaded with sacks of flour that Pashley had clearly intended to deliver; but Lubbock seemed little interested in these. He took a flashlight from his pocket, wormed himself down on the earthen floor, wriggled under the lorry and played the beam around. Then, easing himself backwards with the flat of his hands and a series of grunts and groans, he shuffled round to the Humber and repeated the process.

Once again he seemed content with the results of his inspection. Standing up, he brushed himself down, closed the cartlodge doors and crossed to the cottage. Trying the latch on the heavy wooden door and finding it still unlocked, he pushed his way inside. Familiar with the layout from his previous visits, he walked down the narrow corridor that bisected the house and turned left into the parlour. The room was sparsely furnished: a mahogany table with a couple of chairs; a black leather settee; a half-empty bookcase; a side table with a wind-up gramophone, a small stack of records and a cabinet radio; and, under the window, a knee-hole writing-desk.

There was no sign that the room had been in any way disturbed. The brick-tile floor was swept clean, the two rugs still in place; the polished top of the table held nothing but two copies of *Picture Post* tossed idly at one end, and the writing-desk was clear of all save a blotting-pad and half a dozen letters shelved in one of the otherwise empty pigeon-holes.

Lubbock made for the desk. He seemed to know exactly what he was looking for, and where he was likely to find it. Ignoring the letters, he pulled open one of the drawers at the side of the knee-hole, took out a ledger bound in red rexine, and carried it to the table.

He sat there a while, turning the pages; then he drew a pencil and a folded wad of paper from his inside pocket, and began to jot down a list of names and addresses. This took him at least a quarter of an hour, at the end of which time he checked them by once again working through the ledger. When he reached the last name, he underscored it heavily; then, returning the pencil and paper to his pocket, he slid the book back in the drawer of the desk.

He riffled through the letters, but apparently found nothing to stir his curiosity. He then filled his pipe, lit it and set off to search through the rest of the house. He spent a long time in the bedroom, sitting beside the bed, seemingly deep in thought, before he heaved himself up again and made his way downstairs.

He then retraced his steps along the narrow hallway, moved outside and closed the door behind him. Trudging stolidly round to the back of the cottage, he bent down and removed a loose brick from the wall. From behind it he took a key, and going back to the front, turned it in the lock and then dropped it in his pocket.

He spent much time after that inspecting the mill, shaking the sack chain, peering closely at the toppled millstones, and rooting among the charred timbers that littered the floor. A casual observer, walking past the mill, might have seen him, shading his eyes against the sun, staring up at the blackened stumps of the sail stocks before he turned away and headed for what, in earlier, slower, more methodical days, had been the mill stables.

The old stalls had been torn down some years before, and Pashley had used the space as a workshop for doing such repairs as he could handle himself. There was a bench and a lathe, and a variety of metal tools hung from hooks on the walls. The corners were cluttered. One was stacked with timbers, reared at an angle; another with steel rods, iron bands and cog wheels of various sizes; a third piled high with layers of empty flour sacks. None of these appeared to hold much interest for Lubbock, but when he reached the last corner, he stood for quite a time gazing down at what seemed to be a tumbled heap of stones.

They were all of uniform size, rectangular blocks, the sides roughly a foot by eighteen inches, and some six inches thick. They'd clearly been stacked in piles, waiting to be used for some purpose or other, but now they lay scattered on the floor of the shed as if someone had hurriedly dragged the piles apart and never bothered to restack them in an orderly fashion. Lubbock, so it seemed, knew only too well the limitations of his strength. He made no attempt to lift them, but he counted them carefully, puffing away at his pipe with a kind of controlled ferocity. Then he turned on his heel and plodded out of the shed.

For another ten minutes he prowled round the mill, poking among the debris and here and there stooping to examine the ground; then, evidently satisfied with what he'd discovered, he knocked out his pipe, walked back down the track, wound himself awkwardly behind the wheel of his car, and drove off towards Cley.

He stopped only once – at a phone box in Blakeney – and while Tench's knife and fork were still hovering fitfully above the Boldings' roast beef, he unlocked the door of Umzinto Cottage, brewed himself a pot of tea, flopped down in the armchair, drank half a cupful and promptly fell asleep.

Tench received the message when he and McKenzie got back to Norwich.

The desk sergeant stopped him.

'Mr Lubbock rang, sir.'

Tench gave a barely audible sigh.

'What did he want?'

'Said would you be free tomorrow? As early as possible. Needs to meet you at some place called Kettle Hill. Seems he's got one or two things there to show you.'

'Wants to take me out on a guided tour, does he?'

The sergeant gave a grin.

'Sounded very much like it, sir. Said to be sure you got the message tonight.'

Tench took a deep breath.

'Right then, Sergeant. Get him on the phone and put the call through. I'll be up in my office.'

He turned to McKenzie.

'I told you, Mac,' he said. 'The hounds are out already.'

60

2

WEDNESDAY

'Then read my fancies; they will stick like burrs.'
Bunyan, *The Pilgrim's Progress*

1

Lubbock unlocked the cottage door and handed the key to Tench.

'It wasn't locked yesterday,' he said. 'Locked it myself. That's his spare key. Kept it behind a brick round the back of the house. Told me about it last week in case he wasn't in when I happened to call. You'd better take charge of it.'

Tench dropped it in his pocket.

'What about the other one?'

'Upstairs with all the rest. Found them in a drawer. You'd better take them, too.'

He led the way inside.

'Everything's in order,' he said. 'Pashley tidied up, then it seems he went to bed. Come upstairs and see.'

'Now,' he went on, waving a hand round the bedroom, 'take a look at this. Shirt and underclothes on the chair, trousers draped across the back. The bed's been slept in, but the sheet's thrown back. There's no sign of pyjamas, or of a dressing-gown. Looks as if he might well have left in a hurry.'

'So,' said Tench, 'you've a theory?'

'No, laddie, I haven't. Theories are for later, when we've got more facts.' Lubbock was almost curt in his assessment. 'All we can possibly hope to do at the moment is toss around a few random ideas. My guess would be that young Pashley went to bed, and when he heard the alarm bell he threw back the bedclothes, slipped on a dressing-gown – that is, if he had one – and dashed across to the mill. That would explain why the cottage door was left unlocked.'

'And after that?'

'Who knows? We haven't enough evidence yet to be able to say, but with a wee bit of luck Ledward and forensics may provide a few clues. You haven't heard anything from them?'

'There was nothing when I left. We'll probably hear something later this morning.'

Lubbock scratched his nose.

'Well, it's no good rushing Reg Ledward,' he said. 'He'll take his own time. Now, let's go back downstairs.'

He led the way into the parlour, opened the desk drawer and pulled out the ledger.

'You'd better take this away with you as well.' He laid it on the table. 'This is where Pashley kept a note of his orders. He was pretty meticulous about that sort of thing. If you look here, you'll see.' He flicked back the pages. 'He wrote down the date, the name and address of the customer, and the quantity of flour that the buyer required. Now' – he pulled the folded wad of paper from his inside pocket – 'it was your idea that he could have had a late order: one that caught him unawares and meant he had to work the mill late into the night. Well, I've made a list here of all his regular customers. There are something like a couple of dozen altogether, and the orders are steady. They don't vary much from one week to the next. They certainly haven't varied over the last few days, but there is one new name.' He turned to the last page. 'Here it is. Wickstead. Warborough Road, Stiffkey. That's roughly three miles away towards Wells. It seems he made the order the day before the fire, but it isn't a very big one. It's nothing that Pashley couldn't have met from his stocks. It certainly wouldn't have forced him to run the mill at night . . . All the same, it might be worthwhile to have a word with Mr Wickstead. I've checked in the phone book. He's a baker and confectioner. Small business, I'd imagine. Stiffkey's only a village. It's pretty clear he didn't normally order his flour from Pashley, so it might be interesting to know who his regular supplier was and why he suddenly decided to change. Anyway, laddie, that's your business. It's up to you to decide. Now let's go outside.'

He trudged doggedly ahead past the ruins of the mill; then, reaching the end of the track from the road, he pointed to the ground.

'Look down there,' he said. 'Oil. Quite a lot of it, too, and there's a trail of it all the way up from the road.'

Tench bent down and examined the blackened patch.

'Looks reasonably fresh. Dropped in the last few days?'

'Can't claim to be a forensic expert,' said Lubbock, 'but I'd say so, yes. The rain on the night of the fire was pretty heavy, but it didn't last long. It'd take a hell of a lot of rain to make an impression on thick stuff like that.'

'Couldn't have come from the mill, could it?'

Lubbock shook his head.

'No. Too far away.'

'What about the fire engine?'

'Didn't park here. It was way over there.' He pointed behind Tench. 'Fifty yards away at least. And the fire brigade keeps its engines regularly serviced. Has to. You wouldn't find one of them dripping oil like that.'

Tench straightened up.

'What did Pashley use to deliver his flour?'

'You mean did he have a lorry? Yes, laddie, he did, a new one; and a grand old Snipe saloon he couldn't possibly use. It'd have gobbled up his monthly ration of petrol in less than a week. They're both in the old cartlodge next to the cottage. Neither drops oil. I've crawled underneath them and had a good look.'

The vision of Lubbock's ample buttocks protruding from underneath a flour-dusted lorry was enough to bring a flicker of a smile to Tench's face. He looked away swiftly, down at the oil.

'So ... ' he said.

'So, laddie, it seems that Pashley's had a visitor. Recently, too. Maybe just before the rain when the ground was still hard. The only tyre marks on the track are those of the fire engine. They're clear enough. But some other vehicle's driven up to the mill, and it's my guess that the driver must have lived fairly close. If he didn't, then he couldn't have hoped to get home. He was losing oil too fast.'

'It's odds on then that it was something pretty old. Another lorry perhaps?'

'Could have been anything.' Lubbock pulled out his pipe. 'A lorry, a van, maybe a car, even one of those ancient dilapidated buses that trail round the villages selling farm produce. We've no means yet of telling.'

Tench didn't look at him. He kept his gaze firmly fixed on the oil.

'My own guess,' he said slowly, savouring the moment, 'would be a very old lorry. One with creaking springs and a broken mudguard. And caked up with dust.'

2

'Now,' said Lubbock, 'let's go through this again.' They sat opposite one another at the cottage table. 'This Dixon girl ... She's reliable, is she?'

'Difficult to tell.' Tench gave a shrug. 'You know how it is when people volunteer to give information. You've just got to take them on trust to begin with. We've no other evidence to corroborate what she said, and from all I can see we're not likely to get any ... She seems honest enough. That's as much as I can say.'

'A tasty bit of goods, is she? Full of rich promise?'

'Yes, I think I'd be prepared to go as far as that.'

Lubbock shook his head.

'Young women,' he said moodily. 'Most of them make damned unreliable witnesses. Trouble is, laddie, they can't be objective. Prone to all kinds of illogical emotions. Tend to lose their heads completely when they get into court. Nothing but easy meat to a good defence counsel. He'll pick them off in no time like paralysed rabbits. I've seen it happen too often ... Would this girl of yours be a paralysed rabbit?'

Tench grinned.

'No, I'm pretty sure she wouldn't. She's far too self-possessed.'

'That can be just as fatal.' Lubbock seemed sunk in gloom. 'Ah, well, we'll just have to take her at her word ... Now, she saw this lorry.'

'That's what she says.'

'And the driver threatened Pashley. What were his words again?'

'"I'll get you for this, Pashley. See if I don't."'

'But get him for what? That's the root of the problem. Any ideas?'

'No, not the faintest.'

'Well, let's put it aside for the moment then. Time enough for it later. What have we got so far? A case of suspected arson that might well be murder, and a man who makes threats against the possible victim. That makes him a prime suspect. Wouldn't you agree?'

'If the mill was fired deliberately.'

66

'And you're still not sure it was.'

'Not entirely, no. I think we need something more than mere speculation.'

'Right. Facts are what count. Fair enough, laddie. So what d'you plan to do?'

Lubbock, once again, was all ruthless good cheer. He puffed at his pipe with a near-demented fury, and the smoke swirled away in ever-thickening clouds. The sensation, thought Tench, was like sitting in the heart of a kippering shed.

'It's being done,' he said. 'There's a team out already, searching for the lorry, and once we find that, we'll be on to the chap who drove it.'

'Six foot, you said?'

'Well over six foot. Something of a hulk. Dark hair, and dressed in blue dungarees stained with what looked like oil.'

'Maybe that's a link. Mucked about with his lorry, wiped his hands on the dungarees.'

'Or he could, quite simply, be working in a garage.'

'Yes, of course he could. And, in any case, if I were searching, the first thing I'd do would be to check all the garages. It's an even bet that that lorry's in dock. He'd need to get that oil leak fixed, and fixed fast.'

'Not to worry, sir,' said Tench. 'I think we'll lay hands on him before the day's out.'

Lubbock's pipe began to bubble. The sound was almost obscene.

'Let's hope so,' he said. 'But you may need to do a little bit more than that, laddie.'

Tench looked at him, said nothing. Lubbock crossed to the desk, brought back a battered ashtray, and poked inside the bowl of his smouldering briar with an equally battered penknife.

'Oh, you'll find him, this menacing lout of yours,' he said. 'I've no doubt about that. He and his lorry won't stay hidden for long. They'll stand out like black teeth at a dentists' convention. Someone must have seen them. Yes, as you say, you'll probably have him before the day's out, and that'll be one prime suspect unearthed. But it still leaves the other.'

'The other?'

'Yes, mine. The lorry man's yours. Mine could be someone entirely different ... You see, laddie, there's a slight complication.'

'You know what?' said Tench. 'I thought perhaps there might be.'

'There always is. It's a fact of life. You know that as well as I do. There's always something crops up that turns a case upside down. You think you've got it sorted, and then it goes all haywire and you've got to start again.'

'So enlighten me.' Tench rested his elbows on the table. 'What exactly is this slight complication?'

'Stones,' Lubbock said.

'That's a cryptic answer if ever I heard one.'

'It's intended to be. You're supposed to say, "What stones?"'

Tench raised his eyebrows.

'All right,' he said. 'What stones?'

Lubbock didn't answer till he'd knocked out his pipe, scoured it with the penknife and stowed it away in his pocket.

'Come across to the stables,' he said. 'I'll show you what I mean.'

They stood, looking down at the scattered blocks of stone.

'There were three dozen of these.' Lubbock jabbed out a finger. 'Now there's only about a dozen.'

Tench made a swift count.

'Thirteen,' he said.

'Thirteen, fourteen. What the hell does it matter? Most of them have gone.'

'You mean they've been stolen?'

Lubbock's lips tightened: the old, familiar sign of growing impatience.

'Well,' he said, 'they were all still here the evening before the fire. I know because I saw them. So, unless they've sprouted wings and flown off across the fields, yes, laddie, someone's stolen them.'

'Has the door been forced?'

'No, but yesterday all the doors were unlocked. This one and the cartlodge as well as the cottage. Probably Simon hadn't locked them. Sometimes he didn't. He was careless that way. Said what was the point? The nearest house was Morston Bottom Farm. That was a mile away, and the Boldings weren't likely to want anything he'd got.'

'The granary?'

'He never used it. Never kept enough stock.'

'Did anyone else know about that key behind the brick?'

'Not so far as I know.'

'But somebody stole the stones.'

'Yes. And it couldn't have been your chap in the leaking lorry.'

'Why not?'

'Try to lift one.'

Tench bent down. With a struggle he managed to raise one of the blocks a foot from the ground, then he staggered and let it fall. Lubbock watched him with satisfaction.

'I don't suppose you'd like to carry one of those a hundred yards.'

'Not if you paid me.' Tench flexed his back in obvious discomfort.

'No,' Lubbock said. 'It'd take an exceptionally strong man to do it. And even he'd be flat out before he'd done it very often. He'd be mad to try and do it a couple of dozen times. So work it out, laddie. Your lorry was parked at least a hundred yards away. If your man had been thinking of loading up those stones, he'd have driven it up here and parked it right outside the stables. But there isn't a spot of oil anywhere near. Take a walk round and see. No, this is my man. He's a different one, so he's Suspect Number Two.'

Tench was determined not to yield without a fight.

'From all accounts,' he argued, 'this roughneck of mine was strong enough to do it. He could have had another lorry.'

'If he did have another, he wouldn't have been likely to drive over here in a rattling old wreck spraying pints of oil.'

Tench sighed.

'Maybe not.'

He stared at the tumbled blocks.

'But why on earth', he said, 'would anyone want to steal a load of old stones? Who'd want them, anyway?'

'Ah, well,' said Lubbock, 'that's another tale.' He pulled an ancient gunmetal watch from his pocket. 'Five to eleven, laddie. Time for a cup of tea. Let's go back to Umzinto. I'll explain it all there.'

3

Lubbock downed his tea.

Tench sipped his coffee.

'I suppose', he said, 'this is another of those things that can only be explained by someone who knows about the working of windmills.'

'Let's just say,' said Lubbock, 'that without my undoubted expertise you'd never have noticed that anything was wrong.'

'That's true.' Tench graciously acknowledged the debt. 'So what is it that's wrong? What's the subtle meaning that attaches itself to a pile of apparently useless stones?'

Lubbock poured himself yet another cup of tea.

'Millstones,' he said. 'Let's begin with them. You see, laddie, it's like this. A windmill's a living creature. She's got a heart and lungs, and she also has a belly.'

'She?'

'Yes, "she". Windmills are feminine, just like ships. And women have bellies, just as men do. Have you never heard of a belly-dancer, lad? A girl who performs an erotic dance with abdominal contortions? Or was your academic training so utterly cloistered that you slammed the door firmly on a wiggling navel?'

'We had our moments,' Tench confessed.

'I'm delighted to hear it,' Lubbock said drily. 'Now let's put it like this. A windmill has lungs. They're her sails that catch the wind. She has a heart that beats. That's her drive mechanism: the wheels, cogs and shafts. And she also has a belly. That's her millstones that keep on grinding down the grain. If her belly's full, she's happy. If it's empty, she complains. She gets the rumbles, just like all of us do. When a mill's running true, when she's fed with grain, the runner stone sings in its wooden casing like one of those tops we used to have when we were children. A miller can tell that all's well with his mill by the singing of the stones. But if she runs empty or the bearings run dry, if she hasn't got food and drink, then she grouches and grumbles. The bearings begin to moan, the stones rasp and grate. The mill doesn't sing, she cries out in pain. That was what your Dixon girl heard the other night. She wouldn't normally have heard it from so far away, but the wind was blowing straight towards Morston Bottom Farm. And that, according to her, was at ten to two. A significant time, Tench. More than half an hour before the lightning flash. You follow me? Yes?'

Tench had sat through too many sessions like this to fret over-much at his old Chief's methods. Lubbock, like his longtime associate, Ledward, wasn't to be rushed. He'd take his own time.

70

This was just the prologue. The tale, at any moment, would begin to unwind.

'I'm listening,' he said with an admirable patience.

'Right, then. Millstones. The singing stones.' Lubbock launched himself on a tide of exposition. 'Generally speaking, here in this country, they come in two kinds. The first kind are Peak stones. They're quarried all in one piece from the gritstone bands in the Derbyshire Peak, and they're used mainly for grist milling: that's grinding barley and maize for animal feed. For good-quality flour, you need another kind: burr stones. French burrs they're called because they come from France, the hardest and best of them from a bed of stone that stretches roughly from Paris to Rheims. They're not quarried in one piece, but built up in sections from blocks that are known as panneaux or panes. When you see a millstone made of French burrs, it looks rather like a jigsaw puzzle. The sections are cemented together and smoothed over at the back with plaster of Paris. Then iron bands are fitted round them, like on a cart-wheel, to stop them from bursting apart when they run.'

Tench began to see the light.

'And those in the stables are blocks of French burr?'

'Yes, laddie, they're panes. Cut them into sections and fit them together, and you've got a millstone made of French burrs. The trouble is that nowadays you can't get hold of them. They have to be imported, and the war put paid to that, as it did for a time to most of the quarries. Pashley's uncle had built up quite a stock. Kettle Hill had two pairs of French burrs, but they were already pretty old and he must have known that they'd need replacing sooner or later, so just before the war he had a load shipped from France and stacked in the stables.'

Tench stirred his coffee.

'Had Pashley used any?'

'No, not so far, but he had it in mind. He was thinking of replacing one of his runner stones. He mentioned it to me. You see, laddie, though millstones have fairly long lives, they don't last for ever, and French burrs in particular need frequent dressing. They have to be sharpened up perhaps once a fortnight.'

'So the pile of stones we saw was a vital reserve.'

'Irreplaceable,' said Lubbock.

Tench seemed deep in thought.

'And they wouldn't be any use except to a miller?'

'They can be used for building, but you'd need far more than there were in the stables. No, I think we can be almost a hundred per cent sure that whoever took those stones needed them for a mill: a mill that was grinding flour: one that was working with French burrs, not Peak stones.'

'But surely,' said Tench, 'that must narrow down the search.'

'Oh, it does.' Lubbock drained off the last of his tea. 'That is, if we're right, and he lived fairly close. There aren't so many mills still standing round here. There's Weybourne and Burnham Overy, but they haven't worked for more than a quarter of a century, and both of them were stripped of their machinery in the twenties. Then there's Cley. She had three pairs of burrs, but since she was turned into a holiday home they've been bedded in the terrace. Blakeney's been derelict for many years now. She had two pairs of burr stones. They're still in the mill, but even if a man was in desperate need, he'd have a rare job to shift them. Each of them weighs in excess of a ton. No, laddie, now that Kettle Hill's gone, there's only one mill within easy distance that's still grinding flour, and that's Breckmarsh, just the other side of Stiffkey.'

'Working on burr stones?'

'Has to be, I should think, if she's milling flour. Driven by some kind of oil engine, at a guess. But it is only a guess. I can't say for certain.'

'You mean you don't know?' Tench was mildly astonished. 'What about the expertise?'

'Expertise can't work without evidence,' said Lubbock. 'I've never been able to get inside Breckmarsh to see. The miller over there's the only one who's been awkward. He doesn't take kindly to people like me.'

'He wouldn't let you in?'

'Wouldn't even allow me a sniff inside the door. I went there once. Haven't been back since.'

'What's his name, this chap?'

'Goes by the name of Jacks. Gabriel Jacks. I reckon he's the one who's been supplying our friend Wickstead, the baker at Stiffkey. And if he has, then why did Wickstead suddenly lodge an order with Pashley for flour? Did his supplies fail? Did something go wrong at Breckmarsh? Something perhaps that meant Jacks was desperat0e to lay his hands on a pile of burr stones?'

Tench thought about it.

72

'Look. This lorry of mine,' he said. 'If it was churning out oil, it must have dropped some on the road. Couldn't we trace it back?'

'To Breckmarsh, you mean? No, laddie, it's not on. Of course, you could try. There's nothing to stop you. But have you ever tracked an oil drip along a tarmac road? I have, more than once, and it's a damned sight more difficult than on a clay path or across a stretch of grass. It soon wears away. Seems to blend in with all the rest of the muck. Added to that, the heat's brought up the tar. And it's a main road. A lot of vehicles use it. That won't have helped. If you find any oil, who's to say that it came from your particular lorry? And anyway, I've told you, it wasn't your driver that picked up those stones ... You're still not convinced?'

'He could have come back later on. Used some other kind of transport.'

Lubbock shook his head.

'If you're thinking it was Jacks, lad, forget it right now. He just doesn't square up. I've only seen him once, but he's certainly no hulk. He's a nasty piece of work, there's no doubt about that, but he's as thin as a rake and he can't be more than five foot six in his boots.'

He thumped his fist on the table.

'I'll tell you what, though,' he said. 'I'd give a hell of a lot just to see inside that mill. I've a pretty shrewd suspicion it could tell a few tales.'

4

It had always been one of Lubbock's strongest convictions, impressed more than once on the young Sergeant Tench, that, in dealing with any case, it was prudent to be sceptical of other people's statements. 'Be suspicious,' he'd say. 'Folk rarely tell the whole of the truth; sometimes less than half. Never accept their stories as gospel. Have them checked out, or better still check them out for yourself. You never know, laddie. The chance of a conviction may turn on nothing more than a carelessly spoken word.'

Mike Tench remembered that, and he'd long ago decided that what was sauce for the goose was also sauce for the gander. His old Chief might be right more often than not, but he wasn't infallible, and while he, Inspector Tench, was ready to accept that Simon Pashley's death was still to be explained, he wasn't yet prepared to accept that it was murder. And, moreover, while he was hardly in a position to question Lubbock's newly acquired expertise on windmills, he was only too ready to question what he'd said about oil on tarmac roads.

'Try and trace it for yourself,' Lubbock had told him. 'There's nothing to stop you'; and it was with that in mind that, when he left Umzinto Cottage, Tench didn't take the road to Holt and then cut across country direct to Norwich, but drove down into the village and turned along the coastal road towards Wells.

When he reached the blackened stump of Kettle Hill mill, he parked his car by the kissing-gate and, for a couple of hundred yards, traversed the road on foot, carefully peering down at the tarmac surface. On the bend by Morston Church he did exactly the same, and repeated the process a mile further on; then, following the winding road into Stiffkey, he stopped for the last time on the edge of the village, pulling on to the little green by the deep-sunken church. From there he paced all the way through the straggling village, his eyes on the road, and it was only when he reached a small corner shop which bore the name of Leo Wickstead, Baker and Confectioner, that he finally admitted to himself with a sigh that Lubbock had been right. There was oil here and there, all the way from Kettle Hill, but only wishful thinking could possibly have made any firm connection between such intermittent traces and one among the hundreds of rattling lorries that passed along the road in the course of a day.

He wasted no more time. Pushing open the shop door, he stepped inside.

Wickstead's wasn't large. There was, to be truthful, barely enough space to contain Wickstead himself, his wife (he called her Emmy), two customers, the shelves of crusty loaves and the range of glass-topped cases that seemed to hold every possible type of cake, bun and doughnut known to the world of gastronomical connoisseurs.

This was, first of all, because Wickstead was enormous. With his snub nose, sideburns and square-fronted apron, he reminded Tench of a Cruikshank engraving of a brewer's drayman that he'd once seen in a Cambridge library and never forgotten. It was easy to picture him leaning back against a barrel wlth a tankard of foaming ale resting on his paunch.

Mrs Wickstead, too, red-faced and cheerful, though clearly short of breath, was of comparable girth. She bulged in all the most appropriate places, and it struck Tench of a sudden that, if they shared the same bed, it would need to be a structure that was closely akin to the Great Bed of Ware: eleven feet wide and the same in depth.

It was merely a passing thought. He waited his turn and then produced his card.

'Detective Inspector Tench,' he said. 'Is there somewhere where we could have a quiet word?'

Wickstead adjusted the rimless pince-nez that dangled from his neck on a loop of black ribbon. He studied the card closely, then eased his immense weight from one foot to the other and laid a hand on the counter to steady himself.

'Aye,' he said stolidly. 'Come you wi' me, boy, back o' the shop.'

Since it was impossible for the Wicksteads to pass one another in the narrow space between the counter and the shelves, his wife had to shuffle breathlessiy round to the flap, raise it and back herself into the gap to let him squeeze through. Tench watched the manoeuvre with some fascination, permitting himself the extravagant fancy that, like balloons under pressure, one of them might suddenly explode without warning and devastate the bakery. It was a fear that proved unfounded, though Mrs Wickstead had some difficulty in extracting herself from the vice-like grip of the counter edges, and only freed herself at last with much puffing and blowing and a sound like a cork coming out of a bottle.

The room at the back was even smaller than the shop, and most of the space was given up to a heavy deal table piled wlth bakei s trays. Wickstead nudged them aside, lowered himself perilously on to a stool, handed Tench back his card, wiped his pince-nez on a large scarlet handkerchief spotted in white, clipped them back on his nose, and looked at his visitor with a mild belligerence.

'Right then,' he said. 'What you arter, boy?'

'A little help, Mr Wickstead. Nothing more than that.'

The baker eyed him with a Lubbock-like fund of suspicion.

'Where be Dodds then?'

'Dodds?'

'Ol' Constable Dodds. It be mostly him as come.'

Tench gave what he hoped was a soothing smile.

'This is nothing to do with the local force, Mr Wickstead. I'm from Norwich. We're just following a line of inquiry.'

Wickstead flickered an eyebrow.

'Tha's a long way off. What you come dawdlin' all tha' way fer?'

Tench pulled out his notebook.

'You ordered a consignment of flour from Mr Pashley.'

'Tha's right. It were weekend. Anythin' wrong o' tha'?'

'Not the slightest, Mr Wickstead ... You ordered how much? Sixty stone was it?'

'Aye, six sacks. That were what he say, an' a rum business tha' be. All my young time it were twenty stone a sack. Now it be none but ten. Reckon they young fellers be losin' their spunk. Ol' Grimes at Breckmarsh – him as were there some forty year abye – he could carry a twenty-stone sack on a level like as it mighta bin a bagful o' peanuts. I remember one day – I'd be roun' about fifteen that time abouts – it were blowin' off they marshes like nothin' God made, an' spittin' o' rain an' allsorts...'

'Six sacks, Mr Wickstead?' Tench interposed gently.

'Aye, six he say ... Seem like I'll not be gett'n' 'em though.'

'You hadn't ordered from him before?'

'That ent far wrong.'

Tench wondered whether that meant that Mr Wickstead hadn't or whether it was intended to mean that he had. He decided on the former.

'So,' he said, 'who normally supplied you?'

Wickstead took a tin from his trouser pocket, extracted a pinch of snuff, sniffed it up his nostrils, pulled out his handkerchief, and yielded himself to a thunderous sneeze. He shook like a mountain of shale in an earthquake. His pince-nez fell off.

'Why, ol' Jacks up at Breckmarsh,' he said, wafting the scarlet handkerchief back and forth across his nose. 'He were allus closest ... You got some reason fer askin' these questions?'

Tench admitted he had.

'Then what might it be?'

'Just confirming a few facts, Mr Wickstead, that's all ... Why did you suddenly order from Mr Pashley?'

Wickstead gave a shrug and clutched at the table.

'Had to, boy, had to. Never had no choice.'

'Why was that?'

'Well, he come to see me, didn' he like?'

'Mr Pashley?'

'No, not Pashley. Jacks, boy, Jacks.' His scathing tone implied that Tench could only be one degree short of a moron. 'Said he couldn' let me have none. Wouldn' be able to let me have none fer mebbe three week.'

'Mr Jacks came to see you and told you that he couldn't supply you with flour?'

'Aye.' Mr Wickstead declared once again that that wasn't far wrong.

'Did he say why?'

'No.'

'Did you ask him?'

'Course I did.'

'Then what reason did he give?'

'Didn' give none at all. Said what the hell business were it o' mine? So I told him to get to hell out o' my shop. Said I'd order some place else.'

'He's an awkward chap, then?'

'Aye, a bloody rum bugger, an' tha's fer sure.'

Tench paused for a moment.

'What did he use to deliver his flour?'

'Had a lorry, didn' he?'

'What kind of a lorry?'

'It were an ol' Chevvy, weren' it?'

'A Chevrolet?'

'Aye.'

'You said "old". Just how old?'

'It were scrap, boy, scrap. Ready fer th'knacker's yard. That were plain enough. Had bin fer years.'

'Did it have a loose mudguard?'

Wickstead retrieved his snuff tin and rammed it in his pocket.

'Mudguard?' he said. 'Nay, it were more ner tha'. Runnin' board, tail flap, bonnet, th'lot. Every blasted thing were loose. Rattled like th'clappers. It were a bloody wonder it all stuck togither. Reckon as one good gust o' wind an' th'hull bloody thing'd be arse-uppards in bits.'

77

5

When, half an hour later, Tench drove away from the Wickstead shop, now hot on the trail of his elusive lorry, he had on the seat beside him a cardboard carton containing six of Mrs Wickstead's butterfly cakes, and inside him a coffee that he suspected had been laced with a more than liberal quantity of rum.

Following Wickstead's directions, he climbed the gentle slope that led out of the village, and, a mile further on, turned right towards the marshes and the tall black tower that was Breckmarsh mill.

From a distance it seemed a copy of the one at Kettle Hill: just another tarred brick tower, as most of them were in Norfolk, with the sails painted white and a number of small brick-and-flint-pebble buildings clustered round its base. It was clearly not working – there was no sound of Lubbock's auxiliary engine – but Tench had little doubt that, somewhere close by, he was bound to set eyes on the dilapidated lorry that Wickstead had described, not to mention an undersized, thin, aggressive figure that would unmistakably be Gabriel Jacks.

He was more than ready to confront him. He might well, in Wickstead's words, be a bloody rum bugger, or, as Lubbock had portrayed him in more discreet terms, a nasty piece of work, but Mr Jacks was going to find himself marooned up a desperately mucky creek if he proved rash enough to obstruct a police inspector in the course of his duty.

But if Tench, in his newly promoted role, was resolutely prepared to prove himself in battle with even the most ill-favoured of Norfolk's millers, he was doomed to be disappointed. The mill was locked and so was the cottage, and the windows were shuttered.

He made a tour of the outbuildings. There were three of them. The nearest was a circular brick affair, with a boarded roof that was tarred against the weather. Lubbock would have told him that it was a roundhouse, the base of an earlier postmill, but Lubbock wasn't there, and to Tench it was merely some kind of storeroom. It, too, was locked. He tried to see inside, but the windows were small and covered in grime, and the interior so dark that all he could make out was what looked like a pile of empty sacks in one corner. Even if Pashley's burr stones had been there, it would have been quite impossible to detect them in the gloom.

The second building was clearly the old mill stables. Peering in through the minute windows, Tench could see the stalls, but all, as far as he could tell, were empty, though he did think he glimpsed in the half-light within what appeared to be straw scattered around the floor.

The only one among the three that could possibly have been used to shelter a lorry, or hide it from view, was a long, low brick-and-flint barn that stood some distance apart from the rest. Tench approached it without much hope, and he was right to do so. The heavy double doors were bolted and padlocked, the walls were solid and windowless, and the only way to see what might have been inside was through a series of narrow ventilation slits, and these were set so high that they were way beyond his reach.

He hammered on all the doors, but without result; inspected the ground, but found little that offered him much consolation. There was no sign of the lorry, no trace of the burr stones, no hint that Jacks was anywhere around.

He went back to the car, and sat for a few moments deep in thought. Then he drove off down the lane towards the main road and, turning left, retraced the route that had brought him to the mill.

Reaching Blakeney, he stopped at the telephone box that Lubbock had used on the previous day. From there he rang Norwich and asked for McKenzie.

'That you, Mac?' he said. 'Any sign of the lorry?'

'Not a glimmer, sir, no.' McKenzie's gruff voice came through clearly on the line. 'The whole team's reported. They've searched every listed garage in the area, and no one's seen or heard of the damned thing at all. It's just vanished from sight in a puff of oily smoke. God knows where it's gone.'

'Tell them to keep on trying.'

'They're already doing that, but it doesn't look too hopeful. Pity that girl couldn't have seen the number plate, or maybe a name on the door of the cab. As it is, the lads are just working in the dark, or at least in a kind of twilight.'

'From what I've heard today, it could possibly be a Chev. One of those pre-war models.'

McKenzie made an audible effort to be cheerful.

'Well, that's something,' he said, 'but it still doesn't get us very far, sir, does it? Old lorries of that make aren't exactly scarce, and it isn't going to be much help unless we can get a sight of it. It may not be in a repair shop at all. It could be hidden away somewhere.'

'I'm beginning to think that's exactly where it is ... Any word from Ledward yet?'

'Yep. The reports are in.' McKenzie sounded gloomy.

'No joy?'

'Not a deal. Could be interpreted either way. Nothing firm to go on.'

'I was afraid of that.'

'So what's the next step?' McKenzie waited.

'The trouble is,' said Tench, 'we're not doing much at all. We're just wasting time, fumbling around in your twilight world with nothing more than a candle. It's time we decided whether to blow it out or bring in a few hefty searchlights to help us. We've got to make up our minds, Mac. Is it a case of murder, as the old man suspects it is, or is it quite simply an accidental fire? We can't afford to shilly-shally around any longer. We'd better have a talk. I'll be back in an hour, so give it some thought ... And in the meantime ...'

'Yep?'

'We bring in the press. So far they haven't cottoned on to the case. To them it's been just another fire in a windmill. Well, let's give them something to make a splash about. Get on to Dave Ransome at the *EDP*. Say we're giving him an exclusive. Do it in my name, and ask him to give it a front-page spread.'

'Right. What are we telling him?' McKenzie was more alert than he had been all day.

'Say we think the fire at Kettle Hill may well have been arson, and we're treating young Pashley's death as suspicious. We need information. Give him the details about the lorry. Dark-coloured, caked in dust, loose mudguard, creaking springs. Could well be a pre-war Chevrolet. Give him a description of the driver, too. Well over six foot, thickset, dark hair, dressed in a pair of grimy blue dungarees. Could be stained with oil. Anyone who's seen either of them or knows anything about them, to contact the police. Also anyone who noticed anything unusual in the Kettle Hill area on the night of the fire. And if anybody's seen a vehicle transporting blocks of stone, we want to know about that, too.'

'Blocks of stone?'

'That's right.'

'What kind of stone?'

'Doesn't matter a damn. Just leave it at that. If we get a report, we'll do the detecting. I'll explain when I see you. OK?'

'Will do.'

'Get cracking, then,' said Tench. 'The sooner we get some results, the better. I'm getting a bit tired of holding a candle while Lubbock pokes around for what he thinks are clues.'

6

Back in his office, he pushed aside a couple of letter trays, an inkstand, a paperweight and a clutch of pens and pencils, and replaced them by two yellow soft-backed files.

'Right, Mac,' he said. 'Let's try and probe this murky twilight of yours. First of all, the times. At somewhere round about half-past one in the morning, Gunner Ellison hears a bell ringing from the mill. Then, twenty minutes later, at ten to two, Hilary Dixon hears a grating noise from the same direction. She described it as the sound you get if you rub two pieces of sandpaper together. At a quarter past two friend Lubbock's prowling round and sees a glow in the sky above Kettle Hill. Ten minutes after that, Mrs Bolding's wakened at Morston Bottom Farm by the sound of a pile of buckets rolling about in the wind, and almost immediately she sees a flash of lightning followed by a clap of thunder. That's at twenty-five past two. Walter Bolding gets up and fumbles his way downstairs. How long would it take him? A couple of minutes? Then he calls out that the mill's on fire. Two twenty-seven. She slips on a dressing-gown, makes her way down and takes a look at the fire. The mill's well alight. She said the sky was full of sparks and flames were shooting out of the little slit-windows. Walter described it as looking like a grate full of red-hot coals. She slings on

81

her waterproof, sets off across the yard and shouts to her husband to phone the fire brigade. She's more agile than Walter. Let's say it took her a minute and a half. That makes it nearly twenty-nine minutes past two, and a couple of minutes later, at two thirty-one, the fire station at Holt logs in Walter's call ... Have I missed anything out?'

McKenzie stroked the stubble on his chin.

'No,' he said. 'That seems to be the lot. Except for the time when the Chief saw the lightning flash over Cley.'

Tench nodded.

'That was roughly at two thirty-five, but it doesn't really matter. We're concerned with Kettle Hill, and Agnes Bolding saw the flash at Morston Bottom some ten minutes earlier ... So what do the timings tell us?'

'Seems to me,' said McKenzie, 'they tell us the Chief was dead right in his guesswork. We know lightning struck the mill – the sack chain was welded – but it must have been ablaze well before that.'

'Fair enough. Let's accept it was blazing away at two fifteen when Lubbock looked out of his cottage window. The next question is why? What happened at the mill?'

'Well, if the Chief's right, there wasn't enough grain left in the hopper, the bell alarm sounded, the stones ran dry, and the friction between them sparked off the fire.'

'Yes, but that poses a lot more questions. Why was the mill working at that time of night? According to the old man, it was something that never happened. When he left at six o'clock the evening before, the mill was shut down. Pashley had finished his stint for the day, and he said nothing about starting it up again later on. And he didn't need to, so we're told. He could have met Wickstead's order out of his stocks. And why didn't he top up the grain in the hopper? Why didn't he open the shutters on the sails, and why, as a last resort, didn't he disengage the fantail and quarter the mill?'

'There's one obvious answer.'

'You think so?'

'Yes.' McKenzie was firm. 'I'd be willing to bet a week's wages on it. Someone emptied the hopper, set the mill running, and arranged that Pashley couldn't do a damned thing about it. Didn't the Chief say that, if the mill had been working, the lad would have been there until the moment it stopped? Well, he wasn't there, was he? Looks like he was in the cottage, fast asleep in bed, and dashed out in a panic. My guess would be that someone set a trap for him, knew he'd come running when he heard the bell alarm, and waited inside the mill in the darkness to nobble him.'

'And then what?'

'Your guess is as good as mine, Mike. Hit him on the head? Pushed him down a ladder? That would fit in with what Ledward had to say.'

'All right.' Tench opened one of the files. 'Let's look at exactly what he did have to say ... We gave him an almost impossible job. The body was badly charred, the face burnt away beyond all recognition, but, at least in another sense, it seems we were lucky. The body was on the ground, covered with smouldering timbers, and because of that it escaped most of the roaring heat that funnelled up the mill. So Ledward was still able to deduce certain facts. According to him, there were no obvious signs of death by natural causes: nothing to indicate a heart attack or stroke. There were fractures to the ankles, legs and pelvis, and the neck was broken. I rang him up just now and asked him what, in his opinion, could have caused such injuries. He was cagey about it, but said it seemed to him that the body had fallen from a considerable height. There was a minor fracture at the back of the skull, but that could well have been caused by the fall. He wouldn't commit himself on the cause of death. Referred me back to the report...'

'And that says there was carbon present in the lungs. So Pashley breathed in smoke. That means he was alive after the fire started.' McKenzie was grim. 'Reckon I'm right,' he said. 'Someone did him in.'

Tench pondered for a moment.

'There is another possible scenario,' he said. 'Suppose Pashley heard the alarm bell ringing, dashed across from the cottage, tried to brake the mill, and found the brake wouldn't hold. If he then tried to open the shutters on the sails and found the striking rod had jammed, he'd have to disengage the fantail and turn the cap by hand to quarter the mill. He'd be in a desperate hurry. Suppose he was dashing up the ladders to the fantail platform when he slipped and fell. He might have broken a leg and, when the mill caught fire, been overcome by the smoke. Then, as the fire ate its way through the floors, his body would have dropped to the bottom of the mill.'

83

'Could be,' said McKenzie, 'but then...'

'Yes, I know. It still leaves us with all the vital questions unanswered. Why was the mill working at half-past one in the morning? Why wasn't Pashley there to keep an eye on it? Why did the hopper run short of grain, and why didn't he fill it up straight away?'

'Because someone had made sure that he damned well couldn't ... The forensics report. What about those fibres Ledward found on the body? Could they mean anything?'

Ledward had found some charred remnants of fibre adhering to Pashley's body. He'd passed them to forensics for detailed analysis.

'Wouldn't think so,' said Tench. 'They found cotton and wool, probably burnt remnants of his pyjamas and dressing-gown...'

'And jute.'

'Yes, I queried that with them, and they said it was normal. Used for making flour sacks. They'd expect to find such fibres anywhere in a mill.'

McKenzie sat back, drove his hands in his pockets and tilted back his chair.

'Well, Mike,' he said, 'you can think what you like, but it looks to me like arson and probably murder.'

Tench took a deep breath.

'Right,' he said. 'Let's assume that it is. Then where do we go next? We've got two possible suspects: the driver of a lorry who threatens young Pashley, and another man who comes and carts away his burr stones. The first we can't identify; the second could possibly be Gabriel Jacks. The trouble is there's no physical resemblance between them. The man who drove the lorry was a thickset bloke, well over six foot tall. Jacks, so Lubbock says, is as thin as a lath and no more than five foot six.'

'So what do we do?'

'I think,' said Tench, 'we turn a spotlight on Kettle Hill for the next few days. Unless there's another murder, which Lubbock forbid, the rest of the misdemeanours'll have to wait their turn. We need facts and plenty of them, so let's press ahead and try to root them out. We've already made a start. We're searching for the lorry; Ransome's promised a spread in the *Eastern Daily Press*; and Ledward's taken an impression of the teeth on the body and circulated it to all the dentists in the county. The inquest's provisionally fixed for the day after tomorrow, but it looks like we'll have to press for an adjournment.'

'How about a warrant to search Breckmarsh mill?'

Tench shook his head.

'Not a chance, Mac,' he said. 'So far we haven't anything like enough evidence. No magistrate's going to let us turn the place over just in the hope of finding a pile of old stones.'

'Fingerprints?'

'We're checking the stable door. Apart from that it's likely to be just a waste of time. There's nothing to show that Pashley was assaulted in the cottage, and we haven't a hope in hell of finding anything in the mill. No, first thing tomorrow morning, split up the team. We've got four detective constables working on the case. Keep a couple of them searching for the lorry. Give each of them a particular area to cover. Stretch it out as far as Wells. Send the other two out to visit all the bakers. Find those who dealt with Jacks. See if any of them have had their deliveries cancelled. And if so, why.'

'And after that's fixed? What d'you want me to do?'

'Get out to Morston Bottom and take a statement from that girl, Hilary Dixon. Give the Boldings a ring tonight and tell them you're coming. Then go on to Stiffkey, see Constable Dodds. Get a bit of local colour. Find out what he knows about Gabriel Jacks. After that, see if anyone's around up at Breckmarsh. If there is, then try and wangle your way inside the mill. And poke around the out-buildings. You know what you're looking for.'

'Right. Where will you be?'

'Here,' said Tench. He replaced the letter trays. 'To begin with, I'm simply going to clear the decks. Get rid of this lot. Then I'll be waiting here at the end of a phone to see what Ransome's stirred up. No doubt we'll get a lot of useless information, but there's always the chance there'll be something that warrants a closer look. So give the team a rota. Tell them to ring through. I want someone on the line every half-hour. And I'm going to get Lubbock in. Let him read what Ledward's managed to piece together. See if he's any more gems of detection to lay at our feet. That should please the old boy.'

McKenzie gave a grin.

'Reckon you won't even need to call him,' he said. 'He'll be over here at the double once he's read Ransome's column in the *EDP*.'

3

THURSDAY

'He that tells a secret is another's servant.'
Herbert, *Outlandish Proverbs*

1

At nine thirty next morning Tench was in the Chief Super's office.

'Reporting, sir,' he said.

'Lubbock's windmill?'

'Yes.'

'Any progress?'

'A little. We've two possible suspects. A man who was heard to threaten the victim of the fire, and another who stole some articles from the mill.'

'Not the same chap?'

'Apparently not. The descriptions don't tally, but the one who did the threatening drove up in a lorry. Pretty distinctive. We're searching for it.'

'No names yet?'

'Not for him. We think the other may be a miller called Jacks.'

'Have you had him in for questioning?'

'Not so far, sir, no. We're not too sure of the ground. Sergeant McKenzie's out making inquiries.'

'A press appeal for witnesses?'

'I've already done that, sir.' Tench produced a copy of the *Eastern Daily Press*. 'Ransome's been quite helpful.'

'He's the crime reporter.'

'Yes ... The trouble is ...'

'Go on.'

'Well, sir, Mr Lubbock seems convinced that the case is one of murder.'

'But he hasn't convinced you.'

'Not yet, sir, no.'

'Well, he could of course be wrong. He has been wrong before. Just once or twice ... What do you think it is?'

'Could be just an accident, sir, nothing more. The mill was struck by lightning. The theft might have nothing to do with Pashley's death.'

'And the threats?'

'Could mean something, or could have no connection.'

The Chief Super stroked his chin.

'One of those, is it?'

'Afraid so, sir, yes.'

'Well, it's on your plate, Mike. I've just had a call from Chief Superintendent Erskine.'

Erskine was Hastings' counterpart in Ipswich.

'Some news of Inspector Maitland?'

'Yes. He's not likely to be back till the beginning of next week. Significant developments, so Erskine says.'

He sat back in his chair.

'So it's all up to you ... But don't forget, Mike, it's your decision now. It isn't John Lubbock's.'

Tench gave a wry smile.

'Yes, I understand that, sir,' he said. 'Not to worry. I think we're on the verge of some developments of our own.'

If he spoke more in hope than conviction, he didn't have long to wait.

At ten twenty-eight, just as he was clearing up the last of his paperwork, a call came through from Detective Constable Gregg, one of the two men still searching for the lorry.

Gregg was soft-spoken, thoughtful and never less than sound in the judgements he made.

'I think we may have found it at last, sir,' he said.

'The lorry?'

'Yes.'

'Where is it?'

'It's in Wells, sir.'

Tench pulled a pad towards him and picked up his pen.

'Tell me all about it.'

Gregg explained at some length.

'Found it in a breaker's yard. Small business run by a bloke called Lucas. Seems it was brought in the day before the fire. Driver was a short, thin chap, pretty rough, and dressed in a pair of scruffy dungarees. Said it was bloody useless. Those were his words. Wanted to sell it for scrap. Lucas gave him a fiver. Told him it wasn't worth any more.'

'Does it fit the description?'

'Yes, sir. It's a Chev. Looks to be dark blue, but it's difficult to tell, it's so bunged up with muck. Low sides and tailboard. The near-side front mudguard's ready to drop off, and the whole thing's leaning over at an angle as though the springs have gone. If someone gave it a push, it'd topple on its side.'

'Did he give his name, this chap who brought it in?'

'Oh, yes. Didn't bother to keep it a secret. Quite open about it. Said he was a Mr Jacks and gave his address as Breckmarsh mill, Stiffkey ... It's empty, of course, the lorry, but there's a lot of white dust that's worked into the floorboards. Looks to me like flour.'

'Right.' Tench wasn't slow to act once he had a firm lead. 'Wait there till Sergeant McKenzie arrives. Tell Mr Lucas we'll have to impound the lorry. I'll get it towed in. The boffins at forensics'll have to work it over.'

Gregg gave an almost apologetic cough.

'I've already told him that, sir. Said he didn't mind. If we wanted to keep it, we could for all he cared.'

Tench rang Morston Bottom Farm. It was Walter who answered.

'Inspector Tench,' he said. 'Is Sergeant McKenzie still there?'

'Aye.' Walter was still as cheerful as ever. 'Writin' like mad, 'e is. Reckon 'e'll need a new pen afore long. Want to speak to 'im?'

'Please.'

'I'll put 'im on then,' said Walter.

Tench waited. He could hear heavy footsteps fading away, then a distant mumble, and at last McKenzie's voice.

'Mac?' he said.

'Present.'

'Gregg thinks he's found the lorry.'

'That's a turn-up. Where?'

Tench told him.

'It's close to the Buttlands, on the road to Holkham. I want you to take Miss Dixon over there now. Find out if it's like the one she saw at Kettle Hill ... I suppose you're on that clapped-out old banger of yours?'

McKenzie had a vintage Norton that he swore had once, in the

91

distant past, won a TT race in the Isle of Man. It was incredibly noisy, spat out clouds of smoke, and had been for years his constant pride and joy.

'What d'you mean, clapped-out? She's in flawless condition. Goes like a bird.'

'Well, if Miss Dixon's willing to risk her neck, take her on the pillion. It sounds the perfect mix. All that power between your legs, and a stunning girl wrapping her arms around your waist. What more could a man desire?'

'Depends on the man.'

Tench raised an eyebrow.

'Don't bother to explain,' he said. 'Just get her there.'

'Gregg's standing guard?'

'Yes, I told him to wait.'

'D'you still want me to call at Breckmarsh, see this fellow Jacks?'

Tench was cautious.

'No,' he said. 'There's a bit of a complication. The man who drove it into the scrapyard was Jacks, right enough. But if it's the same lorry that Miss Dixon saw, then who was the hulking brute who drove it up to Kettle Hill?'

'Could have been someone who works for him.'

'Could have been, yes, but we need to get our facts straight before we make a move. No, don't go near the place for the moment. Call and see Dodds. He may be able to throw a bit of light on the subject. If we have to tackle our friend Jacks, then we'll do it together.'

'OK, if you say so.'

'That's the drill, Mac. Just find out what you can, then report back to me. And don't scare that girl to death. We may need her as a witness.'

2

Constable Gregg's discovery was only the first of a number of developments that day that left Tench, by the evening, in a state of some confusion.

Promptly at eleven o'clock, Lubbock announced himself, armed with a copy of the *Eastern Daily Press*.

'See you've been hitting the headlines, laddie.' He revealed an unaccustomed cheerfulness that almost put Walter Bolding in the shade. '"Police believe windmill fire could be murder." Do they believe that?'

Tench eyed him warily.

'Let's just say,' he said, 'that they've accepted that a certain ex-Detective Chief Inspector could possibly, given a hell of a lot more evidence, be on the right track.'

Lubbock laid the paper on the desk and sat down.

'Any results yet?' he asked.

'One old dear who says she saw someone prowling round her dustbin; a young lad from Blakeney, walking his dog, who says it turned up a blackened bone in a ditch; and Tommy Maguire who's confessed to the murder.'

'He always confesses. How many times is that?'

'Six, including that stabbing at Hellesdon. The one he claimed he'd done with a double-bladed hack-saw.'

'And that's all, is it?'

'No. There is something else. We may have winkled out the lorry.'

Lubbock showed no surprise.

'Didn't think it could lose itself for very long,' he said. 'Where did you find it?'

Tench told him.

'When was it left there?'

Tench told him that, too.

'Do we know who the owner is?'

'Yes, your pal Jacks.'

Lubbock stroked his chin.

'Is it, by God?' he said. 'Now that could be interesting.'

'It could be. Perhaps both of us were right after all. If Jacks dumped that lorry the day before the fire, and if he did steal the burr stones, as you think he did, then he must have used some other means to take them away. So he could have had another lorry, or maybe a van. When you were up at Breckmarsh, did you see anything else that he might have used?'

'No. Never had the chance to nose around the place. There's a barn there, of course. What he keeps inside it is anybody's guess.'

'And you didn't see anyone else beside Jacks?'

'Not a soul ... You're thinking of that brute of a driver?'

'Yes, he's the problem.'

'Like as not a hanger-on, a delivery man. Does the heavy work. Easy to find out. Get on to the local flatfoot. Chap called Dodds at Stiffkey.'

'Mac's doing that now.'

'Well, Dodds should know him. Mine of information is old Ezra Dodds. Been there since the Rector was haring off to London to sample his little bits of crumpet in the teashops. There isn't much he doesn't know about what goes on in the village . . . Anything yet from Reg?'

Tench pushed the file across the desk.

'Better read it,' he said.

'Nothing conclusive?'

'I'd say not. Could point to foul play, could be accidental death. Ledward won't commit himself.'

Lubbock read through the report.

'He does make three points that are worth a second thought.'

'You mean the blow on the head?'

'No,' said Lubbock slowly. 'I wasn't thinking of that. I reckon Reg is right not to labour that point. No, laddie, it's the other injuries that strike an odd note. Now I'm not in the business of knocking Reg Ledward. He's good at his job; but he's always been reluctant to offer opinions. Says it's nothing to do with him: that's our side of things. Well, that may be so, but sometimes we need to know a good deal more than simply the bare facts that he sticks in his reports. It's not enough to say that a corpse reveals a compound fracture of the tibia. We need to know how, in his informed opinion, such a fracture was caused.' He tapped the report. 'All he does here is list the broken bones . . .'

'I did ring him up.'

'And what did he say?'

'Looked like the body had fallen from a height.'

'Ah, but did he say how?'

'How?' Tench frowned. 'I'm not quite with you.'

'Well, people can fall in any number of ways. On their heads, on their shoulders, flat on their faces. You name it, they've done it.' Lubbock rummaged in his pocket and pulled out his pipe. 'I'm no expert on this, laddie. Don't claim to be. But from what Ledward says, it seems to me young Pashley fell straight down, feet first. As

94

though he'd been strung up somehow, and the fire had burnt through whatever was holding him.'

'But that's just conjecture. Can't be anything else.'

'At the moment it is, yes.'

'OK,' said Tench, 'maybe it's worth considering. What are the other points?'

'First there's this business of carbon in the lungs. Pashley wasn't a smoker...'

'So he must have breathed in the fumes from the fire. Yes, I'm with you there.'

'And then these scraps of burnt sacking.'

'The jute.'

'Yes, laddie, the jute. When you find it in a corn mill it can only mean sacks. Grain sacks or flour sacks. Take your pick which.'

'Then there's nothing unusual about it, sir, is there?'

'No, but with our particular forensic department we could probably find out a little bit more. Remember Sherlock Holmes. He said his methods were always founded on the observation of trifles. Spoke more than once about the monograph he'd written on the ashes of 140 different varieties of pipe, cigar and cigarette tobacco. I think he mentions it in passing in "The Boscombe Valley Mystery". Well, it's the trifles that sometimes count, lad, take it from me, and like Holmes we can't afford to ignore them. We need every scrap of evidence we can possibly gather, whether it turns out in the end to be relevant or not. Now the boffins here in Norwich have lived for God knows how long surrounded by windmills. They know a lot about jute. Just as Holmes set himself to collect tobacco ash and put it under a microscope, so these lads have had to do the same thing with jute. They've built up quite a formidable dossier on it. They can tell you whether it comes from Bengal or Assam. More than that, they can narrow it down to a matter of miles on the same stretch of river. They can tell you whether it comes from Goalundo or Faridpur or maybe Chandpur; and if you find that you need the ultimate refinement, they'll pin-point the particular mill near Calcutta that processed the stuff. It could be Lawrence or Birla, Albion, Kelvin, Kinnison, or any of a host of others. It might even be some mill by the Tay in Dundee. Wherever it is, they can tell you. They're experts on jute.'

'I'm listening,' said Tench, 'but what's the point of knowing whether it comes from this place of yours – Goalundo was it? – or from somewhere else that happens to be fifty miles downstream?'

'No point at all, laddie, except that we can distinguish one kind from another, and we may need to do just that. You see, there's something else that's worth consideration. When most of the windmills round here were still working, they used a standard sack. Filled with grain or flour, it weighed twenty stone. That's 280 pounds, or two and a half hundredweight. Sounds a lot, doesn't it, to cart around on your shoulders? But in those days millers all over the country used them, and found them easy enough to handle. They had the knack, you see, laddie. But with a youngster like Pashley, new to the business, it was a different matter. He hadn't the same know-how, couldn't hope to have, so he used smaller sacks that were half that size. Found them easier to shift. But it's my guess that Jacks still uses the old type. That's why he pays that hulk of a driver to help him. So it might be interesting to know which kind of sack it was that produced those scrapings Ledward took from the body. It's a fair enough bet that the ones that Jacks uses come from a different mill from Pashley's, and forensics could tell us.'

Tench looked at him narrowly.

'You've got some kind of theory, haven't you?' he said.

'It's only an idea and it may come to nothing, but I'd just like to know whether Ledward's bits and pieces came from the sacks that were used at Kettle Hill, or whether they came from Breckmarsh. The point is that forensics would need samples of both to work on. Well, you can get hold of Pashley's sacks without any trouble – there's a pile of them stacked near the burr stones in the stables – but you'd need to snatch a sample from Breckmarsh as well.'

'But you're not going to tell me why.'

'Pointless, laddie, pointless. It's simply a notion, nothing more than that, and I wouldn't want to wind you up and set you running in quite the wrong direction. No, let it rest for another day or two, but bear it in mind. If you do get the chance to search Breckmarsh mill, then keep your eyes skinned and slip a sack in the car.'

Tench surveyed his old Chief with a quizzical expression.

'There's one thing worth remembering,' he said, 'in all this. We still don't know for certain that the body that was found at Kettle Hill was Pashley's.'

Lubbock dismissed him with a flick of the hand.

'Whose else could it be? Ledward says the man was roughly five foot ten. That's about Pashley's height. And if it isn't his body, then where the devil is he? Swanning around on some Caribbean island?'

He filled his pipe and lit it.

'No, laddie,' he said, 'I think you'll find that it's Pashley right enough. Can't be anyone else ... But there are other things worth remembering, too.'

'Such as?' said Tench.

'The lad himself. Simon Pashley. You see, Mike, I still think you're galloping ahead far too fast. Let's not jump to conclusions. Just because we suspect a man's guilty of theft doesn't necessarily mean that he's guilty of murder. If I'm right, and someone did kill young Pashley, it might perhaps be Jacks, but again it might not. There are all kinds of avenues we've not yet explored. Remember what I said about working on a murder. If you're faced with a murdered man, the first thing to do is find out as much about him as you possibly can. More often than not he'll lead you to the killer. There's nearly always some connection. The most intractable murders are those where there's none. Random killings are the devil to solve, but they're few and far between.'

'Yes, I suppose you're right.'

'Of course I'm right. If Maitland were here, he'd be the first to tell you. Oh, I know he's away. Had a word with the Chief Super. Chasing round Europe, isn't he, trying to sniff out the loot from that Nettlefield affair? Wasting his time, I reckon. But that's beside the point. We're not concerned with Holland, for all that it's got more windmills than Norfolk ever had. We're concerned with Kettle Hill and Simon Pashley. Now I've told you everything that I know about him, and that's quite a lot. But remember, laddie, it's only what he told me. What he chose to tell me. There are other things we need to know. All that money, for instance. Where is it? Who gets it now that he's dead? Did anyone have a motive – anyone beside Jacks – for doing the boy in? Any women in his life? He never mentioned any to me, but then again, why should he? How about this Dixon girl, the one who was painting?'

Tench shook his head.

'I wouldn't have thought so. According to her, she didn't know him very well.'

'He showed her round, didn't he? She dropped in for tea more than once. You said so.'

'Yes, but I can't think...'

'Start thinking, laddie. Was she tied up with someone else who might have been jealous? Was it just a wish to paint Kettle Hill that made her set up her easel close to the place? Or had she some other motive? She spent a lot of time there. Did she see any other comings and goings? There are all sorts of possibilities that we haven't yet probed. Remember, laddie, the two most common ingredients of murder are passion and greed. Sex and money. We know Pashley had money, a great deal of it, and he wouldn't have been nor' .ai if there hadn't been a woman somewhere in his life.'

'You don't know who dealt with his business affairs?'

'No.'

'Or whether he made a will?'

'No, Mike. What he did with his money was nothing to do with me. I don't even know if he had any surviving relatives. He never mentioned any. We talked about windmills and not much else. But you need to know. The boy's dead, may be murdered. We've one suspect already, and possibly two. There may well be more...'

He was suddenly interrupted.

The desk sergeant knocked discreetly on the door and handed Tench an envelope.

'Dropped in the box, sir. No one saw it delivered, but it seems to be for you.'

Tench turned it between his hands.

It was addressed in red ink, in capital letters, to the officer in charge of the Kettle Hill case.

He slit open the flap. Inside was a strip of paper with a single sentence, again in capitals:

'IF YOU WANT TO FIND THE KILLER, LOOK FOR THE CHURCHYARD WATCHER.'

He tossed it across to Lubbock.

'Looks like we've got one already,' he said.

3

'It's a hoax,' Lubbock said.

'You think so?'

'I know so. Shove it in the file along with Tommy's confession and forget all about it.'

'And this is the man', said Tench, 'who told me that every trifle of evidence was vital.'

'Evidence, not nonsense.'

Tench was determined, on this occasion, not to yield without a fight.

'Why should it be nonsense? It could be relevant and it might be significant.'

'Laddie,' said Lubbock wearily, 'how long have you lived in Norfolk? Eighteen months?'

'Thereabouts.'

'Then you've still got a hell of a lot left to learn. D'you know what the hakes is?'

'How d'you spell it?'

Lubbock detailed each letter with a measured precision. Tench shook his head.

'Not the foggiest idea.'

'No, you wouldn't have, laddie. You couldn't, in all fairness, be expected to have ... The evening before the fire I was talking to Zack Brett. He's my next-door neighbour. The weather was cloudless, just like all summer; but somehow – don't ask me how – he knew a storm was brewing up. He looked at the sky and said it was going to turn as black as the hakes. You'd have asked him what he meant. I didn't need to. I've lived in Norfolk now for nigh on sixty years, and that's more than long enough to know all the local twists and turns of phrase.'

'It's a bit of local dialect?'

'That's right. It is.'

'So enlighten me,' said Tench. 'What does it mean?'

'Well, it's like this. A hake...'

'Sounds like a fish.'

'So does a Tench,' Lubbock said drily, 'but some of 'em don't reckon much to life under water.'

'Fair enough. Carry on.'

'A hake's a kind of long hook that sticks out from a cooking-range. The top edge has notches like the teeth of a saw. You turn it over the fire and hang a kettle on it, or one of those old stewpots that folk used to have. It gets black from the smoke, so they use the word in these parts to describe any colour from a mucky kind of grey to a black that's like pitch. If you stick around long enough, you'll be bound to hear some mother tell her grubby little son he's got a face like the hakes.'

Tench pondered the simile.

'Good,' he said. 'That's explained, but what's it got to do with this churchyard watcher?'

'Same kind of thing, laddie. It's a bit of local lore.'

'Something I wouldn't know about? Like sack chains and burr stones?'

'Like enough, yes. Let's put it this way. You wouldn't come across a watcher in the back streets of Manchester. You'd need to be somewhere out in the country where people still cling to legend and superstition. Get out to any of these little Norfolk villages and mention the watcher, and the folk there'll tell you all about him right away. But ask anyone in Norwich, and most'll just look blank and think you've gone mad. It's countryside lore like Farmer Giles' pigs being able to see the wind, like blacksmiths knowing a secret word that gives them power over horses, like the devil moving stones to stop a church being built: things you'd never come across stuck in the middle of that sprawling mass of houses and factories and junk where you were born and brought up.'

'Always willing to learn, sir,' Tench said smoothly. 'But what I want to know is this: why shouldn't I look for the churchyard watcher?'

'You'd be wasting your time, unless you're keen on hunting ghosts.'

'You mean all I'd be doing would be chasing a shadow?'

'More than that, laddie. A spectre, a phantom, a manifestation. A churchyard watcher's always dead. If he were still alive, he could never be a watcher.'

'I'm all ears,' said Tench.

Lubbock grunted.

'So you should be. Stop you wasting time when you're lumbered with another of these useless scraps of paper ... No, to be serious, laddie, the legend of the churchyard watcher's been around a long time, maybe hundreds of years. I don't know that it's simply confined to Norfolk. You can probably find it in some form or other all over the country. It stems from an old superstition about funerals. You see, if there was one thing that always terrified people, it was the thought that they might be the last to be buried in an old graveyard, or the first in a new one. If you suffered that fate, then the devil was sure to make off with your soul, and you wouldn't have any rest until you got it back. Folk went to the most extraordinary lengths to avoid such a calamity. They'd pay the gravedigger to bury a dog first in a new churchyard, or slip him a little something to dig up an old grave to make way for a new one; but if, in spite of everything, the devil succeeded, his victim became what was known as the churchyard watcher. He couldn't get his soul back until someone else was buried in the same churchyard, and he was condemned to tour the village every night in a ghostly cart, seeking out the one who'd be next to be buried ... So, if you want to fritter away valuable time looking for this watcher, you'll need to find a full graveyard, or maybe a new one, park your car in the village once it gets dark, take a flask of coffee, and stay awake all night, propping your eyelids open with a couple of matchsticks and waiting for a ghostly horse and an equally ghostly cart with some strange hooded phantom jerking at the reins ... If you think that's a profitable way to spend tonight, then good luck to you, laddie.'

Tench gave a rueful grin.

'I don't think I'll bother.'

'Glad to hear it,' said Lubbock. 'I wouldn't like to think that the strain of this job was addling that brilliant academic mind.' He knocked out his pipe. 'Well, now that we've seen off Tommy Maguire and the non-existent watcher, let's get back to basics. I take it you found nothing in Pashley's cottage?'

'Nothing significant. Business letters from the customers he dealt with, but nothing that added to what we know already.'

'No copy of a will?'

'Not a trace of one, no.'

'Money?'

101

'Ten pounds in notes and a handful of coppers. All in his jacket pocket.'

'Cheque books?'

'Just one. Lloyds, here in Norwich. Nothing but the normal payments you'd expect.'

'Bank statements?'

'Two recent ones. Deposit and current. Nine thousand pounds in the deposit account and just over five hundred in the current. I rang up the manager. Apparently Pashley opened the accounts twelve months ago when he settled at Kettle Hill. Nothing unusual about the transactions.'

'Then where's all the rest of the money? We need to know.'

'You said you'd no idea who dealt with the sale of his properties?'

'Never talked about it, laddie. If I were you, I'd be ringing round solicitors, here and in Wymondham.'

'That's already being done.'

'Who's doing it?'

'Lock.'

'Well, he's a sound enough lad. Not over-bright, but sound. You'll just have to keep your fingers crossed that he comes up with something ... Let me know, won't you?'

He pushed back his chair and heaved himself up.

'I'm off down to Meg's for a wee spot of lunch. How about you?'

Tench suddenly felt all the stifling weight of his former Chief bearing down upon him.

'Thanks all the same, but I've got to stick by the phone.'

'Canteen spam and chips?'

'More like a sandwich.'

'Won't put any flesh on that delicate frame of yours.'

'I think I'll survive.'

Lubbock gave a shrug.

'Well, please yourself,' he said. 'I'll be there for an hour if you change your mind.'

4

Tench nibbled another sandwich.

He wasn't in the best of tempers.

In the hour that had followed Lubbock's departure, no doubt to regale himself on haddock and egg, he'd taken four phone calls: one from a man who'd seen a very old lorry in a scrapyard at Wells, and three from various people who claimed to have spotted a tall man dressed in oil-stained dungarees. Since the sightings were first at Norwich, then at Swaffham and North Walsham, none within twenty miles of Kettle Hill, he'd thanked the callers for their public spirit, taken their names and addresses and filed them away under the mental heading of no immediate action.

At one fifteen Rayner had rung up from Blakeney, followed promptly at one forty-five by Spurgeon from Wells. They were the two detective constables whose job had been to contact the bakers and interview those who'd traded with Jacks. Neither had had anything fresh to report. They'd found half a dozen shops between Blakeney and Wells that had ordered their flour on a regular basis from Breckmarsh mill. All their orders had either been cancelled by phone, or Jacks had simply failed to deliver. When asked to give a reason, he'd been sullenly taciturn. He wasn't delivering and that was that.

Spurgeon had only just rung off, when Detective Constable Lock had tapped on the door.

'Fisher and Feldgate, sir,' he'd said. 'Castle Meadow.'

'Tell me,' said Tench.

Lock had studied his notebook.

'They handled the property sales for Mr Pashley. June last year. I spoke to Mr Feldgate. Seemed quite distressed. Said he'd better come up and see you, sir. Were you available?'

'And?'

'I said you were, so he's coming at three, if that's all right for you.'

Tench had nodded.

103

'OK. Did you ask about a will?'

'Said as far as he knew, there wasn't one, sir. Said he'd give you all the details once he got here.'

'Right. Tell the desk to keep an eye open for him. When he gets here, show him up.'

Once Lock had left, he'd sent down to the canteen for a cup of coffee. Then at twenty past two the switchboard had put through a call from Wymondham. The caller had given his name as Booth-way: Anthony Boothway. Mr Boothway was a dental surgeon with a practice in the town. He'd searched through his records and was ready to make a positive identification of the body at Kettle Hill. Yes, he was certain. It was one of his patients, a Mr Simon Fren-chard Delisle Pashley, late of Park Lodge, Wymondham. His address had been altered nine months before to Mill Cottage, Kettle Hill, Blakeney. No – Mr Boothway's voice had been affectedly cultured – there could be no possible mistake. He'd done some recent work on Mr Pashley's teeth: capped a left incisor, extracted a wisdom tooth and made several fillings. The impression and the X-rays corresponded precisely with what was in his files.

Tench had once more expressed his thanks, told Boothway the provisional time of the inquest and rung the coroner's office.

He hadn't been surprised to find that his feelings were some-what mixed. Along with his relief that at least one point in the case now seemed to be resolved, went the irritating knowledge that Lubbock had once again proved to be right; and while rejecting the thought that his action might smack of a mild disloyalty, he breathed a silent prayer that somewhere along the line – perhaps in some small unimportant detail – his old Detective Chief Inspector might, simply out of homage to human frailty, draw the wrong conclusion.

His prayer was answered a lot sooner than he had any reasonable right to expect, but not before Mr Feldgate and then Mr Burage had added their measure of confusion to the case.

Mr Feldgate was a short, lean, ascetic whipcord of a man, who came in tight-lipped, with two bulky files that he laid on the desk.

'This is a grievous tragedy, Inspector,' he said, 'but I knew it would happen. I told him so.'

Tench was taken aback.

'Told who what, Mr Feldgate?'

'I warned him more than once that he was playing with fire.'

'Fire?'

'A slip of the tongue, Inspector, but you know what I mean.'

'I'm afraid not, sir,' said Tench. 'Please sit down, and maybe then we can get things clear. You're talking about Mr Pashley?'

'Mr Simon, yes. I always called him that. You see, Inspector, we've been solicitors to the Pashley family for more than fifty years. My father, Henry Feldgate, always acted for Mr Roger.'

'Simon Pashley's father.'

'That's right. You should really have got in touch with us immediately, Inspector.'

'I'm sorry, sir,' said Tench, 'but we'd no means of knowing who dealt with Mr Pashley's business affairs, and it was only half an hour ago that we had the first positive identification of the body.'

Mr Feldgate looked at him sharply across the files.

'Yes, well, let it pass. The whole affair is most unfortunate.'

'Tragic, Mr Feldgate.'

'Yes, tragic indeed. A healthy young man with most of his life ahead of him. Do you know yet who did it?'

Tench decided it was time for a little firm control.

'No, sir, we don't. We're not even sure that it wasn't just a case of accidental death.'

'But I read in the morning paper...'

'Press speculation, Mr Feldgate, nothing more. Now, you say that you warned Mr Pashley. What about?'

'Why, not making a will.'

'He never made one, then?'

'Never, to my knowledge. I kept on at him about it. I told him time and time again that, should anything untoward happen, he'd be leaving his affairs in considerable disarray.'

'And what was his reply?'

Mr Feldgate took from his breast pocket a neatly folded handkerchief, brushed it across his nose and replaced it with care.

'He said he'd no intention of dying for many years yet. Said he'd make a will in his own good time. Irresponsible, I'm afraid. Quite irresponsible.'

Tench felt it unwise to argue the point.

'So he died ... what? Intestate?'

'He did, Inspector, yes.'

'And how much is the estate likely to be worth?'

Mr Feldgate flicked open a file.

'Difficult to estimate precisely, Inspector, but something in excess of half a million pounds.'

'A considerable sum.'

'Indeed.'

'And where is this half a million pounds?'

Mr Feldgate snorted down his nose.

'Not invested as it should be.'

'Meaning what, exactly?'

'Meaning, Inspector, exactly what I say. We advised his father on judicious investments: gilt-edged securities, reliable stocks and shares, high-interest-bearing bonds; and his uncle, Mr Philip, was equally shrewd; but Mr Simon was wayward, very wayward indeed.'

'In what sense, Mr Feldgate?'

'He instructed me to sell them all, as well as the whole of the family property.'

'Then where are the proceeds?'

'In banks, sir. In banks. At low rates of interest. He had deposit accounts in three separate banks. I can give you the figures.' He turned the pages of the file. 'He had some hundred and fifty thousand pounds in the National Provincial; another hundred and fifty thousand in Barclays; and two hundred thousand in the Midland.'

'And ten thousand in Lloyds.'

'His loose change, Inspector. That was what he called it.'

Tench scratched his head.

'But why did he do this?'

'You may well ask,' said Mr Feldgate. 'He told me he didn't want the money tied up. Preferred it to be accessible, without prior notice, should he ever need it ... I really think, between you and me, that he liked to see the rows of noughts in a bank book.'

'And where are the bank books? There were none in his cottage.'

'We have them, Inspector. They're held in our vaults. We had instructions to keep the interest payments recorded, and transfer money as needed to keep the Lloyds' account above five thousand pounds.'

'Was he likely to have kept large sums in the cottage?'

'Most unlikely, I would think.'

'And did he ever make any substantial withdrawals?'

'No,' said Mr Feldgate. 'That at least was in his favour. He seemed to live a somewhat Spartan existence for such a wealthy man. But he was losing a great deal from improper investment. I repeatedly pointed that out to no avail. And not to make a will was an act of dereliction.'

Tench pondered the point.

'If a man dies intestate, then who gets the money?'

Mr Feldgate shrugged.

'There is, of course, a line of priority. First to the father and mother, then to brothers or sisters, grandparents, aunts and uncles, and last of all to cousins.'

'And in Mr Pashley's case?'

'The Pashley clan was not prolific or its members long-lived.'

'So?'

'The only surviving relative, it seems, is a cousin: the son of his father's eldest brother, Mr Francis Pashley. His name is Nicholas.'

'And what d'you know about him?'

'He's considerably older than Mr Simon. In his forties, I believe.'

'And where is he?'

'He owns a sheep station in New Zealand. Waitaki Valley, down in the South Island.'

'Moderately well off?'

'According to reliable evidence, extremely well off.'

'Not in desperate need of money.'

'Hardly that, I'd imagine. I understood from Mr Simon that he owned one of the largest flocks in New Zealand.'

'And he'll get the money.'

'Eventually, Inspector, failing any other claimant as yet undetected. But intestacy is a very long-drawn-out business. Most unsatisfactory. I made that abundantly clear to Mr Simon, but he seemed to have only one concern in his life. That windmill of his.'

'I suppose that, too, if it hadn't burnt down, would have gone to this cousin.'

'As a matter of fact, no.' Mr Feldgate flipped open the second of his files. 'Since he was so consumed by this ridiculous mill, was so concerned for its well-being, I did my best to use it to persuade him to sense. I told him that, if only for the sake of its preservation, he should make some testamentary disposition. And there, at least, I succeeded. He came in to see me a month ago, and made a deed of gift to take effect on his death.'

Tench felt his interest quicken.

'A deed of gift. Who to?'

Mr Feldgate referred once again to the file.

'The only man, so he said, who could be trusted to look after it. Someone called Lubbock. A John Spencer Lubbock of Umzinto Cottage in the village of Cley. He gifted him with the mill, its adjacent outbuildings, and five thousand pounds for running repairs.'

Tench stared at him for a moment. He wondered what he ought to say, or, more to the point, what he oughtn't to say.

'This man Lubbock,' he asked, 'does he know about the gift?'

'Certainly not from us,' Mr Feldgate replied. 'That would be most irregular. Whether Mr Simon saw fit to tell him is quite another matter.'

Tench had little time to ponder this revelation, for, no sooner had Mr Feldgate been shown to the door, still roundly condemning the fecklessness of youth, than a call came through from Sergeant Bates on the desk.

'Yes, Sergeant?' he said.

'There's a man down here, sir, says he needs to see you. Name of Burage. William Burage. Comes from Morston.'

'What's his business?'

'Says he's got some information on the case at Kettle Hill.'

'Not confessing, is he?'

'I wouldn't think so, sir. Seems a down-to-earth bloke.'

'Right,' said Tench. 'I'll see him. Get someone to show him up.'

Burage was a stocky, grey-haired, weather-beaten man who walked with a limp and leaned heavily on a stick. He was, as Tench judged, somewhere in his sixties.

'Mr Burage?'

'Tha's right, sir.'

'Good of you to come.'

'Had to. Thought I'd better like. Might be somethin', might not. An' wife were in, shoppin'.'

Tench held out a hand.

'Sit down, Mr Burage ... You live at Morston?'

'Aye. Winter an' summer.'

'Whereabouts in Morston?'

'Agen the main road, sir. Out Cockthorpe way.'

'Going towards Stiffkey?'

'Mile or so from there, sir, but aye, on the road.'

Burage, so it seemed, had been a fisherman at Wells, until an old war wound, coupled with arthritis, had forced him to retire. His son was still fishing out of the port for whelks, and the two of them had had a boat moored at Morston Creek. They'd used it in the summer to take visitors on trips, but the war years had put paid to such holiday traffic. They were hoping now that the trade would pick up.

'You had something you wanted to tell me?'

'Aye,' said Burage, 'an' tha's a fact. It were like this, sir, see.' He stretched out his leg and tapped it with his stick. 'This leg o' mine, it give me a bit o' gyp like at night, an' what wi' that an' th'arthritis, I'm awake like as not. Doctor, he call it somnia, but then he be one o' they blasted furriners. Birmin'am or some such, an' that in't Norfolk. Reckon he be one o' they know-alls, all blether; an' when it come down to it, empty as a bloody ol' kettle that run...'

Tench did a swift bit of mental deduction.

'You were awake on the night of the fire, Mr Burage?'

'Aye, that I were. Wide awake.'

'What time was this?'

'Nigh on two, mebbe.'

'And you saw something?'

'Aye ... It were cramp i' this leg o' mine. Had to get up.'

'Was it something unusual?'

'It were tha', right enough. Blast, Bill, I say, but tha's a bit rum.'

'What was it, Mr Burage?' Tench was courteously patient.

'Well, it were this here cart like...'

'A cart?'

'Hoss an' cart. Had they rubber wheels as folk has a notion to stick on 'em now.'

'Inflatable tyres?'

'Aye, that'd be right. Dawdlin' down th'road it were. An' this big feller leanin' over forrard an' jerkin' at reins. Seemed in a Gor-blasted fret to get some place, he did.'

'Which way was he going?'

'Up to Stiffkey, I reckon, but he weren't more'n crawlin'. Couldn' see what he were totin' around at that hour – it were covered in one o' they sheets o' tarpaulin – but seem like it musta bin a rare kind o' weight.'

'What makes you say that, Mr Burage?'

'Why, it were common sense.' Burage thumped his stick down hard on the floor. 'Poor ol' hoss he were sweatin' an' strainin' at shaf's, an' bloody cart were barely movin'. I were never one fer all they ol' tales about ghosts. Load o' squit they be. But it give me quite a turn, Gor blast it, it did. It were like that there yarn about churchyard watcher. If I hadn't had more sense, I'd a sworn he were shiftin' all they bloody big gravestones from down at All Saints. I were glad when he drawed out o' sight, an' tha's truth. Had to go an' wet me whistle wi' a totful o' rum.'

5

At three forty-five Tench sent down for another cup of coffee. He felt that he needed it. He was beginning to regret that he'd ever agreed to take on the case.

He sat at his desk for the next twenty minutes, pencil in hand, jotting down notes on a writing pad and trying to make sense of the tangled web of facts and rank speculation that surrounded the fire at Kettle Hill mill.

He didn't get very far. At five past four there was an ear-splitting rattle like a Bren machine-gun that signalled the arrival of McKenzie's Norton, spitting smoke in its normal flawless condition, and a couple of minutes later McKenzie himself, his black mane of hair tossed into wild disorder by the breeze of his passage, slapped his notebook on the desk and flopped down on a chair.

'Guess what?' he said in a poor man's imitation of Lubbock.

'You tell me,' said Tench. 'I suppose she couldn't identify the lorry.'

'Who? Your ravishing little artist from Morston Bottom Farm? She's a dainty piece of bric-à-brac if ever I saw one ... No, she identified it as best she could. Said it looked like the one she saw at the mill. That's the most we can hope for. After all, she was never closer to it than a couple of hundred yards. The girl isn't dim, but she hasn't exactly got microscopic eyes ... No, I wasn't thinking about that. I took a statement from her, and one from Lucas, the chap who runs the scrapyard; then I dropped her off at the farm, and went on to see our man Dodds at Stiffkey.'

'A mine of information, according to Lubbock.'

'Oh, he was that all right. Cackled his head off and told me we'd been barking up a couple of empty trees.'

'Go on,' said Tench. 'Tell me the gory details.'

McKenzie brushed back his hair.

'Well, to begin with,' he said, 'it seems our friend Jacks has got a criminal record. Grievous bodily harm. Sent down for six months at Ipswich Assizes in June last year. Took on three lads in a pub down at Beccles. Broke a couple of arms and laid the third out for nigh on twenty minutes. Seems he got off lightly. Said he was provoked. Came out in November.'

'Dodds must have got it wrong. Lubbock said Jacks was only five foot six and thin as a rake. What were they? Circus midgets?'

'All six-footers. Worked in the docks at Lowestoft.'

Tench closed his eyes. It seemed a painful process.

'I don't believe it,' he said.

'Neither did I until Dodds explained. Said he was amazed we didn't know all about it.'

'So,' said Tench wearily, 'what have we missed?'

'We haven't exactly missed anything at all. We took the Chief at his word, and for once he slipped up.'

Tench seemed in a daze.

'Impossible,' he said.

''Fraid not. It's true. He only went up to Breckmarsh once. Isn't that what he said?'

Tench nodded.

'Just the once.'

'And Jacks told him to beat it.'

'Yes, that's right.'

'And being by that time nothing more than an ordinary law-abiding citizen, he took himself off and never tried again.'

'Never even sniffed around. That was what he told me.'

'And this chap who gave him the brush-off was the same scraggy little sod who drove the lorry into Lucas's scrapyard.'

'Must have been, yes.'

111

McKenzie took a deep breath.

'Well,' he said, 'we can't blame the old boy. It was a simple enough mistake. He probably saw this scrawny fellow hanging round the mill and asked if he was Jacks. And the bloke said yes, so what? And the Chief just assumed that he'd been speaking to Gabriel.'

'And he hadn't?'

'No, he hadn't. That was his brother, Raphael. There's two of them. The long and the short of it, Dodds likes to call them. Gabriel's the hulk. He's the one who goes about breaking dockers' arms...'

'...And the one who threatened Pashley and maybe pinched his burr stones.'

'Got to be him, hasn't it? And from what I've heard, he wouldn't find himself averse to a nice bit of arson and probably murder.'

Tench was suddenly angry.

'We should have checked with Dodds before.'

McKenzie shrugged.

'Well, we didn't.'

'No, we damned well didn't.'

'So where do we go from here?'

Tench had already made up his mind about that. He had a lead at last, and after sitting at his desk in some frustration all day, he was ready to seize on the chance for a spot of action.

'We go to Breckmarsh,' he said. 'It's time we paid Mr Gabriel Jacks a visit.'

'And turned his place over.'

'Sacks, bins and hoppers, roof tiles, the lot. I'll see the Chief Super and we'll get an application for a search warrant now. Take it over to Colonel Morland and get him to sign it. There shouldn't be any trouble. We've more than enough evidence with what Dodds has told us. Reasonable suspicion that we'll find stolen goods, even if they're nothing more than a few blocks of stone.'

'Right.' McKenzie rubbed his hands. 'Do we clobber the brute tonight?'

Tench considered the matter.

'No,' he said slowly. 'We'll leave it till tomorrow. Make it straight after the inquest. We need daylight to search. And we'll need someone with us who knows what he's looking for. That means your friend and mine: John Spencer Lubbock. I'll give him a

112

ring. We can pick him up on the way. Let him expiate his sins. He'll jump at the chance.'

McKenzie turned thoughtful.

'Strange how they still stick to biblical names in these out-of-the-way places. There's Dodds. He's an Ezra. Then Gabriel and Raphael.' He chuckled to himself. 'Wasn't Gabriel an angel?'

'Yes,' said Tench, 'he was. The prince of fire and thunder, and the angel of death.'

'That fits,' McKenzie said.

'Maybe.' Tench was cautious.

'Something I don't know?'

'I'm still not happy about Lubbock's theories.'

'He seems to know his windmills.'

'He's got a smattering of knowledge,' said Tench. 'Can't be more than that. I'd like to check his ideas with someone who's actually worked in one. D'you know who the miller was at Kettle Hill before Pashley took over?'

'Not the foggiest idea. Doesn't the Chief know?'

'I haven't asked him,' said Tench, 'and I don't really want to.'

'You don't want him to think that you're checking him out?'

'Something like that.'

'Well, Dodds'd know for sure.'

'Yes, he would,' said Tench, 'wouldn't he? Did he mention anything about Gabriel Jacks owning a horse and cart?'

McKenzie shook his head.

'Why d'you want to know?'

'Chap called Burage saw one. Crawling through Morston and going towards Breckmarsh. Two o'clock in the morning on the night of the fire. It was loaded with something heavy, and the time fits all right. The driver was a big fellow. Could have been Jacks.'

'Most likely was. Check it out tomorrow morning ... You didn't see any sign when you were up there yesterday?'

'No. But I couldn't see inside the barn and I'd be willing to swear there was straw on the stable floor.'

'Well, he could have one,' McKenzie said. 'The trouble is, like lorries, they're not exactly scarce. The Boldings have got one. Saw it down at the farm ... Anything else turned up?'

'Nothing that makes much sense at the moment, except that we've got a firm identification.' He explained about Boothway.

'Well, at least that's one point cleared up,' said McKenzie.

113

'And Lubbock's the owner of a burnt-out mill.'

'He's what?'

'Apparently Pashley wanted him to have Kettle Hill. Left it to him by a deed of gift.'

McKenzie looked bemused.

'What's he going to do with it?'

'I don't think he knows anything about it yet.'

'But you do?'

'On the quiet.'

'Are you going to tell him?'

'No. Neither of us are.'

'Why not?'

'Two reasons, Mac,' said Tench. 'If he hasn't been told, then it's not our place to tell him. And if he does know, then he'll tell us sooner or later . . . Probably later, but you know Lubbock. He won't be able to keep it a secret.'

6

Left on his own, Tench stared at the phone. Then he lifted the receiver, referred to a list of numbers and dialled the operator.

'Give me Stiffkey double two,' he said.

Five minutes later he was driving through Norwich and out on the road to Holt.

The police house at Stiffkey was the usual brick-and-flint cottage with a white wooden porch. The garden was immaculate: a narrow gravel path edged with rounded flints, and two small circular lawns, each with a standard rose in the centre. There wasn't a weed to be seen, and the bush roses in the flower beds were aligned with an almost regimental precision.

Constable Dodds was equally impressive. He was not merely the arm of the law in Stiffkey, but its trunk as well, and a sturdy trunk at that. A good six feet tall and broad round the waist, he reflected the weight and dignity that only a man in full command of his parish could possibly do, and Tench approached him with every bit of the respect due to a man who was twenty years his senior, infinitely more experienced and likely, as Lubbock said, to prove a mine of information.

'Good evening, Constable,' he said. 'Inspector Tench from Norwich. You had my sergeant in to see you earlier today.'

'Aye, that's a fact, sir.' Dodds all but smiled. 'Wanted to know about Gabriel Jacks. Reckon I put him right.'

'You certainly did that. We should have come to you before. Are you willing to share a bit more of your local knowledge?'

'Do my best, sir,' said Dodds. 'Step inside for a spell.'

He ushered Tench into a parlour as immaculate as the garden, sat him down in a massive high-backed armchair and took the other one himself.

'Now, sir,' he said. 'How can I help?'

'You know we're investigating the fire at Kettle Hill and the theft from there of a number of burr stones?'

The constable nodded.

'So Sergeant McKenzie told me.'

'I'm looking for someone who knew the mill machinery and exactly how it worked.'

Dodds didn't hesitate.

'That's easy enough, sir. The chap you want to see is old Josh Randall. He knows more about the mill than any man living.'

'Randall?'

'He was miller afore that young lad Pashley. Ran the place for nigh on twenty years, he did.'

'And he's still alive?'

'Aye. Getting a bit frail. Must be seventy by now. Been a miller all his life. Afore he came up here, he ran a mill down in Suffolk. Linstead Green, near Halesworth.'

'He was the man young Pashley pensioned off.'

'That's right, sir. Set him up in a cottage at Binham.'

'And he still lives there?'

'He does, sir, yes. Two miles up the road.'

'What sort of a man is he?'

Dodds stroked his moustache.

'Josh? He's a stumpy little chap, five foot six or seven...'

'I mean what's he like to talk to? Approachable?'

'I'd say so.'

'And reliable?'

'Oh, no doubt about that, sir,' said Dodds. 'I've known him

115

ever since he came to Kettle Hill. Never put a foot wrong. Trust him with your life, and he wouldn't let you down.'

'Right, I'll go up and see him ... By the way, Constable, does Gabriel Jacks own a horse and cart?'

'Never seen one, sir, no. Just that mucky old lorry. Been running around in it as long as I remember.'

'What about this brother of his?'

'Raphael?'

'That's the one.'

'Just helps him part-time. Lives over at Warham. As far as I know, the only thing he's got is an old bike he bought in a sale down at Wells.'

'Would either of them steal those burr stones?'

'Aye, more than likely. Light-fingered as Fagin. One's as bad as t'other.'

'And it seems that Gabriel's got a bit of a temper.'

'Aye, more than a bit.'

'And he's strong.'

Dodds chuckled.

'With all due respect, sir, he'd crack you across his knee.'

Tench nodded slowly.

'So in one of his fits of temper he could easily kill someone.'

'Could do, sir, yes. Doesn't know his own strength, that's Gabriel's trouble.'

'You know we're treating Pashley's death as suspicious?'

'I'm aware of that, sir.'

'From what you know of this man, d'you think he could have killed the lad? Suppose he did steal those stones and Pashley caught him in the act ...'

Dodds leaned forward, spread his hands upon his knees.

'Let's put it this way, sir. If he did, then it wouldn't have been deliberate.'

'Not premeditated?'

'No.'

'Would he throw him down a ladder in the mill?'

Dodds scratched his head.

'It's difficult to say just what Gabriel would do if his temper was roused, but whatever he did, it wouldn't be with any intention of killing the lad.'

'That could have been the result.'

'It might have been, yes, but let's go carefully, sir. From what Sergeant McKenzie said, you've got some idea that the mill was fired deliberately.'

'Just a suspicion. It's nothing more than that.'

'You think Gabriel killed the lad and set the mill ablaze to cover his tracks.'

'It could be a possibility.'

Dodds shook his head.

'That wouldn't be my reading of Gabriel,' he said. 'He's a bully and a liar and I wouldn't put it past him to make off with those stones, but he's a desperate coward and he doesn't think too fast. If he found he'd killed the lad, he'd be off like a shot. He hasn't got the brains to do anything else ... You think he's hidden the stones at Breckmarsh?'

'If he took them,' said Tench, 'then yes, he must have done. We're searching the place tomorrow. I'd like you to be there.'

Dodds got to his feet.

'Aye, sir,' he said, 'that might be a good idea ... Any special time?'

'We've got the inquest at ten. Say half-past eleven?'

'I'll be there, sir. Don't worry.'

Tench pushed himself up.

'Right. Thank you for the help, Constable,' he said. 'Now whereabouts in Binham is this cottage of Randall's?'

7

It was flint, with a pantiled roof, possibly a worker's cottage from one of the old farms.

He walked up the path and knocked on the door.

Randall was, as Dodds had said, a stumpy little man, but broad of shoulder, and Tench could well imagine that, in his younger days, he might have handled a twenty-stone sack with some ease.

He introduced himself, and Randall led him down a dingy hallway, past a flight of stairs and a branching hatstand into the cottage parlour. There was a Welsh dresser hung about with crockery, and a heavy oak table and two oak chairs. Randall took one and motioned Tench to the other.

'Ye say it were Ezra Dodds as sent ye to see me?'

'That's right, Mr Randall.'

'An' ye're all the way from Norwich?'

'Correct.'

'Then it mus' be a mite important, this business o' yourn?'

'You could say that, yes, but this is just a friendly visit. I need some advice.'

Randall's eyes narrowed.

'Advice?' he said. 'From me? There's little enough I know ye'd find useful in Norwich.'

'Oh, there may be quite a lot, Mr Randall. You'd be surprised. According to Constable Dodds you're the man I need to see. He says you're the expert.'

Randall's eyebrows, heavy and silvery-grey, flicked upwards a fraction.

'Owd Ezra, 'e ramble on a bit. Can't say as I ever thought I were an expert. Far from it.'

'Not even on Kettle Hill mill, Mr Randall? Surely you must know a great deal about it. After all, you worked there for ... how long was it?'

'Nigh on twenty year ... Aye, well, maybe I do know a bit about the mill, though if ye're lookin' fer me to tell ye what happened there las' Tuesday I'll not be makin' much sense.'

'You'll make more than I can, Mr Randall, that's for sure. I know nothing about windmills.'

Randall was laconic.

'There's not many as does.'

'No,' Tench said smoothly, 'I'm quite sure you're right. That's why I need some expert assistance. We're investigating the fire and the death of Simon Pashley, and we think there may be something suspicious about both.'

'Then I reckon ye're wastin' time.'

'You do?'

'Aye, the lad were pleasant enough. I've no complaints about 'im. Treated me fair. Set me up in this cottage. But 'e 'adn't got the nous to run a mill on 'is own.'

'You think not?'

'Stands to reason, lad. Never worked a mill till 'e come to see me. Offered to stay on, I did, teach 'im 'ow to go about it. But no, 'e were all fer learnin' on 'is own.' Randall shook his head. 'Can't be

118

done that way o' things. Them as takes on a mill needs prenticin' first.'

'You think he made a mistake?'

'More ner one from the look o' things.'

Tench seized on the point.

'You've been up there?'

'Aye.'

'When was that?'

'Reckon it were Wednesday. Didn't stay long, mind. Wandered up, took a look, saw enough an' come back.'

'So you don't think the mill was set on fire by lightning?'

'Oh, there were lightnin' right enough. Sack chain were welded.'

'But it didn't cause the fire.'

'Helped a bit, mebbe. Reckon that were all.'

'Then how did the fire start?'

'Mill were runnin'. Must a bin. Then she run dry.'

'What makes you say that?'

'Stones was all scratted. Run out o' grain.'

'So what d'you think happened?'

Randall eyed him for a moment: a calculated pause.

'Wind were pretty strong. Reckon 'e were workin' late an' tried to ride out the storm. Kept 'is shutters closed an' mill ran away.'

'You mean the brake wouldn't hold it?'

'Like as not it caught fire.'

Tench seemed to hesitate.

'But isn't there some method of turning the sails away from the wind?'

'Aye, quarterin' the mill.'

'Couldn't he have done that?'

'Takes time, lad. 'E'd be workin' down below. By the time 'e got up top, 'e'd be blinded by smoke. Looks like 'e panicked, tried to disengage fantail an' were trapped at top by the fire. That'd be the time when the stones run dry.'

'So you think the fire started at the top of the mill?'

'Aye, more like than not.'

'Not by sparks from the millstones?'

'Nay. If lad 'ad bin down below, 'e'd 'ave fed in more grain.'

'Isn't there some means of telling when the grain's running low?'

'Aye. Bell alarm'd ring.'

'But you think he was trapped at the top of the mill when the bell alarm rang.'

'Must a bin, aye.'

Tench took a deep breath.

'Mr Randall,' he said, 'you told me your explanation wouldn't make much sense. It sounds feasible enough to me.'

'Oh, it's that right enough.' The old man thumped the table. He seemed suddenly angry. 'But it still don't make sense, not to them as knows 'ow a mill should be run. Lad weren't seasoned enough. 'E were plain daft to try an' ride out that wind.'

'Not what you'd have done.'

'Last thing I'd 'ave done.' Randall pushed back his chair. 'One sniff o' that storm, an' I'd 'ave opened the shutters, closed the mill down, quartered the sails an' gone straight to bed.'

Tench drove back to Norwich in a thoughtful frame of mind. Once there, he rang up Morston Bottom Farm and spoke to Hilary Dixon. After that he rang Lubbock.

'Well, laddie? What?'

Tench told him about Boothway, Mr Feldgate and Burage; and then, with as much tact as he could reasonably muster, explained about Gabriel and Raphael Jacks.

Lubbock's comment on that opened his eyes a fraction, though, thinking about it later, he wasn't really surprised.

'And we're searching Breckmarsh tomorrow morning after the inquest. We're going to need help, so we'll pick you up at Cley.'

'Good. About time. Anything else to report?'

'I don't think so,' said Tench.

He didn't mention his evening trip to see Dodds or the talk he'd had with Randall.

As he'd told Meg Dennison, little boys grew up, and when they grew up they tended to keep some secrets to themselves.

4

FRIDAY

'Watch the wall, my darling ...'
Kipling, *A Smuggler's Song*

1

Tench appraised her across the desk. She was just as attractive: lithe and slim, a white skirt and jumper, pony-tail swinging, a gold charm bracelet circling her wrist.

'Thank you for coming so early,' he said.

'No trouble.' She smiled. 'I had to come in anyway. Needed a new wash brush.'

The dark eyes looked up at him, bright with inquiry.

'Have you found him then?' she asked. 'The man with the lorry?'

'Well, we think we know who he is.' Tench was guarded. 'We've a little way to go before we can prove he did anything more than threaten Mr Pashley.'

'But you're making investigations.'

'Yes, Miss Dixon, we're certainly doing that.'

'And you think I can help?'

'It's possible.'

'Then, of course, I'll do anything I can.'

'It's just a matter', said Tench, 'of clearing up one or two odd little points ... I have to ask you this, so please don't take offence. You told me you didn't know Mr Pashley very well. Was that strictly the truth?'

She seemed unperturbed.

'Yes, as near as I could honestly get to the truth. I met him three or four times. We had tea together twice. He showed me round the mill. We talked. And that was just about all there was to it.'

'What did you talk about?'

'Windmills and painting. The obvious things.'

'Nothing ... more intimate?'

She gave a little laugh.

'You mean did he seduce me? No, Inspector, he didn't. He never

123

even tried. We chatted to one another. I liked him. He was interesting, but that's as far as it went.'

Tench nodded.

'Fair enough. Have you made any other friends here in
Norfolk?'

'Only Walter and Ag.'

'No young men dancing attendance on you?'

'No.' She seemed mildly amused. 'I came up here to paint. There
isn't much in the way of night life round Blakeney and Wells.'

'What about Norwich?'

'I've only been here twice, and that was to buy colours.'

Tench felt that to press any further would be pointless.

'Did Mr Pashley tell you anything about himself?'

'Very little. He said an uncle had left him the mill. He was trying
to keep it running because there weren't many left.'

'Did you know he was very wealthy?'

'Who? Simon?' She seemed completely taken aback. 'No, he
never mentioned money. Just what d'you mean by wealthy?'

'He had a fortune of more than half a million pounds.'

She stared at him.

'Come again.'

'He was very rich indeed.'

'Surely not.'

'Yes, it's true.'

'But he seemed such a very ordinary young man. No, Inspector,
I hadn't the faintest idea. I don't normally mix with the millionaire
set ... You think somebody may have been after his money?'

'There's no reason yet to think so, but we can't entirely rule out
the possibility. Please think hard, Miss Dixon. While you were
painting, did you ever see anyone else round the mill?'

'You mean anyone suspicious?'

'Anyone at all.'

She furrowed her brow.

'Well, there was the postman. He came on a bicycle. Walter
brought the milk from the farm every day. And a delivery man
came with the bread from Suttons in Blakeney. He parked his van
on the road and walked up the track.'

'No one else?'

'I don't think so ... Yes, wait a minute. There was one strange
man. The day I started painting.'

124

'How long ago was that?'

'Oh, a month ago now.'

'Tell me about him,' said Tench.

She hesitated.

'Well . . . Simon had gone out delivering flour in the lorry. I saw him loading up and then he drove off. I was trying to make up my mind which was the best angle to paint the mill from. I was quite close, I remember, but kneeling down by a clump of gorse, when this man came out from behind the cottage. He unlocked the door of the mill and went in . . .'

'And after that?'

'I didn't really think anything of it. I'd only met Simon once, and I just assumed it must be some friend of his. I simply carried on with what I was doing.'

'Did you see him come out?'

She nodded.

'Yes, about ten minutes later. He went across to the cottage and disappeared inside.'

'Did he unlock the door there?'

'I think he must have done, yes.'

'And how long did he stay?'

She shook her head and the pony-tail swung.

'I don't honestly know. I didn't stay very long myself. Made a few quick sketches, and then I was off to Blakeney. I didn't see him leave.'

'Did you ever mention this to Mr Pashley?'

'No, it didn't seem that important.'

'What was he like, this man?'

'Youngish, I'd say. Fairly tall and slim. He walked with a limp.'

'You never saw him there again?'

'No, just that once.'

'Is there anything more you remember about him? What was he wearing?'

'That's difficult,' she said. 'An open-necked shirt? I think it was a check.'

'Smart, was he?'

'Oh, no.' She shook her head again firmly. 'Far from it. Looked as if he hadn't had a shave for quite a time.'

'Scruffy?'

'Decidedly.'

'Anything else? What about his hair?'

'Cut short. Very dark. Could well have been black.'

'And you've never seen him anywhere else around here?'

'No. Mind you, I haven't really looked out for him ... You think it might be worthwhile following him up?'

'Anyone who lets himself into Kettle Hill with a key is worth following up. If we find him, we'll want to know what he was doing there.'

'So it might be a good thing if I kept an eye open.'

'More than that,' said Tench. 'Keep both eyes open. If you see him again, let me know straight away.'

'Any luck?' said McKenzie.

'Depends what you mean. Know any men who limp?'

'One or two. Why?'

'Only that we've now got a limping man with a key to Kettle Hill. Hangs around the place, waits till Pashley goes out, then opens up the mill and after that the cottage and takes a sniff around.'

'That's interesting.'

'It is. We'd better start looking. Who's going with us to Breckmarsh?'

'Rayner, Gregg and Spurgeon.'

'That leaves Lock. Tell him to track down the postman who delivered to Kettle Hill, and the man who drives the bread van from Suttons in Blakeney. Ask them if they've seen a limping man around. At the moment it's all conjecture, but he might turn something up. Not that it really alters the case against Jacks. The signs still point to him.'

'They pointed that way for me,' McKenzie said drily, 'ever since Dodds broke his little bit of news, and that was before all that tale about the cart. It's a pity we've got this damned inquest this morning. We could have been down at Breckmarsh a couple of hours ago and winkled him out.'

Tench gave a shrug.

'First things first,' he said. 'We've another job to do, so let's get it done.'

'Right.' McKenzie pushed aside his chair; then he bent down and picked up something from the floor. 'Looks like your little artist's lost a bit of her bric-à-brac.' He turned it between his fingers. 'Appropriate, too. A windmill.'

Tench took it from him: a tiny gold windmill set with pin-points of light that sparkled in the sun.

'It's a charm,' he said. 'Must have come off her bracelet. Yes, look. The link's opened up.'

He slid out a drawer in the desk, and dropped it inside.

'Better save it for her. I'll give her a ring later and tell her we've found it.'

2

The coroner, a grey man in a grey suit and tie, seemed determined to deal with the case as swiftly as possible. After a few words with Tench, he announced that they were present to inquire into the death of one Simon Frenchard Delisle Pashley at Kettle Hill, Norfolk on such and such a date, and set the inquest in motion without further delay.

The fire officer in charge on the night of the incident was called upon briefly to state how the body had been discovered and then removed from the mill. He was followed by the dental surgeon, Anthony Boothway, who gave evidence of identification based on the impressions, the X-ray plates and his own dental records. A young man, sporting a pink shirt and red tie as if in deliberate defiance of convention, he detailed the work he'd performed on Pashley's teeth in the previous twelve months. Speaking in precise but supercilious tones, he listed the fillings he'd made in both upper and lower jaws, the capping of a left lower incisor, and the extraction of an upper right molar, a wisdom tooth. He had, he admitted, been forced to leave a part of the molar root still in position, and he pointed out the presence of this residual root on the X-ray photographs. He also produced a diagram and explained its correspondence with the prints and impressions the police had provided. In answer to the coroner, he declared that, in his opinion, there was no doubt that the body was that of Simon Pashley. The dental data recovered from the victim of the fire at Kettle Hill matched precisely the information in his files.

The pathologist's report was then read out, and Ledward, in the voice that Lubbock had once described as like crackling parchment, answered a number of supplementary questions. No, at this stage he was not prepared to be conclusive about the cause of death. The evidence proved that the deceased had survived the outbreak of fire, and the injuries were consistent with a fall from some considerable height, but he was not, of course, in any position to say how such a fall might have happened. Yes, the deceased could well have been overcome by smoke, but there was insufficient evidence to say that this had caused his death. Nor was it clear whether the injuries had been sustained before or after death.

The fire officer was then recalled, and, while conceding that his initial conclusion had been that lightning caused the fire, he acknowledged that certain evidence had since come to light which cast doubt on that assumption. No, he would prefer not to say what this was. The police, he knew, had the business in hand.

It was then Tench's turn. Yes, he said, in answer to the coroner's questions, there were certain circumstances connected with the fire which led him to believe that he might well be dealing with a case of arson. This, as the coroner would appreciate, could carry with it more serious implications. No, with all due respect, he would, at the moment, prefer to say nothing more. The police were making inquiries, and any further revelations might prejudice the course of the investigation. He therefore asked that the inquest be adjourned.

The coroner said he fully appreciated the situation. He commented on the tragic nature of the fire, expressed his sympathy with any relatives of the young man concerned, wished the police success in their inquiries and, without further ado, granted the adjournment.

The court then dispersed. Tench told the reporters that he'd issue a statement later in the day, and took Ransome aside and promised him that if there were any developments he'd be the first to know. Then, after another few words with the coroner, he drove off with McKenzie down the road to Holt.

The sergeant flexed his arms.

'Well, that's that,' he said. 'Gives us time to nail our friend Jacks to the wall ... What did the Chief say when you rang him up last

128

night and told him that that awkward little bugger he met wasn't Gabriel at all?'

Tench grinned.

'He offered me his warm congratulations.'

'Did he, by God?'

'He did,' said Tench. 'Told me he was glad to see I was following his instructions. Hadn't he warned me more than once to be suspicious of people's statements? They always needed checking. Even those that seemed to come from an impeccable source.'

McKenzie shook his head. Then he lit a cigarette and tossed the match through the window.

'What did you expect?' he said. 'A confession of guilt?'

3

In the first car were Tench and McKenzie; in the second the three detective constables, Rayner, Gregg and Spurgeon; behind them, Lubbock in his toiling three-wheeler; and at the bottom of the track that led to Breckmarsh mill stood Constable Dodds, leaning on his bike.

'Glad to see you've brought a full posse, sir,' he said. 'You'll maybe be needing it. This Gabriel Jacks, he's not the sort of chap to be tackling on your own. Best let me go first and do the explaining. He knows me from way back, and I know him. Had to deal with him before, and that may be a help.'

Tench pulled his warrant from the locker by the dashboard.

'Right, Constable,' he said. 'You lead the way. If there should be any trouble, we've more than enough back-up to quieten him down.'

Dodds shook his head doubtfully.

'I wouldn't be so sure about that, sir,' he said. 'If I were in your shoes, I'd step a bit wary. He's a big man is Gabriel, all muscle and sinew, and when he's roused he's a temper like one of those wild bull-elephants in must. Get him going and he's likely to do something more than twist a few arms. Those three he took on in that pub down in Beccles were a good lot weightier than anybody here.'

'We're not looking for a confrontation, Constable,' said Tench, 'but we've a warrant to search the mill and it's going to be searched. Any trouble from Mr Jacks and he'll find himself spending the night in a cell.'

Dodds tugged at his moustache.

'Understood, sir,' he said, 'but I wouldn't want any of your bright young lads to be ending up tonight in a hospital bed.'

The mill door was shut. Dodds knocked without response.

'Gabriel,' he called.

There was no sound from inside. He called again, louder.

'Gabriel. You in there? It's Constable Dodds.'

There was a clattering and swearing from somewhere up above; then a voice shouted down.

'What the hell ye want?'

Tench took a step back. Some twenty feet up, leaning on the railing of the stage round the tower, was a bullet-headed man in a fisherman's jersey.

'Are you Gabriel Jacks?'

The man rested his arms on the rail, and spat out a stream of brown tobacco juice.

'What ye blarin' away at?'

'Is your name Gabriel Jacks?'

'Mebbe, mebbe not. What ye wantin' to know fer?'

'I've a warrant to search these premises, Mr Jacks.'

'Have ye, Gorblast it? An' who the hell are ye? Who's this long streak o' mungey ye've brought wi' ye, Dodds?'

'This', said Dodds, 'is Detective Inspector Tench. He's come all the way from Norwich. Best get down, boy, and sharp. A warrant's a warrant.'

'An' what'll ye be lookin' fer?'

'Never you mind, boy. Just you come down.'

'We've reason to believe', said Tench, 'that there may be stolen goods somewhere on the premises.'

'Stolen goods? Tha's a lie.'

'If it is, boy,' said Dodds, 'you've no reason to stop the inspector from searching. Best come down and open up. Then you'll be in the clear.'

'Can't be wastin' bloody time wi' a load of owd dickeys. Got work to do.'

130

'Maybe so, but so have we. Come on now, boy. Get down those ladders and open the door. We don't want to have to force it.'

'Mr Jacks,' said Tench, 'you're obstructing the police. That's a dangerous thing to do. You could well be arrested.'

Jacks grinned down at him.

'Ye reckon so, manny? Now ent that too bad? An' who'll be a-doin' it?'

'If necessary, I will.'

'Tha's a bloody laugh.'

'Mr Jacks, I'm giving you an order. Open up.'

Jacks spat for a second time on the planking.

'Open up yerself,' he said. 'Door's on th'sneck. If ye want to search, search, an' stop bettyin' about.'

They searched, all seven of them. Rayner, Gregg and Spurgeon combed the roundhouse, the stables and the brick-and-flint barn; McKenzie worked through the cottage; Dodds and Tench scoured the mill; and Lubbock, enveloped in acrid smoke, devoted himself to each of them in turn; while from time to time Jacks, like a menacing thunder cloud, hovered around them, grunting mono-syllabic answers to questions and making it clear in no uncertain terms that they were wasting his bloody time and wasting their own.

At the end of an hour, Tench began to wonder whether he wasn't right. Despite all their efforts, they'd found nothing at all: no trace of a burr stone, no sign of a horse and cart, no indication that any form of transport, apart from the lorry, had been used around the mill. The barn was empty, the stables swept clean, and the round-house held nothing but the normal clutter of sacks and chains, dressing tools and timber wedges.

There was a large double trap let into the floor of the mill, and Lubbock said it led to a basement storeroom. It had to be that, because of the block and tackle suspended above it. He raised one of the flaps, borrowed Tench's torch and climbed down the ladder, but once again to no avail. The only things he could find were a dozen sacks of grain and three badly worn Peak stones reared against the wall.

Tench followed him down.

'Anything here?' he said.

131

'Not a damn thing.'

Frustration began to show. Tench slapped his thigh.

'Then where the hell are they?'

'The burr stones? God knows, but they're somewhere about. We need more time, laddie. Given the time, we'll find them.'

'You're still sure that he took them?'

'Who else would need them?'

Tench shrugged his shoulders.

'You're the expert,' he said. 'We're not even sure that he needed them, are we?'

Lubbock straightened up.

'Not yet, but we could be. There are one or two questions I'd like to ask our friend Jacks. Come up to the stone floor. I'll show you what I mean.'

They trudged up the ladders. The stone floor was empty. There was no sign of Jacks, or any of the other searchers.

Lubbock pointed to an octagonal wooden case on a plinth.

'See that?' he said. 'That's a stone vat. Inside you'll find the millstones. Now, laddie, if I'm right, Jacks must have at least one pair of burrs. The others may be Peak stones. He'll use them for grist.' He laid his hand on the casing. 'It's my bet,' he said, 'that this one holds the Peak stones.'

Tench peered at it closely.

'How can you be sure?'

'Can't be sure, laddie. Not till the vat's removed. But look over here.' He dragged aside a tarpaulin cover. 'This is the other pair, and from the look of it Jacks has been doing some work. There's no vat over this pair. The stones are exposed.'

Tench looked at them; ran his hand across the top one.

'Meaning?' he said.

'Meaning that there's something strange going on. Look, laddie, there's hardly any grist milling these days; farmers grind their own barley for animal feed; so Jacks must be turning out flour and little else. That's what his living depends on, and for quality flour he needs to use burrs. Am I making myself clear?'

Tench gave a sigh.

'Transparent,' he said.

'Right.' Lubbock was unruffled. 'Let's move on from there. He's

132

stopped his deliveries. He's told his customers they won't be getting any flour for maybe three weeks. Now, you're not telling me that's just because his lorry's given up the ghost. He could have hired one, borrowed one, bought a second-hand one if he'd needed to keep his customers supplied. No, something's stopped the mill. It's not his auxiliary engine. That's in good nick. So, if I'm right, something's happened to put his burrs out of action. It's not often that a burr stone disintegrates, laddie, but it has been known to happen. And more than once. After years and years of dressing, the band can wear down and snap if it's not replaced. A piece of metal in the grain can do even more damage. Now if that's what's happened here, it wouldn't merely stop Jacks from grinding his flour, it'd wreck the vat as well, blast it into pieces ... And there isn't any sign of a vat around, is there? Or am I going blind?'

'No' – Tench was puzzled – 'but the stones are still in place.'

Lubbock nodded.

'That's true. Two stones are still in place. But I'd like to ask Jacks one very simple question. That bedstone's a burr, but the runner – the one you've got your hand on – that isn't. It's a Peak stone ... They're incompatible, laddie, at least to some extent. They just don't fit together. You can't grind anything much at all with a combination like that. Rough grist perhaps, but not quality flour. Now Jacks is a flour miller. He knows what he's doing. So why's he mounted a Peak stone on top of a burr? It just doesn't make sense.'

'Desperation?' said Tench.

'No, there's more to it than that. There's something very odd going on at this mill, and the sooner we find out what it is the better.'

McKenzie had wandered in from the cottage. He'd been listening intently.

'Let's take the bugger in,' he said, 'and give him a grilling.'

Tench looked towards Lubbock.

'And what would you advise, sir?' he murmured very sweetly.

Lubbock struck a match and relit his pipe.

'Take them both in,' he said. 'Him and that nasty little whelp of a brother. Where is he, by the way?'

'Dodds says he's only a part-time helper. Lives down at Warham.'

'Then round him up as well. Stick them both on the griddle. You need answers, laddie. Not that I think you're likely to get very

133

many, but at least you can hold Jacks himself on suspicion. Cool him off in a cell. That'll give us the time to poke around a bit more.' He picked up an empty sack. 'And if I were you,' he said, 'I'd get this to forensics. And one of Pashley's, too. They may tell us more than our shifty friend here's ever likely to tell us.'

4

Tench assembled all his forces.

'Gabriel Jacks,' he said, 'I'm making inquiries into the fire at Kettle Hill and the theft from there of a number of valuable blocks of stone. I've reason to believe that you may be connected with both these incidents. I'm therefore taking you back with me to Norwich for questioning.'

Jacks eyed him with contempt.

'Tha's a load o' squit. Ye couldn' make a fist o' draggin' me as fur as ye could spit a bloody cobble.'

'Are you refusing to come?'

'An' what if a be?'

'Then,' said Tench stiffly, 'I shall have no alternative but to place you under arrest.'

'You an' who else?'

'I'm warning you, Mr Jacks...'

'Warnin' me, ye grit babby? Ye couldn' stop a pig in a passage, an' tha's a fact.'

'I'm warning you, Mr Jacks – any violence against my men and, with your prison record, you'll find yourself serving a much longer sentence than the one you served in Ipswich. Now what's it to be? Are you coming, or are you not?'

Jacks glowered. He seemed to be weighing the odds against him. Then he suddenly shrugged and turned towards the door.

McKenzie drove him back to Norwich with the three detective constables. Dodds pedalled off on his bike towards Stiffkey.

Tench lingered behind with Lubbock.

'Any ideas?' he asked.

Lubbock lit his pipe and sat down on a grain sack.

'One,' he said, 'but it needs testing out.'

'You still think it was murder, not just plain, straightforward theft?'

'Don't you?'

Tench wasn't to be drawn.

'To tell you the truth, I don't honestly know.'

Lubbock ground his pipe stem.

'Oh, yes,' he said, 'it was murder right enough ... Any more developments since you rang me last night?'

'I sent Lock out to Wymondham to make some inquiries about young Pashley. He came up with some answers, but all of them negative.'

'No attachments?'

'Nothing serious. Seems to have played the field a bit. Two or three girls who knew him. Took them out once or twice, but none of them lasted for any length of time ... Gregg went down to see the Boldings. Walter delivered the milk every day, but he'd never seen any women around the mill. Apart from Miss Dixon.'

'And what about her?'

'Had a word with her this morning.'

'Sticks to her story?'

'Yes, says he was nothing more than a casual acquaintance. Cups of tea and chats. She certainly didn't know anything about his money. He doesn't seem to have talked very much about himself.'

'No, he wouldn't,' said Lubbock. 'And she didn't see anyone else except Jacks?'

'Ah, well' – Tench paused – 'that's where there's one of your slight complications.'

'What kind of a complication?'

'A man with a limp.'

'Go on.'

Tench explained. Lubbock puffed at his pipe.

'And he had a key, this chap?'

'Apparently so.'

'And she said he came out from behind the cottage?'

'That's what she told me.'

'Sounds as if someone else knew about that key Pashley kept behind the brick.'

'Yes, I had thought of that.'

135

'But I'm pretty sure he didn't tell anyone else about it.'

'Then maybe our limping man just happened to see him hide it.'

'That's possible, laddie. It's more than possible. But there's another complication. You say Miss Dixon saw this man unlock the mill. She was sure about that?'

'Very sure. Why?'

'Well, that key behind the brick was only to the cottage. The mill had a different one. So had all the outbuildings. The granary, the stables, the cartlodge, the mill: they all had separate keys. You know that. You took them all away. So if what Miss Dixon says is true, and this limping man used a key on the mill...'

'He must have had more than one, perhaps all the lot.'

'Well, he must have had two.'

Tench was suddenly thoughtful.

'Suppose he had all the lot. He could have opened up the stables and taken the burr stones. You said that all the doors were unlocked the day after the fire ... D'you know any limping millers?'

Lubbock wandered to the mill door and knocked out his pipe. Then he stuffed it in his pocket and sat down again.

'Let's slow down a bit, laddie. You're moving too fast, jumping to conclusions ... First of all, no, I've never seen a lame miller, and now that I've seen Jacks I've seen every one in Norfolk. Second, Jacks is the only one who might have needed those stones; and third, he's got a Peak stone mounted on a burr. So, before we go chasing the stones somewhere else, let's make sure he hasn't got them stowed away here.'

'But we've searched the place already from top to bottom.'

'We've searched the mill floors, the cottage, the outbuildings, yes, but I still think they're here, so let's not get sidetracked till we're certain they aren't. All right, think about this man with a limp. Get someone out searching, trying to track him down...'

'Lock's doing that now.'

'Good. But in the meantime concentrate on Jacks. Give him a good grilling. See if he's got any plausible answers. And leave me here for the moment. I want to have a look at that vat that's still sealed. I'll call in at Dodds' place on the way back and drop off the keys. Will that be all right?'

'I should think so,' said Tench. 'Once everything's locked up, Dodds is the chap to keep an eye on the place. They'll be safe enough with him.'

136

'Right.' Lubbock was already at the foot of the ladder that led to the stone floor. 'The point is, laddie, I'm not entirely convinced by your little artist girl. She could have been mistaken. It's not easy to tell if someone's turning a key or picking a lock. And they're easy enough to pick, these locks on old mills. One turn and you're inside ... She didn't mention a bunch of keys?'

'No, she didn't,' Tench admitted.

'You see, Mike, there's only one man I can think of who just might have a set of keys to the mill. That's the old miller, Randall, and I'd rule him out straight away. I've never met him, it's true, but according to Simon he was sound as a bell. Honest, reliable, the best type of miller. He wouldn't be one to hang on to a bunch of keys, let alone use them to turn the place over. And in any case this limping man that she saw was far too young to be Randall ... No, for the moment at least, lad, I'm sticking to Jacks. You put him through the mincer, I'll test out this little notion of mine, and I reckon that between us we'll uncover those stones.'

He began to climb the steps, then half-way up he stopped.

'I'll give you a ring,' he said, 'if anything turns up ... Oh, and don't forget to pick up that sack from Kettle Hill.'

Tench drove away slowly through Stiffkey and Morston. Beyond Morston Bottom he turned up the track that led to Kettle Hill and stopped by the burnt-out ruin of the mill. Then he unlocked the glove compartment in the car, took out a ring with a cluster of keys and walked round to the stables.

He examined the lock and chose what he thought was the appropriate key. It turned with an easy, satisfying click and he pushed the door open.

He rummaged through the pile of empty sacks in a corner, picked out a couple and took them back to the car. After that he made a tour of the rest of the buildings – the granary, the cartlodge, and last of all the cottage – testing each of the locks in its turn. As Lubbock had implied, they were all warded locks, simple devices, meat and drink to the casual thief. The only door with any refinement at all was the one to the cartlodge, where Pashley had garaged his lorry and the old Snipe saloon. That, in addition to the warded lock, was fitted with a Yale.

He couldn't test the mill itself: there was no door to test; but the one remaining key seemed no different in essence from those that unlocked the rest of the buildings.

Back in the car, he sat for some moments staring at the smoke-blackened tower of the mill. Then he drove off down the track, turned towards Blakeney, and there took the road that led back to Norwich.

5

They faced one another across the stark wooden table in the interview room. McKenzie lounged in a corner.

'Now, Mr Jacks,' said Tench, 'let's get down to business. Why did you drive up to Kettle Hill mill and threaten Simon Pashley?'

Jacks looked at him stolidly.

'Ye're dawzled,' he said.

Tench restrained an impulse to ask him what he meant.

'The mill was burnt down in the early hours of Tuesday, the ninth of September. Two days prior to that you owned a Chevrolet lorry, colour dark blue, registration number CL 7536.' He paused. 'Am I right?'

'Ye could be.'

'Then I'm to assume that you did?'

'Assume what ye bloody well like,' said Jacks.

'Right, then,' said Tench. 'Let's assume a bit more. Let's assume that on the afternoon of the seventh of September, you drove up to Kettle Hill in that identical lorry. Let's assume that you were seen to get out of the cab and enter the mill. Let's assume that when you came out a few minutes later, you were heard to threaten Mr Pashley.'

'Tha's all bloody lies.'

'You didn't visit the mill?'

'Not sayin' as I didn'.'

'What are you saying, then? Were you at the mill, or weren't you?'

'Mebbe I were.'

'You were there, but you didn't use threatening language?'

'Course I bloody didn'.'

138

'You didn't say, "I'll get you for this, Pashley. See if I don't."?'

'No, nothin' like. Who be sayin' as I did?'

'That's no business of yours.'

'I'll be wringin' his bloody neck if I find him, the bugger.'

'You'll do no such thing, Mr Jacks,' Tench said smoothly. 'Interfering with a witness is a criminal offence ... Why did you go to Kettle Hill?'

'Jus' passin'. Tha' were all.'

'All, Mr Jacks? All? Is it your usual practice just to turn off the road and threaten a man with violence?'

'No, it bloody ent.'

'But someone heard you quite clearly.'

'Then someone's lugholes needs pokin' wi' a pritch.'

'You mean they misheard you? Got it wrong, what you said?'

'Arse-uppards in a delf'd be more bloody like.'

'Then, when you left the mill, exactly what was it you said to Mr Pashley?'

'Told him I'd get'n fer him, didn' I?'

'Get what?'

'Sacks like. It were sacks.'

'What did he want sacks for? He'd got his own, hadn't he?'

'Aye, rummuns they be. Duzzy little buggers. He be wantin' some bigger uns. Try 'em out like.'

'He wanted some of your twenty-stone sacks?'

'Aye, an' that ent wrong.'

'So what did you say?'

'Said I'd get'n fer him, didn' I?'

'Your actual words, if you please, Mr Jacks.'

'"I'll get'n fer ye, Pashley. See if I don'."'

Tench frowned.

'Why did you say, "See if I don't"?'

Jacks brought his fist down hard on the table.

'Blast an' ye're a worritin' little bugger,' he said. 'How much more ye be wantin'?'

'Just answer the question, please, Mr Jacks. Why "See if I don't"?'

'He were sayin' as I'd ferget like. Allus sayin' tha', th'little bugger were. Were a regler joke atween him an' me, weren' it? So I say to him like, "I'll get'n fer ye, bor. See if I don't." So he'll not be a-moithered.'

139

'And did you get them?' Tench asked.

'Weren' no blasted chance. Owd lorry, she give out. An' afore ye could as much as say tha's a bloody rummun, th'poor little bugger were frizzled to dead.'

6

McKenzie took over, according to plan. He was quite prepared to play Jacks at his own little game.

'Gabriel,' he said, 'you're a bloody poor liar.'

The big man scowled at him.

'And not only that. You're as thick as two millstones.'

Jacks still said nothing.

'My mistake,' said McKenzie. 'Two pairs of millstones.'

'What ye bibblin' on about?'

'You think you can get away with a tale like that? You know damn well you drove up to that mill and threatened young Pashley.'

'Ha' ye gone shanny?'

'You're a fine one to talk about being shanny. You couldn't tell a bee from a bull's arse, and that's no more than the God-honest truth.'

Jacks' eyes glinted dangerously.

'Ye're jus' talkin' a lot o' squit.'

'Am I? We'll see. You know Mr Wickstead, the baker at Stiffkey?'

'Aye, that I do. Great lummox, he be.'

'You supplied him with flour on a regular basis?'

'Aye, an' tha' too. Now ax me another.'

'That's just what I'm going to do.' McKenzie leaned forward, his elbows on the table. 'Why did you suddenly cancel his deliveries?'

'What d'ye wan' to know tha' fer?'

'Just tell me why.'

'Ent no business o' yours. Tha's my affair.'

'You want me to suggest a reason?'

Jacks glowered at him.

'Do what ye bloody well like.'

'Right, then. You couldn't deliver because you hadn't got a lorry. Would that be correct?'

140

'Happen it might be.'

McKenzie sat back.

'You're as wooden as a wormeaten old pump, Gabriel,' he said. 'You'd lie the skin off that horse you've got hidden away somewhere.'

'Ye're all up at bloody Harwich. Niver had no hoss.'

'You never had a horse?'

'Said so, din' I?'

'You'll be telling me next that you don't have a cart.'

'Aye, an' tha's truth enough.'

'Then how d'you account for the fact that you were seen driving a horse and cart through Morston village on the night of the fire?'

'Dorn' know nothin' about tha'.'

'A cart loaded up with stone.'

'If someone say I done tha', he be romentin', tha's fer sure.'

'It's a fairy-tale, is it? You weren't carting Pashley's burr stones back to Breckmarsh mill?'

'No, I bloody well weren'.'

'Then tell me this, Gabriel. What was it happened to that runner stone of yours?'

'Yew tell me, ye great load o' pig wash. Why should anythin' be a-happenin'?'

'For one simple reason. No one grinding high-quality flour would ever mount a Peak stone on top of a burr.'

'Tha's a fact?'

'It's a fact. So why did you do it?'

'I ent a-gorn to tell yew all o' my know, ye great mardlin' bugger.'

'You're not going to say?'

'Course I ent. Why should I?'

'Then you don't mind spending the night in a cell?'

'Ye dassn't bloody keep me.'

'Oh, yes, we dare. You're obstructing the police. You're refusing to answer questions.'

'Tha' dorn' signify.'

'Oh, but it does, lad. It certainly does. You see, we're anxious to hear just what you've got to say, and we're quite prepared to lock you up till we get a few answers.'

'Are ye now?'

'We are.'

'Ye primmicky owd blowbroth...'

'You've got a fine flow of language, Gabriel, for a miller. It's a pity it's so restricted. Have you never thought of using it to give a straight answer?'

'Ent answerin' nothin'.'

'You aren't going to tell us what went wrong with that runner stone?'

'No, I bloody well ent.'

'You're not going to say why you, an experienced miller, fitted a Peak stone on top of a burr?'

'Right agen. I ent.'

'Nor what you were doing with that horse and cart in the middle of the night at Morston?'

'Niver was no hoss an' cart.'

'Not even a little one?'

'No, there blasted well weren'.'

McKenzie looked across at Tench.

'I think it's time we shared a mite of our knowledge with Mr Jacks. Don't you, sir?' he said.

Tench nodded.

'I'd say that was fair enough, Sergeant. If he plans to be awkward, then he'd better know the score.'

'You see, Gabriel,' McKenzie said – he was deceptively gentle – 'we're a busy lot here in Norwich what with one thing and another, and we don't have time to wait until illiterate, fumble-fisted oafs from the swamps make up their minds that it's time to confess. We can't just sit around listening to string after string of unimaginative lies. We've got other, far more important jobs to do. So we're going to make things a little bit easier for you. We're going to tell you what happened. We're going to lay bare the truth of all the comings and goings between Breckmarsh mill and the one at Kettle Hill ... Are you comfortable in that chair? Or would you like a cushion?'

'Get on wi' it, ye slinky bugger.' Jacks had reached the snarling stage.

'Hardly a kind invitation,' said McKenzie, 'but I'll accept it nonetheless ... Sometime last week the runner stone in that pair of burrs you've got down at Breckmarsh split apart at the seams and smashed through the vat. Now that was a disaster. You'd contracted to supply good-quality flour, and to grind it you needed

142

burr stones. You hadn't got a replacement, nor could you get one. Your whole livelihood was at stake. So what did you do? You knew Pashley had some blocks that he kept in his stables, so you drove up to Kettle Hill in that rattling old contraption you liked to call a lorry and told him, in your own inimitable way, that he'd better hand them over. And then, when he said, justifiably enough, that he couldn't really spare them, you flew into one of your dependable tempers and threatened to do him in.'

'He axed me fer sacks. I told him I'd get'n.'

McKenzie raised his bushy eyebrows.

'I think we can conveniently forget that little tale. It's not even worthy of your poor endeavours. Let's continue, shall we? You were determined to get your hands on those blocks of stone, so, on the night of the fire, you went back to Kettle Hill. Not in the lorry. You'd sold that for scrap. You drove up there with your horse and cart...'

'Dorn' know nothin' about any hoss an' cart.'

'You went up there with your horse and cart. You broke into the mill. You set it running and fixed it so that the alarm bell sounded. Then you waited in the dark for Pashley to come running from the cottage, and once he was inside the mill you hit him over the head, tied him up and probably gagged him. You then loaded up the burr stones and drove back to Breckmarsh, knowing that Pashley was helpless, that the mill would catch fire and the evidence of what you'd done would be completely destroyed.'

'Ye think so?'

'No, Gabriel, no. We don't think so. We're sure.'

Jacks bunched his fists. His knuckles stood out white.

'Then yew prove the bugger.'

'We intend to do just that,' McKenzie said gently. 'That's why tonight you'll be sleeping in a cell. You're a thief, an arsonist and a murderer, Gabriel, and before the year's out you'll be dangling from a gallows.'

Jacks kicked back the chair and crashed his fist on the table.

'Ye slummockin' great mawther. Ye'll not be keepin' me.'

'And how are you going to stop us?'

'Ye want me to show ye, blast ye?'

He swept up the chair and swung it back across his head.

Tench was on his feet.

'Sit down, Mr Jacks.'

143

The big man turned towards him.

'Git yew out o' the way, ye botty little bugger, or I'll gi' ye such a clout ye'll be winnickin' like a babby.'

Tench took a step forward.

'Sit down,' he rapped, 'now. I mean now, Mr Jacks.'

For a moment Jacks stood, the chair raised above his head, then he flung it as hard as he could against the wall.

In an instant, McKenzie had wrenched the door open, and the room was alive with uniformed men. Before Jacks could move, he was pinioned and handcuffed.

Tench gave him a look of withering distaste.

'Take him down,' he said tersely.

They watched him go, still sullen and scowling.

Tench leaned on the table. He took a deep breath.

'Mac,' he said, 'don't ever let me do that again.'

7

Lubbock was engaged in more peaceful pursuits.

Left alone in the mill, he climbed up to the stone floor and spent some time removing the vat and inspecting the stones. After that he sat down on the casing and appeared to be deep in thought. Then he lowered himself carefully down the ladder, locked up the mill and, stopping at Dodds' cottage to hand over the keys, drove back to Umzinto.

Once there, he predictably boiled a kettle, made a pot of tea, settled himself in his deep armchair and stoked up his pipe.

He sat for some moments, wreathing himself in smoke. Then, opening his bookcase and selecting a file, he turned to the section that held his notes on millstones, and stretched out a hand for the telephone directory that he kept on the floor by the side of his chair.

He made two calls, one to a firm in Ipswich and another to a second at Wickham Market. They were both inquiries, identical in content, and both, so it seemed, left him passably content. He then knocked out his pipe, backed his three-wheeler on to the road, and set off towards Norwich.

A couple of miles short of the city, he turned left and drew up by a renovated cottage. When he knocked on the door, it was opened by a tall, gaunt man with a mop of ginger hair, who greeted him much as a long-lost friend and led him into a spacious room at the back which contained a wall of books, two wide armchairs and a heavy broad-topped desk. The desk was submerged in a white sea of paper from which a typewriter rose like a great black rock, and the wall shelved hundreds of volumes on Norfolk that embraced every aspect of life in the county.

Lubbock planted himself in front of them.

'Lawrence,' he said. 'Remember when I came to see you six months ago about that business at Elsdon Hall, and you told me about the curse on the Wilder family? Well, I've got another query. This time it's something quite different, but I'm pretty sure you can help.'

He went on to explain.

'Do they really exist?' he said.

'Oh, yes. They must do.' His host was quite adamant. 'The evidence is overwhelming, but to pin-point exactly how and where they lie, that's a different matter. And you've got to be wary. Practically every village within two or three miles of the coast around here's reputed to have one. Stand the locals a couple of drinks and they're only too eager to tell you where it is. Most of the tales sound plausible enough till you come to examine them. Then they turn out to be nothing but legend: the products of ale and some vivid imagination.'

'But they're not all like that.'

'No, some do have substance. There are all sorts of tales about Blakeney, for instance. There's supposed to be one there that runs from the Guildhall right up to Baconsthorpe, seven miles away, and there are signs that something of the kind existed, though how far inland it ran is quite another question. The Guildhall's a rather peculiar building. Its construction suggests that it could have been a merchant's house with an undercroft used for storage, and Mariner's Hill adjoining it appears to be man-made. So there could have been one that ran from the undercroft straight through the hill ... And Blakeney's not the only place where signs have been discovered. One thing's for sure: a couple of hundred years ago the trade was a money-spinner. Well organized, too, so there must have been a network of transportation lines. The trouble is they were abandoned so long ago that it's difficult to trace them.'

145

'Any rumours about the coast between Stiffkey and Wells?'

'Oh, yes. They keep surfacing. One last autumn. Just about a year ago. Farmer near Warham. Chap called Thober, ploughing his fields...'

He described what had happened.

'You must have a map somewhere here,' said Lubbock. 'Can you show me the place?'

'I think so, roughly.'

Lawrence pulled an ordnance sheet from his desk, and spread it on the floor. He and Lubbock knelt beside it.

'Round about there,' he said, pointing with a pencil.

'How far from Breckmarsh mill?'

'Oh, a quarter of a mile.' Lawrence measured the distance. 'No more than that.'

'And on a straight line from Wells.'

'Yes, almost dead straight. More than likely it ended up at the mill. Many of the windmills in those days were used as secret distribution points. The millers were quite often in on the racket. Used their sails for signalling. If they got news that the preventives were around, they'd stop their sails in a diagonal position, at what was known as St Andrew's Cross; and once the coast was clear, they'd stop them again at the square position, St George's Cross. If there wasn't any wind, they'd even send a boy to climb up a sail and turn it with his weight. The message was passed from mill to mill: a kind of semaphore signal. The millers reckoned that, if there was news of a search. they could pass a warning message from Yarmouth to Horsey mill in a quarter of an hour, and that was much faster than a customs man could ride.'

Lubbock heaved himself up.

'Lawrence,' he said, 'you're a perennial marvel. Never fail me, do you?'

The ginger-headed man folded up his map.

'Always willing to help the forces of law and order,' he said. 'And now, I suppose, you'll be needing a cup of tea. Or are the pores leaking caffeine by this time of day?'

An interested observer, tracking Lubbock's movements later that afternoon, might have seen him, in the company of a squat, bearded man in an old tweed jacket and frayed leather gaiters, tramping doggedly to the middle of a turnip field. There the two of them paused and examined the ground, and Lubbock's companion swung his arm to and fro to indicate a line and then pointed towards the black tower of Breckmarsh mill.

Half an hour later that same observer would have sighted his quarry standing outside the mill, shading his eyes in the direction of Wells. At that point he might have lost him, for Lubbock turned and went inside. Lifting the trap in the floor of the mill, he made his way down to the basement storeroom. There he stood for a moment as if trying to regain his sense of direction; then, with a sudden decisive movement, he walked towards the mill-stones reared against the wall and began to examine each of them in turn, poking the rims with the tips of his fingers and pressing his nose against them as if he were anxious to see what lay behind.

Then, lowering the trap and closing the mill door behind him, he drove back to Cley.

Back in his chair, he picked up the phone and demanded a Norwich number.

'Lubbock,' he said curtly. 'Put me through to Inspector Tench.'

8

As far as Tench was concerned, it had been a bad day.

Gabriel Jacks had not merely proved to be obstructive and violent. He'd stolidly refused to admit that he'd even threatened Simon Pashley, let alone removed his burr stones, set fire to the mill or contrived his murder. Added to which, his brother Raphael, dragged under protest from his cottage at Warham, had revealed himself as equally stubborn. Apart from driving the lorry to the scrapyard at Wells, he knew nothing about anything. How the bloody hell could they expect him to know? He hadn't been anywhere near Kettle Hill on the night of the fire.

Where had he been, then?

He didn't see what bloody business it was of theirs, but he'd been over at Yarmouth, hadn't he? His local pub had had a darts match there. A cup final, weren't it? He'd been in the team.

And what time had he got back?

He hadn't damn well got back at all, had he? He'd stayed the night in Yarmouth. Hadn't come back till the following morning.

And where had he stayed?

Had a friend who ran a boarding-house down there, didn't he? Aye, of course he could give the name of the place if they wanted it. And the name of his friend. But he didn't for the life of him see why the hell he should.

Two phone calls, one to the pub at Warham and another to Yarmouth, had been sufficient to prove that he was telling the truth, and Tench had had no option but to pack him off back to Warham with a salutary warning to watch his behaviour and an intimation that he might have to answer more questions should the need arise.

Then Lock had reported back from his search. Neither the postman nor Suttons' delivery man had seen any sign of a limping man, and that left Miss Dixon's elusive intruder as nothing but an uncorroborated complication.

'Well, at least', said McKenzie, 'we've got Gabriel where we want him. We can do him for assault. It doesn't matter a jot that he didn't happen to brain you when he picked up that chair. Threatening behaviour likely to cause alarm. That's enough to put him in the dock. Assault on a police officer in the execution of his duty. Section 38 of the Offences against the Person Act, 1861. Maximum two years. And serve the bugger right.'

'Oh, we'll charge him,' said Tench, 'and we'll get him sent down, but that won't please Lubbock. He's got a thing about this case. He's convinced himself that Jacks set fire to the mill, burnt Pashley to death and made off with the stones. He may get two years for common assault, but that's not enough. Lubbock wants to see him on the end of a rope.'

'And he's damn well right. That's where the bugger should be. I've said all along that he did young Pashley in.'

Tench rested his elbows on the table and stared at his hands.

'But we've got no evidence, Mac. All we've got is a series of wild suppositions about mill machinery. We've no proof that he was anywhere near Kettle Hill on the night of the fire.'

'Ah, but where was he?'

'We've still to find that out, but it's pretty clear what his tale's going to be, if he ever sees fit to tell us. He'll say that he was snugly tucked up in his cottage, snoring his head off, and we can't prove him wrong. We can't even prove that he was guilty of theft. There weren't any prints on the stable door; looks like he wore gloves. And we don't even know for sure that he was the one who was driving that cart. No, unless we can find some link between him and the stones, we'll have to think again about going any further.'

'The lorry?'

'No help. Forensics found nothing but flour dust and grain. And in any case he couldn't have used it that night. It was stuck in a scrapyard.'

McKenzie stroked the stubble on his chin.

'The Chief seems to be sure that those stones are in the mill.'

'Yes, but where? We've had seven men who've ransacked the place from top to bottom. We've searched the cottage and the outbuildings. There isn't a trace. There aren't any floorboards. All the ground floors are stone, and that includes the storeroom underneath the mill. If they are there, then God only knows where he's hidden them.'

'Scour the place again?'

'Is it worth it?'

McKenzie shrugged.

'That's for you to decide, sir, isn't it?' he said.

Tench got up from the table and paced to the window.

'We can't afford to squander time and resources on vague suspicions that Lubbock may be right. No, Mac, unless something turns up before the day's out, I think we'll have to call it off.'

'Well, there's logic in that.' McKenzie took a deep breath. 'But it's a pity, all the same. I'm a bit like the Chief. I've a feeling deep down that that ham-fisted brute's as guilty as hell.'

'If it's any consolation' – Tench closed all the files – 'I feel much the same way. But instinct's not enough, and Lubbock'd be the first to tell you it's not. We need facts, and so far we haven't a single scrap of evidence that'd stand up in court.'

It was ten minutes later that the telephone rang. McKenzie lifted the receiver, then covered it with his hand.

'It's the Chief,' he murmured.

Tench took the call and listened.

'Right, sir,' he said at last. 'We'll be with you in an hour.'

149

He stood holding the receiver for a moment, then he slammed it on its hook.

'What now?' said McKenzie.

'Wants to see us at Meg's. Says he's pretty sure he knows where the burr stones are.'

'Been nosing around again?'

'Seems very much like it.'

'Well, it was always on the cards.'

Tench shook his head slowly.

'You know, Mac,' he said, 'there are times when I wonder who's running this show.'

'Forget it.' McKenzie yawned. 'You're the boss and he's not. Take all that's on offer, then go your own way ... And never, never, never look a gift horse in the mouth, even if it's got a pipe stuck fast between its teeth.'

9

'You've heard of Lawrence Bell?'

Lubbock threw out the question between puffs of smoke.

'The author?' said Tench. 'Doesn't he live somewhere out Horsford way?'

'Newton St Faith. Has a cottage out there.'

'Writes murder mysteries?'

'That's right.' Lubbock nodded. 'All set in Norfolk. He's published something like a couple of dozen. They've made him a tidy packet.'

'Must have,' said Tench. 'Kath's read one or two of them. Thinks they're pretty good.'

'Well, she's not on her own. He's got quite a reputation. But he's more than just a weaver of intricate plots. He's made himself something of an expert on the county. I doubt if there's anyone knows more about Norfolk than Lawrence Bell.'

'He's a friend of yours?'

'Yes, laddie, I think you could say so. We've known one another for more than fifty years. Went to school together. He was a clever lad, was Lawrence. Won a scholarship to Oxford. I used to crib his homework, and in a way I've been cribbing his work ever since.

Whenever I've had a case that's needed local knowledge, I've paid him a visit, and more often than not he's come up with something useful. You remember Old Mother Craske, the woman at Elsdon, who called down a curse on the Wilder family? Well, it was Lawrence who first put me on to the tale.'

McKenzie leaned forward.

'And now he's put you on to something about Kettle Hill?'

'No. Not Kettle Hill. But I went to see him this afternoon. I'd got an idea that had been niggling me ever since we couldn't find those burr stones, and I wanted to check it out.'

'And did he help?' said Tench.

'Yes, I think he may have done. It's still only an idea, and I may be wrong, but it's worth delving into ... Let me say first of all that I checked the other pair of millstones at Breckmarsh. I was right. They're both Peak stones, so Jacks had only the one pair of burrs for grinding his flour ... But maybe I'd better start at the beginning.'

Tench allowed himself the merest flicker of an eyebrow. It seemed likely to prove yet another lengthy session.

Lubbock re-stoked his pipe.

'It seemed to me,' he said, 'that if Pashley's burr stones weren't at Breckmarsh mill, there were only two other places where they could possibly be. You see, laddie, making up millstones from blocks of French burr is a highly skilled business. It's not something that a man like Jacks could attempt. If he stole those blocks from Pashley – and I still believe he did – he'd have to send them away to some reputable firm to be made into a millstone. They'd have to be trimmed, then cemented together, bedded on plaster of Paris and banded with iron. They'd be no good to him just lying around as blocks. So the question was: were they already lodged with a millstone maker, or had he stowed them away somewhere in the mill until he could get them moved? Now, seventy years ago, there were perhaps a dozen firms making up millstones. Not in Norfolk, but in places like London and Leeds. Suffolk had a handful, mainly in Ipswich. Most of them have gone, but there are still a couple that Jacks might have used: Masterton and Grainger who have a works in Ipswich, and George Rogers at Wickham Market. I rang up both of them. Neither had had any recent orders for French burr millstones, so I could only conclude that the stones were still somewhere at Breckmarsh mill. The question was where?'

'And that's still the question,' McKenzie said grimly.

'Yes, but now there's just a chance that there may be an answer.' Lubbock edged his chair back from the table and stretched out his legs. When he spoke, it was to Tench.

'Remember, laddie,' he said, 'when I sent you to Italy to root out the truth about that business at Elsdon? You learnt what it was from that professor chap in Naples. What was his name?'

'Visco?'

'That's the fellow, yes. He told you all about the catacombs underneath that church. Well, it was remembering what he said that started me thinking; that and seeing those millstones reared against the wall in that underground storeroom at Breckmarsh mill.'

Tench frowned.

'Don't tell me we've got catacombs underneath the mill.'

'No, laddie, not quite. But there may be something much the same.'

McKenzie slapped the table.

'Of course,' he said. 'Tunnels. Smugglers' tunnels.'

Lubbock nodded across his pipe.

'Mac's right. He's lived in Norfolk longer than you have. You see, laddie, a couple of hundred years ago, this coast was one of the prime centres for smuggling. It was still going on when my father was a boy, and there are all sorts of tales about tunnels that lead from points on the shore to places inland where contraband was stored. There's supposed to be one at Blakeney. Starts from the quay and runs towards Baconsthorpe. That's what I went to see Lawrence about. I wanted to know whether there was any evidence at all of tunnels near Breckmarsh.'

'And is there?' said Tench.

'According to Lawrence, there is. Came to light last year. It seems there's a farmer called Aaron Thober lives down at Warham. His fields extend right across the main road, and one of them lies between Wells and Breckmarsh. Last autumn Thober was ploughing that field when there was a rumble behind him and the ground fell away. He went back to look and found himself staring down at a hole – it must have been ten feet deep – and at the bottom what looked like a barrel roof of brick. Next morning he went out again with his son, and took one of his labourers. They shifted the bricks and broke into what was clearly a tunnel. They shone a flashlight around, but thought it was far too dangerous to explore, so they simply climbed out again and filled in the hole. That was just about all that Lawrence could tell me, so I drove across to Warham and saw this chap Thober. He took me out into the field and showed me the spot. It's on a straight line from the end of the quay at Wells to Breckmarsh mill and, from what Thober said, the tunnel itself seemed to follow that line.'

'So it's possible it may end up at the mill.'

'Lawrence thought it more than likely. Windmills, he said, were often used as hidy-holes, places where the smuggled goods were stowed away in secret until they could be moved ... And that's where we come to the basement storeroom.'

'But surely ...' Tench intervened.

Lubbock raised a hand.

'No, laddie,' he said, 'don't bother to tell me. They wouldn't just be left in the storeroom itself. It's not secure enough. Access through that trap-door's far too easy. But there's one peculiar thing about that underground room. All the floors in the mill are circular. They have to be: they follow the contour of the tower. But that room's a square. One side faces Wells, and there are three old Peak stones reared against the wall. Now why on earth would anyone lower a millstone down there, let alone three? It's not as if they could ever be used again. They're worn out, finished ... No, it's my guess, laddie, that they're hiding something, and that something's the entrance to Thober's tunnel.'

Tench was silent for a moment.

'And that's where you think the burr stones are hidden.'

'It's the only possible place.'

Lubbock knocked out his pipe.

'So what I'm suggesting,' he said, 'is this. Borrow three of the heftiest men in the force, and drive them out to Breckmarsh first thing tomorrow. Get them to roll those stones to one side, and I'm ready to wager my next month's pension you'll find Pashley's blocks of burr somewhere behind them.'

'I reckon that's a gamble worth taking,' McKenzie said. 'If we find them, we've got Jacks on the end of a skewer.'

'If we find them.' Tench was doubtful. He glanced across at Lubbock. 'How much did you say each of those millstones weighed?'

'Upwards of a ton. Some more than that.'

'It's a pretty tall order, to shift one of those. And we'd have to shift three.'

'Jacks must have done it.'

'Maybe Jacks has got the knack like those millers of yours that hump twenty-stone sacks, but it's not a job I'd like to give to an ordinary copper. Suppose one of them keeled over. It could smash a man's legs. Cripple him for life.'

'What men have we got?'

'We've got Wally,' said McKenzie.

'Wally? Who's Wally?' Lubbock racked his memory. McKenzie explained.

'Constable Walters. You wouldn't know him, sir. He's a new recruit, signed up in June. Bit of a character is Wally. All solid muscle. Six foot eight and eighteen and a half stone. Eastern Counties weight-lifting champion. Rolling a ton of millstone should be right up his street.'

'Sounds the sort of chap we need.'

'Yes, you could be right. I'd forgotten about Wally.' Tench was suddenly more cheerful. 'He might fit the bill.'

'Then get him,' said Lubbock, 'and a couple of others, and let's see just what's behind those stones.'

10

It was half an hour later.

McKenzie had stormed away on his Norton to his bachelor flat on the outskirts of the city, and Lubbock, in somewhat more leisurely fashion, had trundled off to Cley at the wheel of his Morgan.

Tench was left alone. The sun still streamed through the window of the office. He looked at his watch. It showed half-past six. Time for him to be going, too; but somehow, that evening, he didn't relish the prospect of facing the empty house out at Costessey. Kath wouldn't be there, and without her it seemed no more than a lodging: a place to go to bed and wake up in a morning.

He felt a sudden need to talk to her, and knew it wasn't possible. If he rang her parents' home, that too would be empty. She and her father would be out at the hospital. They wouldn't be back for a couple of hours.

He was restless. Lost. In the middle of a case that seemed to be making no headway at all. It could still be a murder. It might be nothing but a simple case of larceny, and even if it were and Jacks were the man responsible, there was still no evidence likely to convict him unless Lubbock was right and Pashley's blocks of burr lay behind those millstones at Breckmarsh mill. As for murder, the evidence, if any there were, lay still locked tightly inside Lubbock's head.

He wondered why the old man was still so certain that Pashley had been cold-bloodedly killed. The points that he'd made about mill machinery were logical enough, but they were open to other, very different interpretations. Randall, for instance, had seen them in an altogether different light. He'd been logical, too; yet he, again, was almost certainly wrong. His theories about the fire didn't tally with what other witnesses had said. It was his idea that Pashley had been trapped at the top of the mill when the bell alarm began to ring, but Ellison had heard the bell clearly enough and he'd seen no sign of fire. And there was Hilary Dixon, too. According to her, as late as ten to two there hadn't been any trace of a fire, and the grating sound she'd heard must have meant that the millstones had run out of grain. If that were the case and Ellison's times were correct, then the bell must, by then, have been ringing for something like twenty minutes.

Tench shook his head. He could only conclude that a knowledge of mill machinery endowed its possessors with a wholly unjustified sense of conviction. Lubbock could well be just as wrong as Randall. He was, in point of fact, more likely to be wrong. He hadn't, like Randall, run the mill for twenty years.

He stared at the files on his desk and flicked one of them open. Then he closed it again firmly, pulled out a drawer and dropped them all inside. As he felt at that moment, he wasn't likely to find himself any more advanced if he read until midnight.

He was just about to shut the drawer when he noticed the charm: the tiny windmill that had somehow unhooked itself from Hilary Dixon's bracelet. In the midst of all the hectic business of the day, he'd completely forgotten it. If only he'd taken it with him, he could have dropped it off on the way back from Breckmarsh. He picked it up and turned it between his fingers. Gold, yes, but commonplace enough. He'd seen many like it in jewellers' windows all over Norwich. The pin-points of light glistened as he turned it. Diamond chips? Possibly. He slipped it in his pocket. He was going that way tomorrow. He'd call in at Morston Bottom...

But he didn't. He changed his mind.

Five minutes later he swung the police car out of the station yard, and in less than an hour he was pulling to a halt by the Boldings' farm.

What had prompted his sudden decision to go there, he didn't quite know. Frustration with the case? The empty house at Costessey? The need to talk to someone?

Maybe that was it. The urge to talk to someone different. Different from Lubbock and McKenzie and Dodds and all the rest of the knowledgeable, theorizing specialists who seemed so certain that their ideas were right. If Kath had been at home, he'd have slumped back after dinner and talked away to her.

Someone with fresh ideas. Someone who might provide the clue that he needed? Perhaps. He wasn't sure. But Walter and Ag and their delightful young artist lived closer to Kettle Hill than anyone else...

He climbed out of the car and, skirting the liquid cow dung again, pulled on the bell-toggle. This time there wasn't any sound of heavy boots. He waited, pulled a second time, but still got no answer. He wandered round to the side of the farm. The old Austin Seven was parked by the window, as it had been before, but there was nothing to be seen of Hilary Dixon or either of the Boldings.

He walked further on, round the back of the house. The sun was setting now in its early autumn splendour, banding the clouds with colour, casting its golden light on the twisting creeks that threaded the marsh. He shaded his eyes, and almost at once he saw her. She was down on the causeway, painting. Experimenting, he supposed, trying to overlay the colours.

He made his way down.

When she saw him, she turned the picture round on the easel, hiding it from view.

'Is it so bad?' he said.

'Bad enough, Inspector.' She smiled. 'I'm still learning.'

'I rang the bell,' he said, 'but nobody answered.'

156

'They're both out. Walter's taken the cart to Wells to pick up some seed, and Ag's gone to Blakeney. There's a dance on there, and she's doing the catering.' She looked up at him expectantly. 'Well, then,' she said. 'Have you found the lorry man?'

'As a matter of fact, yes.'

'Who is he?'

'A chap from Breckmarsh. Gabriel Jacks. You wouldn't know him.'

'You've arrested him?'

'Not exactly. We've detained him on suspicion.'

'Is that all?' She was disappointed.

'I'm afraid so, at the moment. There isn't any doubt that he was the man you saw, and we think he may have stolen something from the mill. But he says that he didn't, and unless we can find the goods in his possession, we haven't evidence enough to charge him.'

She laid down her paint brush.

'What d'you think he stole?'

'Some stones.'

She stared at him.

'Stones?'

Tench explained.

'So they were valuable?'

'They were to Pashley, and we think they were to Jacks.'

'You're looking for them?'

'Yes. We've already done one search. We're doing another tomorrow.'

'And what about the fire?'

'Nothing more yet. There's nothing to connect him with it at all.'

'And the man with the limp?'

'We're still looking,' he said.

She began to gather up her tackle.

'You're not getting very far, are you, Inspector?'

Tench had to be sanguine.

'Oh, I think we'll find them both. The stones and the limping man. It's just a question of time... By the way, have you lost anything?'

'No, I don't think so.'

'You haven't mislaid a windmill?' He drew the charm from his pocket and held it out on the palm of his hand.

She took it from him and looked at it.

'Where did you find it?'

'On the floor of my office.'

'Then it must be mine,' she said. 'It must have come off my bracelet. I hadn't noticed it was missing. When I got back from Norwich, I just slipped the chain off and locked it away. I'll have to be more careful ... Thank you for bringing it. I wouldn't have liked to lose it.'

'Sentimental value?'

'Yes, in a way.'

'A gift from someone, was it?'

She gave a little laugh.

'You're fishing again, Inspector.'

'I'm a policeman. I have to.'

'All right,' she said. 'I'll tell you. I wouldn't want to keep the CID in the dark ... No, it wasn't a gift. I bought it in Norwich, the first time I was there.'

'So what kind of sentimental value can it have?'

She folded up the stool and the easel, and handed them to him.

'You don't give up, do you?'

'Not easily, no.'

'Then you'll have to come back to the farm,' she said. 'I'll have to show you the bracelet.'

11

She unlocked her trinket box, took out the bracelet and handed it to him.

Tench ran it between his fingers. It was heavier than he'd thought: a chain of gold links with a tiny hasped lock, and attached to the links a series of charms.

'It belonged to my aunt,' she said. 'If you look on the back of the lock, you'll see her initials. She had them engraved: ERM. She left it to me when she died earlier this year. I'd always been fond of it, and she'd promised it to me. It's a record of her travels.'

Tench was puzzled.

'Travels?'

'Yes. When she visited a place, she tried to buy a charm that had

158

some connection. See. There's a leprechaun. That was when she went on a holiday to Ireland ... That's a Clovelly donkey, and there's a Cornish pisky.'

Tench examined them.

'An archer?'

'Robin Hood,' she said. 'She had a sister in Nottingham. She used to go and visit.'

'What's this one?'

'A Cockney sparrow. She got it in London. And there's one of the *Queen Mary*. She bought it on board ship when she and my uncle sailed to America ... They had a house in Suffolk, and I used to go and stay with them both in the summer. She'd bring it out and show me the latest one she'd added ... I was very fond of the old dear. She was my mother's eldest sister, but it was a very big family and there was twenty years between them. She used to make a fuss of me, I think because she never had children of her own '

'So when it came to you, you thought you'd do the same. Keep on adding charms.'

'I promised her I would. That windmill was the first. I saw it in Norwich and thought it was just the thing.'

He picked it up from the table.

'Are these diamond chips?'

'Yes, I could have got a plain one, but I wanted the diamonds. It cost me a good deal more, but I bought them for her because she lost her own.'

'How d'you mean, lost?'

'She had them stolen.'

'So you thought you'd replace them with diamond chips.'

'Yes, not quite the same, but all I could afford.'

'Well, it's a start,' he said, 'anyway.'

'Not much of a start, really, but I'd have hated to lose it.'

'It hadn't been fixed on very firmly,' he said. 'You'd better take it back to the jeweller and get a stronger link.' He looked at his watch. 'What time are Mr and Mrs Bolding due back?'

She put the bracelet and the charm in the box, and turned the key.

'Walter shouldn't be very long, but Ag may be late. She's got to help with the clearing up.'

Tench stroked his chin.

'I don't think I'll wait ... Tell me a bit more about this man with the limp. Which leg was it?'

'The one that was damaged?' She gave it some thought. 'It's hard to remember. I think it was the right.'

'He unlocked the mill door. Are you sure he didn't pick the lock?'

'Didn't seem to. He just put a key in the door and turned it.'

'A key. Not a bunch of keys?'

'No.' She was sure about that.

'Did he use the same key when he unlocked the cottage?'

She was silent for a moment.

'That's difficult to remember. I'd only be guessing. When he locked up the mill, he put the key in his pocket and walked across to the cottage. Then he took it out again.' She paused. 'I suppose it could well have been a different one.'

'If it had been the same one, wouldn't he just have kept it in his hand? Wouldn't that have been the logical thing to do?'

'I suppose so,' she said doubtfully. 'If he was a logical kind of man.'

Tench gave a sigh.

'Like you say, it's all guesswork ... Is there anything else about him you've remembered?'

'I haven't really thought about him much since I told you.'

'You said you went from there to Blakeney.'

She nodded.

'That's right. The tide was low that afternoon. I was painting the boats that were stranded on the mud.'

'So you drove down the Blakeney track from the mill. You didn't see a car?'

'No,' she said slowly. 'Wait a minute. Let me think ... Yes, I did see something. I remember it now. There was a bicycle ...'

'Where?'

'Down on the main road. By that little kissing-gate. It was reared against a hedge. I saw it as I was driving to the mill from the farm.'

'What colour was it?'

'Black.'

'Old or new?'

'Rusty,' she said. 'If Noah had ridden a bike, it could have come out of the Ark.'

* * *

160

It was on his way out, just short of the road, that Tench met Walter Bolding driving his cart.

He pulled to the side and stopped. Walter reined in the horse. He was still as cheerful as ever.

'Evenin', Mr Tench, sir. You bin to see us?'

'Just having a word with Miss Dixon', said Tench.

'You stayin' to see Ag?'

'Not tonight, no. Too busy, I'm afraid.'

'Tha's a pity,' said Walter. 'She'd have been fair pleased. She were only sayin' las' night as it were more'n time you be payin' us another visit.'

'Sorry about that, Walter.' Tench eyed the cart. 'You didn't tell me you drove one of those,' he said.

'Oh, aye.' Walter nodded. 'Bought'n a year back from owd Moses Chenery down at Bilsey Bottom. Do me fine, she do. Wi' they rubber wheels she go smooth as a kitty witch. Better'n they topsy-turvyin' tractors a-spittin' muck about.'

Tench got out of the car. He was suddenly curious. He walked across the track and patted the somnolent nag between the shafts.

'Ever lend it to anyone, Walter?' he asked.

Walter's eyes opened wide.

'Funny as you should be axin' tha', Mr Tench, sir,' he said. 'Never lent'n not once till a day or two back. An' it weren' so much lendin'. Paid 'andsome, 'e did.'

'Who did?'

'Why, owd Jacks, lives up at Breckmarsh.'

'Gabriel Jacks?'

'Tha's right, Mr Tench. Ag, she get 'er flour from 'im, once a month maybe ... Come knockin' on the door one mornin', 'e do, sayin' as 'ow 'is lorry's bruck up fer good, an' 'e need to fetch 'is grain from some place i' Wells. So would I be loanin' 'im Nancy an' the cart?'

'Nancy?'

'Aye, Nancy's th'owd mare.' He slapped her rump fondly. 'Good owd skivvy, she be.'

'So you hired out the cart to Gabriel Jacks.'

'Aye, an' Ag were none too pleased. Call me a great lummox, an' tell me I be shanny. Well' – he grinned – 'shanny be as shanny do, Mr Tench, I allus say, an' I be two quid better off'n I were afore 'e come.'

'Mr Jacks hired your horse and cart for two pounds?'

'Aye, an' paid on the nail.'

'When was this, Walter?'

'Why, it were the day afore you come to see us, weren' it, Mr Tench?'

'The day before the fire?'

Walter took some time to puzzle out the dates.

'Aye, that'd be right,' he said.

'And when did he bring it back?'

Walter frowned again.

'It were arter you druv off back agen to Norwich. Reckon it musta bin round about ten. It were dark, an' Miss Dixon she'd gone up to bed.'

'So he borrowed it the morning before the fire, kept it overnight, and returned it the evening after?'

'Reckon so,' said Walter. 'An' when 'e brung it back, Ag get into a rare owd passe at me, she do. Ye see, Mr Tench, Nancy she come back fair knackered out like. Seem as 'ow that bugger Jacks, 'e load up a ton 'o grain, an' then drive 'er aroun' till she bloody nigh drop. Ag, she call me a string o' names as'd make yer lugs blush, Mr Tench, an' tha's a fact. Ever you lend this cart out agen like, she say, I'll gi' ye such a ding as'll mek yer eyes rattle like cobbles in a tin. Wild as a polecat, she were.'

He shook his head in wonder.

'She be a rare un, be Ag, when she get a bit riled. Should a bin in a tank at that Alamein battle. She'd a scared 'alf they Jerries back to Berlin afore they much as fired off a single bloody shot. Fearsome, Mr Tench, tha's what she be. But get 'er atween the sheets an' she mew like a kitten.'

He shook his head again.

'Rummuns wimmin,' he said.

'You're right there, Walter.' Tench nodded his head in solemn agreement. 'Still, she did have her reasons.'

'Aye. She did. Mebbe.'

'You do use the cart a lot.'

'Aye. Every day like. Loads 'er up wi' milk.'

'You delivered the milk to Kettle Hill, didn't you?'

'Tha's right, Mr Tench.'

'Did you ever see a man with a limp around the mill?'

Walter scratched his head.

162

'When be you a-meanin', Mr Tench, sir?' he said.

'Oh, in the last few months.'

'Nay.' Walter was firm. 'Not fer long enough sin'.'

'But you have seen one?'

'Aye, tha' be fer sure. There were a time, Mr Tench, when I be seein' one mos days.'

'When was that,Walter?'

'Why, when owd Randall be miller up there.'

'Josh Randall?'

'Aye.'

'But he hasn't got a limp.'

'Tha's right, Mr Tench.'

'Then who has?'

'Why, the lad. It be Randall's lad.'

'You mean he's got a son?'

'Aye, an' tha's truth. An' I reckon there be times when 'e'm wishin' 'e'd not.'

Tench stared at him. Walter stared back. He cocked his head on one side.

'You be lookin' fair dawzled, Mr Tench, sir,' he said. 'Ent you never bin a-hearin' about young Davie?'

'No,' said Tench, 'I haven't. Go on, Walter. Tell me.'

163

5

SATURDAY

'What should be spoken here, where our fate,
Hid in an auger-hole, may rush, and seize us?'

Shakespeare, *Macbeth*

1

Once again two police cars swept along the narrow, winding road through Stiffkey. In the first were Tench and Lubbock with the redoubtable Walters; in the second McKenzie and two other constables who, though not of Walters' commanding stature, appeared to be sufficiently broad and well-muscled to move at least one Peak millstone between them.

At the bottom of the track that led to Breckmarsh mill stood Constable Dodds leaning on his bike.

He poked his head into Tench's car and surveyed the weightlifting champion with evident satisfaction.

'We could have done with this lad of yours yesterday, sir,' he said. 'He'd have frog-marched Gabriel down to the car without any trouble.'

'That's true enough, Sergeant. But Jacks won't give us any trouble this morning. He's on bread and water ... You've got the keys to the mill?'

Dodds tapped his pocket.

'Right here, sir,' he said. He turned towards Lubbock. 'Sorry I wasn't in when you brought them back, Chief Inspector. Bit of a shindy in the village. Old Merryweather smashing up glasses in the pub. Seems the beer's getting stronger since the end of the war.'

He unlocked the mill, Lubbock raised the trap, and one by one they climbed down into the storeroom.

As Lubbock had said, the walls formed a square. Built of whitewashed brick, which had long since declined into a dirty shade of grey, they were cluttered with grain sacks. All except one. This was clear apart from the three massive millstones poised on their rims.

They stood side by side, touching one another, as if the two outer ones were standing sentinel over the one in the centre.

Walters considered them first from a distance, then inspected them more closely. After that he stepped back, stripped off his jacket, and hung it on a nail.

'Chicken feed, sir,' he said. 'Where d'you want me to start?'

'Let's make it the left,' said Lubbock. 'Which of these two strapping lads d'you want to help you?'

Walters eyed them with something approaching contempt.

'Neither of 'em, sir, thank you. They'd only get in the way. Just move everyone back as far as they can go, and leave it to me.'

He rolled up his sleeves, revealing two swarthy forearms, one tattooed with Atlas holding up the world, and the other with a bleeding heart pierced by an arrow.

He flexed them self-consciously.

'Don't mean a thing, sir,' he said apologetically. 'Picked 'em up in the army. Back o' the shop in Cairo. Nothing much else to do once the war was over.'

He stepped forward and placed his hands round the rim of the millstone, his fingers in the grooves.

'For God's sake be careful, Constable,' said Tench. 'The floor there's uneven. If that stone tips over, it'll smash your foot to pulp.'

Walters wasn't to be deterred.

'Not to worry, sir,' he said. 'Just testing the grip.'

He stepped backwards again and took a second look.

'Seems a shame to move 'em, don't it, sir?' he said. 'Bit artistic, they are. Like the doors to one o' those Egyptian tombs, seal inscriptions an' all. What's behind 'em? A mummified body in a box?'

'Let's hope not,' said Tench. 'We've got one body and that's quite enough. No, we're hoping to find ourselves a load of precious stones.'

'Oh, another jewel snatch.' Walters gave a shrug. 'Well, I suppose it's maybe as good a place as any to stash away the loot.' He turned back to Lubbock. 'How far d'you want it moved, sir?'

Lubbock took a step towards him.

'It's only a guess, Constable, but I think what we're looking for's behind the middle stone. That's the one we need moved.'

'Best shift both the end ones then, sir,' said Walters. 'Give us room to get at it.'

168

He clamped his hands round the rim of the stone once again. Then the muscles in his arms visibly tightened as he leaned forward and pushed. The stone moved a fraction, then rolled back with a crack against the one in the centre.

Walters spat on his hands.

'Right,' he said. 'Stand clear.'

He gripped again and leaned forward. The muscles tightened a second time. The stone began to move. Slowly, with a sound like distant thunder, it rolled outwards from the centre, scraping along the wall, showering flakes of brick dust over Walters' boots.

He let it roll to a stop. Then, edging himself into the gap that he'd made, he gripped it a third time, set the sole of his boot against the centre stone, leaned again and heaved. As it began to move, he slid his hands down the rim and gave it a second heave, and after that a third.

Lubbock watched the gap widen and measured its width.

'Hold it there,' he said. 'That's far enough.'

Walters stood back and looked.

'One down,' he said. 'Two to go.'

Five minutes later, the centre stone stood bereft of its sentinels.

Walters slumped on a grain sack, and mopped his forehead with a blue silk handkerchief.

'How d'you feel?' Tench inquired.

'Could do with a pint, sir.'

'And I'll stand him one,' said Dodds. 'It's given me a thirst just standing here watching him.'

Tench looked at his champion with a dubious concern.

'How about letting the others have a go at this one?'

Walters sprang to his feet.

'Not a chance, sir,' he said. 'Those two lads'd be sweating and straining for an hour. Let's get it done quick, that's what I say. After that you'll maybe line me up a second pint. It'll not take me long to get rid of the first.'

He took hold of the stone, placed his heel against a rut in the floor, and gave one last heave. The great millstone began to move. Then, suddenly seized by a life of its own, it gathered pace a fraction, canted on its rim and fell sideways with a crash that seemed to shake the whole fabric of Breckmarsh mill.

Walters, with surprising speed, had flattened himself against the wall. He stared at the cloud of dust rising from the floor.

'Well, that's shifted the bugger an inch or two,' he said.

The others seemed stunned into speechlessness. They gazed down at the stone as the dust began to settle and the echoes died away.

'Bloody hell,' said McKenzie.

He spoke for everyone there. Except perhaps for Lubbock.

The ex-Chief Inspector seemed to have dismissed the little contretemps from his mind. He was staring intently at the place on the wall where the millstone had been.

Tench raised his eyes guardedly, and looked in the same direction.

'Oh, no,' he said. 'Not more.'

Where the Peak stone had stood was yet another one, a fourth. It was smaller than the rest and set into the wall, its edges flush with the bricks.

Walters looked at it, too.

'Well, one thing's for sure,' he said. 'We can't roll that one out.'

Lubbock ran his fingers across the minute gap between the rim and the bricks. Then he went down on his hands and knees, and squinted underneath it.

'You won't need to, lad,' he said. 'I reckon it's on a pivot and the bricks have been cut away at an angle behind. All you need to do is push on one side. You'll find it'll swing.'

'Think so, sir?' said Walters. 'Right. Let's give it a shove and see.'

He planted the sole of his foot against the edge of the stone, bent his knee and pushed. There was a grating noise and the stone slowly turned, one rim disappearing somewhere into darkness, the other swinging outwards into the room.

Walters steadied it with his hand and peered into one of the gaps.

'See anything?' said Tench.

'Not a damn thing, sir, no. Anyone got a torch?'

Lubbock took one from his pocket, and Walters flashed it around.

'Looks like a tunnel, sir. Widens out inside and the roof slopes upwards. Reckon a man could stand up in it without a deal of trouble.

'Not me though,' he added. 'I'd need to bend a bit.'

'Well, come on, lad,' said Lubbock. He showed signs of impatience. 'Is there anything there?'

Walters swung the beam round.

'Doesn't seem to be much, sir. Just a pile of old stones. Looks to me like the roof might have fallen in sometime.'

'What kind of stones are they?'

'Hefty-sized blocks from the look of 'em, sir. Must have made a hell of a clatter when they fell.'

'Let's have a look,' said Lubbock.

He took the torch from Walters and edged through the gap. The beam wavered, then steadied itself, pointing down.

'Well, what are they?' Tench called.

The light snapped out suddenly, and Lubbock's head emerged. He seemed pleased with himself.

'Burr stones,' he said. 'What did you think they were, laddie? Liquorice allsorts?'

2

They travelled back as they'd come: Tench and Lubbock in the first car with Walters, suitably refreshed by three foaming pints of best Stiffkey ale; McKenzie and the two supernumerary constables following in the second.

They dropped Lubbock at Cley to pick up his Morgan and trail them into Norwich, and once back at the station Tench and McKenzie made their way upstairs.

There was a buff-coloured envelope lying on Tench's desk. He picked it up, slit it open and took out the two closely typed sheets.

McKenzie slumped in a chair.

'Well,' he said, 'not a bad morning's work. At least we've got the evidence to charge Jacks with theft. We know he used Walter's cart, and we've found Pashley's stones tucked away in his mill. That's two steps to stringing him up where he belongs.'

Tench was reading.

'Could possibly be three.'

He tossed the sheets across the desk.

'Report on those sacks from forensics,' he said.

McKenzie stretched his arms and yawned.

171

'I think Wally's worn me out shifting those stones. Just tell me what's in it.'

'No surprises.'

'The Chief was right?'

'Spot on.'

'The sacks were different then?'

'The sacks were different, Mac. The one we collected from Pashley's place was made of jute from a place called' – he reached for the report – 'Goalpara. That's Assam.'

'And the one from Breckmarsh?'

'Chandpur in Bengal. And they were made up at different places. Pashley's at the Rashiewell Mills in Dundee, and the one we took from Jacks at the Kinnison Mills. They're close to Calcutta.'

McKenzie waited.

'And...?' he said.

'And the fibres that were found on Pashley's body matched the sack that came from Breckmarsh.'

'So the question is,' said McKenzie, 'how did a sack from Breckmarsh come to be at Kettle Hill?'

'And why did burnt fragments adhere to Pashley's body?'

'So it seems the Chief's been right all along the line.'

'So far,' said Tench.

'And for him that's far enough. You won't get him to throw up the case at this stage.'

Tench stared at the report.

'No. That's what I'm afraid of.'

'What's to worry about? If he comes up with the answers, you take the credit. Case Number One wrapped up in short time by Detective Inspector Tench.'

'Yes, but how's he going to do it?'

'Meaning what?' said McKenzie.

'Meaning that we haven't the foggiest idea just what's in his mind. He's convinced himself that Jacks not only stole Pashley's burr stones, but killed him by some cold, calculated method that covered up his tracks. Well, he's right about the stones, and it is still possible he may be right about the murder. But how's he going to prove it? So far it's all hypothesis, nothing more than that. He's worked out what might be a possible scenario based on what he knows about the working of windmills, but the only solid piece of evidence gleaned from that fire was the weld in the sack chain, and that can only suggest that the mill was struck by lightning. He talks blithely about bells and striking rods and fantails, but the fire's consumed all his clues. So what's he got in mind?'

'God knows,' said McKenzie. 'I never could read the Chief. Gave up trying long ago.'

'But you know him,' said Tench. 'You've worked with him long enough. All these dark mutterings about sacks and fibres: I suppose, at a pinch, they could mean something. On the other hand, they may mean nothing at all. You know as well as I do that Jacks isn't going to yield us one single point. Oh, we'll have him for theft, but murder's a different matter. All we've got so far is circumstantial evidence, and not much of that. It's not going to be enough to convince a jury ... No, Mac, the only way we're going to nail him is to force a confession, and with a chap like Jacks that's not going to be easy. We could grill him for weeks and still make no headway. So just how does Lubbock think he's going to pin the murder on him?'

'There's only one thing to do,' said McKenzie. 'That's to ask him.'

'And as soon as he gets here,' Tench said grimly, 'that's what we're going to do. First item on the agenda. He can read this report, and then he can explain. I'm not prepared to blunder around any longer in a twilight world of Lubbock's contriving. I want to know what he's up to.'

'Perhaps he doesn't know himself.'

'Oh, yes, he does.' Tench flattened the report sheets out on the desk. 'He knows damn well, and we need to know too, if we don't want to find ourselves with egg on our faces.'

3

Lubbock read the report. Then he handed it to Tench.

'Good,' he said.

'Confirmation?'

'You could say so, laddie, yes.'

'But what does it confirm?'

'What I've thought all along. That young Pashley was murdered.'

'But how?'

'How what?'

'How was he murdered, and how does what you've read confirm what you think?'

Lubbock blew out a rolling thunderhead of smoke.

'Ever heard of Long Meg?'

'It's a gun,' said Tench, 'isn't it?'

'You're thinking of Big Bertha, that German gun that was used to shell Paris. The French named it after one of the Krupp family women.'

'No.' Tench shook his head. 'There's a gun called Long Meg in the Tower of London.'

'Well, there may be,' said Lubbock drily. 'I wouldn't question your undoubted scholarship, laddie. But it's not the Long Meg that I had in mind. Mine's a trifle more feminine, if only a trifle.'

'You mean she was a woman.'

'Possibly, though doubts were expressed at the time. Long Meg of Westminster was a noted virago back in Tudor days. A giant of a woman with the strength of an ox. I'd say she was very much a female Walters. You're a student of history. I'm surprised you haven't heard of her.'

'Not my period,' said Tench, 'but go on. I'm all agog.'

'Well, she was a rare old termagant was Meg. Fought in the army at the siege of Boulogne, and was well known in peacetime for banging heads together and creating the sort of mayhem that made her name a byword across the length and breadth of London. When she was mentioned, men, so it was said, went all of a tremble and dashed off to hide behind their wives' skirts.'

'She belaboured one or two, did she?' said Tench.

'More than a few, laddie. More than a few.'

'And she's been dead, I suppose, for what? Nearly four hundred years?'

'Something like that.'

'So what's she got to do with the case at Kettle Hill?'

'Quite a lot, laddie. Don't be so impatient. Let the tale unfold.'

Tench glanced at McKenzie and raised his eyebrows.

'Right, sir,' he said. 'Carry on. I'm still listening.'

'Well, it seems that one day – a bitter cold day according to the

174

record – Meg was out on a jaunt with some of her friends. All of them were women – the husbands were at work – but one of them had a boy and she'd brought him along. He was just about fourteen and a bit of a scamp, and they were walking past Epping mill...'

'A windmill?'

'One of the oldest.'

'I thought it might be,' said Tench. 'So what did this fearsome gang of harridans see? Did they find the mill ablaze?'

'No,' said Lubbock, 'they didn't. There was a stiff breeze blowing, the sails were turning at a fair rate of knots, and the miller was leaning on the rail of the stage, sniffing at the air. What happened then – so the story goes – was that the boy looked up and gave him a right old mouthful of cheek, and the miller, a short-tempered devil by all accounts, stormed out of the mill and gave the little sod a whack with a stick.'

'And serve him right,' said McKenzie.

'Maybe, but Meg didn't see things in quite the same way. She told the miller to lay off, in no uncertain terms, and with that he upped and clobbered her. Well, she made no more ado but she grabbed the stick, wrenched it out of his hand and set about him good and proper. I think the phrase was "she beswinged him well". Then she got him in an arm-lock, and sent the boy off to find an empty sack. When he brought it, she tied the miller up with a piece of rope, dumped him inside it, fastened it to the hoist, hauled him up a couple of floors and left him hanging there.'

'So we're back again to the sack chain,' said Tench.

'Back as far as we can go. It's the earliest historical reference to a sack hoist. *The Life of Long Meg of Westminster*, written, I'd imagine, soon after she died.'

'And it's all in your notes.'

'I knew about it, yes. Came across it once when I was reading up about windmills. So I looked it up again, and it set me thinking. You see, laddie, the story ends in a rather revealing way. It says that the miller cried out for help, and if his wife hadn't luckily arrived on the scene, he might well have died because the mill "for want of corn" could have gone up in flames.'

Tench was suddenly serious.

'And you think that's what might have happened to Pashley?'

Lubbock shrugged.

175

'Ledward found scraps of burnt sacking on the body. The signs were that Pashley fell straight down, feet first. And he breathed in smoke...'

Tench slid the report into a file, pulled open a drawer, dropped it inside and slammed the drawer shut. Then he looked straight at Lubbock.

'With all due respect, sir, these are inferences, aren't they? Little more than that. I'm prepared to accept them, but they hardly add up to a cast-iron case.'

'You rarely get a cast-iron case,' replied Lubbock. 'You just press on regardless.'

Tench nodded.

'I know, but I can't help feeling that I need something more. I'm not questioning your logic, sir. Don't think that. And I wouldn't dare to query your expert knowledge. But there's nothing to prove that Jacks was anywhere near Kettle Hill on the night of the fire. No one saw him there, and while we may be pretty sure that he was the man who was driving the cart through Morston village, we haven't a hope of proving it. All that Burage saw was a big man leaning forward and jerking at the reins. Even if he identified Jacks as the driver, any self-respecting counsel would cut him to ribbons in the witness-box. The light was too poor for him to see that distance; the man was hunched over, and he was looking from above, from a bedroom window...'

Lubbock picked up his matches.

'Don't go on, lad,' he said. 'You're just wasting breath. Jacks stole the burr stones, that's clear enough, but he didn't murder Pashley.'

Tench stared at him.

'You mean it was an accident after all?'

'No.' Lubbock wreathed himself once again in smoke. 'It was murder, a particularly vicious kind of murder. But Jacks didn't do it. He couldn't have done it.'

4

'Then who did?' McKenzie asked.

'No,' said Tench. 'Wait. Why couldn't he have done it?'

176

'You want me to spell it out step by step?'

'If possible, yes.'

'Right, laddie.' Lubbock pushed back his chair. 'I'm ready to do just that, but it won't be here in this office. I'm not at home in these bleak surroundings any more. Can't get used to sitting this side of the desk. I suggest we take a breather. Let's go down to the Riverside. I'll stand you both lunch. It's more comfortable there.'

Three-quarters of an hour later, he pushed aside his plate, poured himself a cup of tea, stretched out his legs, filled and lit his pipe, and surveyed them both through the swirling smoke.

'Now, laddie,' he said, 'let's begin from the beginning. Whoever contrived this murder was fiendishly clever. My guess would be that on the night of the fire he drove to Kettle Hill, probably in a car. Now, there are, as you know, two tracks that lead up from the road to the mill. There's one on the Blakeney side, the one Ellison used. That's just a farm gate. But there's another a couple of hundred yards towards Morston where you have to squeeze through a narrow kissing-gate. If you go that way, it's a short climb up the slope, but traffic has to use the gate nearer to Blakeney and that's a longer way. I think that this man, whoever he was, parked his car on the verge by the kissing-gate, and then walked up the track. He made sure that all the lights were out in the cottage, opened the mill door and made his way inside. Then he set to work.'

Tench poured himself a coffee, and one for McKenzie.

'You mean he had it all planned?'

'I'm pretty certain he did.'

'OK,' said Tench. 'Carry on. What did he do?'

'He set to work to lure Pashley from the cottage. He wouldn't have dared to switch on any of the lights, but he may not have needed to. There was a fitful moon that night, and he'd probably brought a pocket torch. He emptied the hopper of grain to a dangerous level, removed the light bulbs from their sockets and set the mill running. Then he waited behind the door in the dark. When Simon heard the alarm bell ringing, he flung on his dressing-gown and dashed to the mill. Once inside, he was clobbered.'

'That's what I reckoned from the start,' said McKenzie.

'Yes' – Lubbock tamped down the tobacco in his pipe – 'but according to my reckoning there was more to it than that. Our

177

unseen murderer knew what he had to do, and after that he worked fast. He'd brought with him a length of rope and maybe an old scarf. He stopped the mill, trussed the lad up, gagged him with the scarf and, like Long Meg of Westminster, dumped him in a sack. Then he fastened it to the hoist, jammed the bell alarm, set the mill running again, hauled him up two or three floors and left him. After that he applied the brake, and possibly, to be on the safe side, wedged the striking mechanism so that it wouldn't automatically open the sail shutters. He could have done all that in a matter of minutes. The rest would be easy. He'd just empty the remaining grain from the hopper, set the mill running, lock the brake into the "off" position and walk away down the hill.'

'And though the hopper was empty, the bell wouldn't ring.'

'Right,' said Lubbock. 'It was a million to one chance that anyone would pass by the mill at that time of night. He'd set it running, the stones were starved of grain, Pashley was trussed up and gagged in a sack, and, left to its own devices, the whole place would shortly go up in flames. The wind was gusting strongly. Ellison said so. If he left the mill door open, the tower itself would act as a blast-furnace. That was what he banked on. Pashley wouldn't stand a chance. The smoke alone would probably be enough to kill him. Then the rope between the sack and the chain would burn away, and the body would drop to the floor of the mill. There'd be no evidence left to prove conclusively just how Pashley died. Simple enough. All the forensic evidence would point to the fact that the mill had caught alight, Pashley had tried to save it and been overcome by smoke. The lightning was a bonus. It couldn't have come at a better time. To an untrained observer, it was obvious what had happened. The lightning had struck the sails and set the mill ablaze.'

'The elements', said McKenzie 'in league with the devil.'

'You could say so, yes. If I'm right, he was a devil and a clever one, too. He had it all worked out, and it could well have gone unnoticed...'

'If a retired Detective Chief Inspector', said Tench, 'hadn't spent the summer poking around windmills.'

'Your words, laddie, not mine.' Lubbock struck a match and rekindled his pipe. 'But yes, at a pinch they could be close to the truth.'

5

Tench frowned.

'Supposing you're right, then Ellison must have been passing the mill at the very moment when the bell began to ring. Just before Pashley heard it and dashed out of the cottage to see what was happening.'

'Yes.' Lubbock nodded. 'A cruel twist of fate. If he'd been half a minute later he'd have seen him, and all that happened after would have been very different.'

'But even so' – Tench was determined to prove every point – 'it seems strange he saw nothing.'

'Not really, laddie, no. Think how the mill and the cottage lie in relation to the track. In half a minute Ellison would have been well down the path towards the main road. Even if he'd turned round, he wouldn't have seen a thing. Anyone running from the cottage to the mill would have been hidden by the tower, and Ellison didn't look back till he got to the gate. He was facing downhill, and all he was bothered about was getting back to Cley before the storm broke. And he wouldn't have seen the car because it was a couple of hundred yards away on the Morston side. Once on the road, he'd have turned towards Blakeney.'

'All right,' said Tench, 'but what about Jacks? If he lifted the burr stones, he must have been around at much the same time.'

'Yes, he must, but if I'm reasoning correctly, he'd already done the job and left. He was on his way back to Breckmarsh. I think we've been overestimating the speed of that cart. How far is it from Kettle Hill to the far side of Morston? Taking the Blakeney track, it can't be far short of a couple of miles. The cart was heavy laden – you know the weight of one of those blocks of stone – and Burage said it was crawling: the horse was sweating and straining at the shafts and the cart was barely moving. If Jacks was making more than three miles an hour, I'd be very much surprised. What time did Burage see it? He was vague, wasn't he? Nigh on two o'clock. He doesn't seem to have checked. Five to, ten to, might even have been a quarter to. To get there by that time, Jacks would have had to leave Kettle Hill somewhere between five past and quarter past one. Ellison's time was speculative, too. He heard the bell, he said, somewhere round about half-past one. No, to my mind, laddie, Jacks was already on his way back home when the murderer walked up that track to Kettle Hill.'

'You're assuming', said Tench, 'that he could have driven up to the mill and loaded up the stones while Pashley was still asleep.'

'And why not? He'd drive up the Blakeney track to the back of the stables. They're well away from the cottage. The cart had rubber tyres, and he'd almost certainly have laid something down, sacking or blankets, to deaden any sound as he loaded the stones. And you know how soundly young people sleep the first two or three hours. Oh, yes, he could have done it all right.'

'One point,' said McKenzie. 'You reckon the killer was waiting in the dark behind the mill door, and his aim was to get rid of Pashley for good. Right. That was my idea. But what you're implying is that he just clobbered him gently and knocked him out for a spell. Why didn't he kill him straight away? Why just lay him out and go to all the trouble of stringing him up in a sack?'

'It's only conjecture, lad, but I'm reasoning like this. This man was clever, devilishly clever. He wouldn't have wanted to leave any trace of what he'd done. If he'd shot him, stabbed him, beaten him to death or even used a chopping stroke, he might have left some vital trace on the body that a skilled pathologist would have seized on right away. One broken bone that didn't fit into the pattern of a fall might have been enough to send him to the gallows. As it was, the only scrap of forensic evidence that might have suggested foul play was that minor fracture at the back of the skull, and Ledward had to admit that even that could have been caused by the fall. No, if I'm thinking right, this man was too clever to do the killing himself. That would have been too risky. And of course he didn't need to. The fire would do it for him.'

Tench stared at his cup.

'What you're saying is that he was far too clever to be Gabriel Jacks.'

'Right, laddie, he was. Oh, Jacks knew all about mill machinery and he had a clear motive: he needed the burrs. But let's face it, he's as thick as one of his own Peak stones. He may have a mite of animal cunning, but he hasn't enough up top to plan a murder like this. The very fact that he thought he could get away with stealing those stones and cover his tracks simply by mounting a Peak stone on top of a burr proves how thick he must be. How long did it take you to trace back that lorry? Less than twenty-four hours. Would the man I'm thinking of leave such an easy trail? Would he be dumb enough to stand outside the mill and yell threats at Pashley for anyone to hear? No, lad, he wouldn't. Jacks stole the burr stones, but his involvement ends there. We're looking for someone else.'

'But who?'

'I don't know. But one thing I do know: he's got to be found.'

Lubbock suddenly leaned forward, his elbows on the table.

'What I can't get out of my mind,' he said, 'is this. I can see that boy strung up there in a sack. Can you possibly imagine what he must have felt when his senses came back? Trussed like a chicken, hanging there helpless high in the mill and hearing the sound of those empty stones throwing off the sparks that he knew must eventually roast him to death? And smelling the smoke, watching it slowly curl up from the stairway, feeling the heat rising up from below; writhing from left to right in the sack in what he must have known was a vain attempt to work himself free? No, you can't imagine it and neither can I. It's beyond contemplation.'

There was silence for a moment. It was McKenzie who spoke.

'Then we're back where we started.'

'Not entirely,' said Lubbock. 'We've got Jacks on two charges, theft and assault. All we need to do now is get someone for murder.'

6

They sat in the car in the police station yard: Tench and McKenzie.

'He's right,' said Tench, 'but I've a shrewd suspicion that on one point he's wrong.'

McKenzie shifted in his seat.

'You think, at a pinch, that Jacks could have done it?'

'No, not if it was planned as Lubbock says it was.'

'But you think he had a hand in it.'

'Probably not. If we accept Lubbock's theory.'

McKenzie's eyes narrowed.

'But you still say he's wrong. Whereabouts is he wrong?'

181

'I don't think the murderer came in a car. I think he came on a bike.'

'You've lost me there. Why?'

'Something Miss Dixon told me. I was asking her last night about that man with the limp. Trying to get her to remember a bit more about him...'

'And what?'

'She said that when she was driving to the mill that afternoon, she saw a push-bike reared against the hedge by the kissing-gate.'

McKenzie stared at him.

'Are you saying that this limping man was the killer?'

'Not yet. But he could be.'

'You've got a theory.'

Tench shrugged.

'That's all it is, so far. I'm just thinking aloud.'

'Then let's think a bit more.' McKenzie was suddenly the diligent sleuth. 'Who is he, this man? If you're right, we need to find him. Where the hell do we start to look?'

'The first question', Tench said slowly, 'is do we accept Lubbock's method of murder?'

'It seems feasible enough.'

'All right, it's logical, as one would expect. So what kind of man are we looking for?'

'An ingenious devil with a murderous mind.'

'That goes without saying, but he must possess other characteristics too.'

'Meaning?' said McKenzie.

'He's a man, first of all, who's well versed in the workings of mill machinery. Second, he can lay his hands, without much trouble, on one of the old flour sacks: a twenty-stone sack. And third, unless I'm very much mistaken, he's got keys to both the mill and the cottage ... Now, Mac, let's do as you suggested. Let's think. Who might know about mill machinery, have an old flour sack lying around, and also a set of keys to the mill?'

McKenzie pondered the question.

'Are you thinking what I am?'

'More than likely, yes.'

'The old miller? The one who was there before Pashley?'

'He's the obvious suspect.'

'Then who is he? Did you check him out with Dodds?'

182

'He's a chap called Josh Randall, lives out at Binham.'

'Has he got a limp?'

'No, he hasn't, but his son has.'

'Go on,' said McKenzie. 'Tell me the rest.'

'Well, it was last night, when I was talking to Walter. I knew he delivered the milk to Kettle Hill, so I asked him whether he'd ever seen a man with a limp. He said yes, he had: Randall's son, Davie; and he went on to tell me a good deal more. Apparently he's been a pain in the neck to old Josh. In and out of trouble. Walter called him a nowty bugger. And there's more to it than that. According to him, the lad's just out of clink.'

'Is he, by God? Have you checked him in the files?'

'Came back here last night.'

'So what was he sent down for? GBH? Arson?'

'I couldn't find him,' said Tench. 'There's no record of anyone called David Randall.'

'You're sure?'

'Yes, positive.'

'Maybe Walter was wrong.'

'That was what I thought. Then I said no. Physically, Walter may be a bit out of kilter, but he's sharp enough up top. No, Mac, there has to be some other explanation.'

'He lived at Kettle Hill?'

'Yes, with Randall.'

'And where is he now?'

'At Binham.'

'Then, if he's been inside, he must be somewhere in the files.'

'Yes, he must be. I got as far as that.'

' So ?'

'It seemed to me that there was only one man who was sure to know the answer.'

'The Chief?'

'No, he told me he'd never met Randall, and it was pretty clear he knew nothing about any son. No, if anybody knew, Mac, it had to be Dodds, so while you and Lubbock were topping up Wally with Stiffkey ale this morning, I took him off to the snug and asked him about Davie Randall.'

'And what did he say?'

'He looked at me,' said Tench,' like he must have looked at you when you asked him about that little runt, Gabriel Jacks. No one of

183

that name in Binham, he said. Maybe I was thinking of young Davie Burns.'

McKenzie stroked his chin.

'Name rings a bell. Can't remember why ... What did Dodds say about him?'

'To begin with, he limps.'

'But if his name's Burns, he can't be Randall's son, so Walter was wrong.'

'Only half wrong. He's the son of a woman called Mary Latheron.'

'Never heard of her.'

'No, you wouldn't have.'

'Who is she?'

'She isn't any longer. She's been dead for thirteen years.'

'All right, then. Who was she?'

'A Scots girl, so Dodds said, born on the edge of the Gorbals.'

'Then how did Davie get down here?'

'She got herself with child by a Clydeside riveter, and the family insisted she married him. That was just before the 1914 war.'

'This riveter's name was Burns.'

'That's right. They christened the boy David, but inside three years the father drank himself to death. Mary had to go out to work as an office cleaner and leave the boy with her parents. Then her mother died, and the lad began to run wild. You know what the Gorbals is like.'

'From all accounts, it's a tenement hell.'

'With a devil on every floor. Not the kind of place for a child to run loose. Mary couldn't do much – not with having to work – and things went from bad to worse. At last, in desperation, she wrote to her mother's sister who lived at Halesworth in Suffolk. She offered to take them in, so Mary packed up and came down here with the boy.'

'And where does Randall come into it?'

'She got a job at what in Scotland would be called The Big House. Largely through her aunt. She was a housemaid. She lived in and took her son with her. Then, some twenty years ago, she met and married Josh Randall. At that time he was miller at Linstead Green post mill, a mile or two from Halesworth.'

'So our Davie Burns is Josh Randall's stepson.'

'Yes, he's his stepson, and from what Dodds said he's been the bane of his life.'

'Burns ... Davie Burns ...' McKenzie tapped his forehead. 'I've come across that name, Mike, somewhere before...'

'That's because you've seen it. It must be in the files.' Tench got out of the car. 'So the first thing to do', he said, 'is go upstairs and check.'

7

'Burgess ... Burgin ... Burke ... Burkitt ...' Tench flicked through the files. '... Burlace .... Burn .... Burnham ... Burns. Burns, David. Got him.' He pulled out the yellow-backed folder and dropped it on the desk.

'Burns, David,' he read. 'Born Glasgow, 1915... That makes him thirty-two ... Five feet eleven. Hair, black. Scar on right cheek. Extensive scarring, right knee...'

'That's our man,' said McKenzie. 'What's his record?'

'Arrested at Harleston, December '45, and handed over to the Met. Convicted at the Bailey, February '46, of complicity in a liquor-smuggling operation between Harwich and The Hook. Also of assaulting a customs officer. Sentenced to eighteen months. Served his term at the Scrubs. Released on good behaviour June this year.'

'No bells ringing yet. Must be something else.'

'Yes,' said Tench, 'there is. Seems he'd been hauled in a couple of months before from the same address – 42 Abercrombie Street, Harleston: a lodging-house – and handed over for questioning to the Suffolk police. Suspected of involvement in the Nettlefield robbery.'

'That's it, Mike.' McKenzie slapped the desk. 'I remember him now. We turned him over to Jock Connors in Ipswich.'

Tench looked up from the file.

'This Nettlefield business. It happened before my time. Tell me about it.'

McKenzie gave a shrug.

'Diamond pendant. The Star of Nettlefield. Property of Lady Masterton at Nettlefield Hall. Twenty-five diamonds. Centre

185

stone, the Star, reputedly cut from the famous Cullinan. Priceless, so they said. Normally kept in a bank vault. Taken out to wear at a London reception and stowed away overnight in a safe at the Hall. Stolen in the small hours. Never seen again.'

'When did it happen?'

'October '45.'

'And Maitland thinks he's got a lead?'

'Some source in Amsterdam, but the Chief always said it'd never turn up. Too well known to be sold as a single piece. Must have been broken up ages ago. He thinks Maitland's wasting his time if he reckons he's going to lay his hands on the loot ... Any more in the file about Burns and this involvement?'

'No, that's the lot. Handed over for questioning. No mention of what happened.'

'I'll ring up Jock Connors.' McKenzie reached for the phone. 'He'll be bound to remember.'

'No, don't do that yet.' Tench put out a hand and stopped him. 'Before you ring,' he said, 'let me tell you the rest of what Dodds had to say.'

'OK, I'm listening.'

'Well, he's known Randall ever since he first came to Kettle Hill, and that was almost twenty years ago. Sound as a bell, he said. Never put a foot wrong in all that time. Had a quiet sort of life till he met Mary Latheron. After that things changed.'

'I can imagine,' said McKenzie.

'No need to. Dodds told me pretty well everything. Apparently Randall thought a lot of his wife. She seems to have been a gentle, simple sort of girl; but the boy was a handful from very early on. Inherited from his father rather than his mother. Bright but wayward. Had a vicious streak in him, and once he'd mixed with those schoolboy gangs in the Gorbals it came close to callousness. He was always in trouble. Oh, nothing too serious. Stealing odd things, getting into scraps, mixing in general with groups of lads that his stepfather disapproved of. Sulky, rebellious, refused to toe the line.'

'Needed a good cuff round the ear,' McKenzie said.

'Probably so, and according to Dodds he should have got more than one, but that was where Randall made his mistake. He tried to keep the peace for the sake of his wife, and put up with more from the boy than he should. Then, in 1929, when the lad was fourteen, they moved to Kettle Hill, and three years later Mary was stricken with infantile paralysis. She lingered a couple more years and then died. Randall, so it seems, took her loss very badly. For Mary's sake he felt he ought to see the boy right, so he took him on as an apprentice and taught him about milling in the hope that they could settle down and run the mill together.'

'But it didn't work out.'

'No,' said Tench, 'it didn't. Not that Davie wasn't sharp. Dodds said it didn't take him all that long to learn. He could soon do everything Randall could do, but it was a stormy relationship. They quarrelled more than once, and when they did young Davie used to take off without any warning and get himself a job doing something else miles away. In a couple of months' time he'd turn up again and Randall would take him back. Then they'd have another fight and the lad would go off again into the blue. And it went on that way till the war broke out and Davie was called up.'

'Just what he needed: a bit of army discipline.'

'Yes, Randall thought so, too. Wasn't sorry to see him go. I asked Dodds what he knew about his time in the army, but he didn't know much except that he was mauled a bit. Normandy or some place ... That wasn't enough. I needed more than that, so I did a bit of phoning ... You remember, Mac, when Lubbock packed me off to London earlier this year to winkle out some facts about the Elsdon case? I had to go to Army Records and see a chap called Clyde. Well, I rang him up from the pub and asked him to do a bit of swift investigation. He rang me back and gave me the facts about Davie Burns' career in the army.' Tench took out his notebook. 'He was called up into the Suffolks in 1940. Seems that when he registered for service, he'd got a short-term job, probably in Ipswich, and registered there. He volunteered for the Commandos and was transferred early in 1942. Served with them that August in the raid on Dieppe and got a shell splinter through the cheek. Hence the scar. In 1943 he did ninety days in the glasshouse at Aldershot. Assaulting a sergeant. He was then returned to the Suffolks' depot at Bury St Edmunds for redeployment, was drafted to the 1st battalion, went on the Normandy invasion in June '44 and was wounded at Colleville. Shot through the knee. That's why he limps. Invalided out in December that year and returned to Kettle Hill. Dodds knows he did, because he saw him that Christmas.'

'I bet Josh was glad to see him. What after that?'

'He stuck it at Kettle Hill for three or four months, then Randall told Dodds they'd had another blazing row and he'd taken off again. I reckon that was when he started lodging at Harleston. Dodds said he got a job in a pub somewhere there.'

'Then in October we were asked to pick him up because Connors thought he might be mixed up in the Nettlefield business, and two months after that he was nobbled for something entirely different – this smuggling racket – and sent down for eighteen months. Bright little bugger to have for a stepson.'

'Bright's the word, Mac. And it could be Davie Burns is even brighter than we think. When was he hauled in for that Nettlefield business?'

McKenzie spun the file round.

'October the thirteenth.'

'And the robbery was when?'

'Three days before. October the tenth.'

'And when was he arrested for the smuggling racket?'

'December the twenty-first.'

'Well, he was back at Kettle Hill between those two dates. He was there in the November. Dodds had to check on some grain nicked from Wells. Thought it might have been sold to a local miller, so he went up to Breckmarsh and then Kettle Hill. Davie Burns was there. According to Randall he'd been back there a week.'

McKenzie closed the file. Then he looked across at Tench.

'You've got something in mind, Mike,' he said. 'Spell it out.'

Tench hesitated.

'Well,' he said, 'suppose we've all been wrong. You, me and Lubbock, even the Chief Super. Suppose the very thing that Maitland's been looking for's been under his nose for the past three months ... You see, Mac, we've all of us assumed that the Nettlefield case and Pashley's death had nothing whatever to do with each other; that they were two distinct happenings, entirely unrelated. But just suppose they weren't. Suppose there was some connection.'

'And Davie Burns was that connection?'

'It's possible, isn't it? You see, Mac, there is another link, too. Something else that Dodds told me. The Big House where Mary Latheron worked as a housemaid was Nettlefield Hall.'

McKenzie breathed deeply.

'Did you say what I think you said?'

'Yes, her aunt wangled her a job with the Mastertons. So maybe now's the time' – Tench handed him the phone – 'to ring up Connors in Ipswich, and see what else he can tell us about Davie Burns.'

8

McKenzie was right. Jock Connors remembered Burns well enough. They'd picked him up because he'd been seen around Nettlefield the day before the robbery. When they'd questioned him, he'd been completely self-possessed. Said he'd lived there as a boy when his mother was in service there at the Hall. All he'd been doing, so he claimed, was trying to trace an old friend, a girl who'd moved away. They'd checked up at the Hall and everything he'd told them appeared to be true, but just to make sure they'd searched his room at the lodging-house in Harleston and then sent a team to scour the Three Tuns at Halesworth where he worked as a barman. They'd drawn a blank at both places, so they'd had to let him go.

'Was there anything in their files about Kettle Hill?' Tench asked.

'No, not a thing. Jock had never even heard of the place. As far as he was concerned, Davie Burns' connections were all around Halesworth and Harleston, the Norfolk-Suffolk border.'

'Right,' said Tench, 'let's go back to this man that Miss Dixon saw. He walked with a limp, and so does Burns. According to the records Burns was shot through the right knee, and that tallies with what she said ... She told me he was youngish: Burns is thirty-two ... Fairly tall, she said: Burns is five eleven ... His hair was very dark – she said it could have been black – and the file corroborates that ... We know that Burns lived at Kettle Hill, and he must have had access to Randall's keys ... And that afternoon, when he was nosing round the mill, Miss Dixon saw an old black bike by the kissing-gate. When I spoke to Dodds he said he'd seen a bike like that up at Binham, at Randall's cottage. So all the evidence points to Burns as the limping man.'

'It must have been him.'

'Then let's assume it was. What did he do? He waited till Pashley was out delivering his flour, and then let himself into the mill with a key. He spent some time there, then moved on to the cottage. So what was he doing?'

'Searching, I'd imagine.'

'Yes, Mac, but what was he searching for?'

For a moment or two McKenzie said nothing. Then slowly, deliberately he lit a cigarette and leaned back in his chair.

'You think it's possible?'

'Why not?'

'Go on,' said McKenzie softly. 'The Chief's had his say. Now it's your turn.'

Tench closed his notebook, screwed the cap on his pen and slipped it in his pocket.

'You remember that little charm you picked up off the floor? The windmill with the sparklers?'

McKenzie nodded.

'We thought it might be a bit of the Dixon girl's bracelet. Did you ask her about it?'

'Yes, it was hers all right. I gave it back to her last night. Those sparklers were diamond chips.'

'Well, it fooled me,' said McKenzie. 'I thought they were bits of glass. So ... a diamond-studded mill.'

'A windmill,' said Tench, 'set with precious stones. I looked at it lying on the table at the farm, and it started me thinking. You see, Mac, out of all the things I've heard people say this last week, two things have stuck and they seem to fit together. First of all there was Lubbock's friend, Lawrence Bell. Windmills, he said, were often used as hidy-holes, places where smugglers used to stow goods away until they could be moved. And then there was Wally. You remember when he was shifting those millstones? He asked us what we were hoping to find behind them, and when I told him we were looking for a load of precious stones, he jumped to the conclusion that we were talking about a jewel snatch. "I suppose," he said, "it's as good a place as any to stash away the loot." Well, I've got an idea that both he and Bell were right. I reckon our friend Davie Burns could be Lubbock's clever killer, and he could also be the man that Maitland's searching for.'

McKenzie reached for the file.

'So what d'you think happened?'

'Let's try and reconstruct. Let's take a look at Burns. According to Dodds he's sharp.'

'Sharp enough, and twisted.'

'Right. So he's devious. Let's delve a bit deeper. He comes from a poor background, the slums of the Gorbals. He soaks up as a child all the attitudes common to those who live in such a hell-hole: bitterness, frustration, resentment of authority, and envy of those more fortunate than he is. We don't really know what his father was like, but if he drank himself to death it's a pretty fair bet that he roughed up the boy on more than one occasion.'

'Then the father dies and he's left with his mother.'

'Yes, he's left alone with her, but she has to work to keep them both alive, and she can't do that and keep an eye on him too. So she hands him over to the grandparents. And what chance do they have?'

'Little, I should think.'

'Oh, probably the grandmother tries to do her best, but she's already ill, and once she's gone he runs loose. Teams up with the gangs of light-fingered lads who terrorize the streets. His mother gets desperate. She makes off with him to Suffolk – to Halesworth, remember – lands a job with the Mastertons at Nettlefield Hall and takes him there with her. Now, Mac, let's speculate a bit. The Mastertons are rich. What does he feel when he finds himself lodged in a place like that?'

'Greed, at a guess.'

'Envy? Resentment of the wealth all around him? He almost certainly gets to know about the diamonds. Hears his mother talk. Hears the other servants talk. Then his mother marries Randall.'

'And saddles him with a stepfather.'

'And not only that. A very different sort of father from the one he had before. According to Dodds, Randall's a man of principle. He doesn't take kindly to young Davie's antics, or to his attitude. Finds him hard to understand.'

'Should have clobbered him,' said McKenzie.

'Maybe so,' said Tench. 'I wouldn't argue with that, but he's torn between his love for the woman and his need, all the time, to keep the son in check. That's where the woman wins, and the son, in a sense, loses out again. It's the classic situation, Mac. It's the kind of background to criminality that we've both of us met with time and time again. It's a wonder the lad steered clear of the law. Perhaps

191

Randall did help, at least for a while. Learning the miller's trade may just have roused some spark of interest in the lad, and then, when he got bored, the war and the army came just in time. Disciplined his wildness. Seems he did quite well for a time in the Commandos.'

'Till he walloped a sergeant.'

'Yes, the old resentment bubbled up again ... Now, let's move on a pace. In December '44 he's discharged as unfit. He goes back to Kettle Hill and works along with Randall for maybe a month or two, but he's not the sort of chap to be content with a pittance for the rest of his life, and he doesn't get on with his stepfather any better than he did before he went in the army. So he takes off again. Now it could be that he's had an eye on those diamonds for long enough. So what does he do?'

'Nicks them,' said McKenzie.

'Fair enough. But how?'

'You tell me. You're the brains of this outfit.'

'I'm only guessing,' said Tench.

McKenzie stubbed out his cigarette.

'Then guess a bit more,' he said. 'I never was a great one for logical thought.'

9

Tench pushed himself up and crossed to the window. He stood for a moment, staring out. Then he turned.

'Well, let's start off with something we know for sure. We know he goes to Halesworth. That's a logical step. It's close to Nettlefield ... He gets himself a job at the Three Tuns hotel.'

'And lodgings at Harleston.'

'Right. So he's working at Halesworth and lodging at Harleston. That's what? Ten miles away?'

'Something like that.'

'And Nettlefield's half-way between the two. Just what he wants. He must pass it every day.'

'Hang on,' said McKenzie. 'His mother's aunt lives at Halesworth. Why doesn't he stay with her?'

'Because he must know she's dead. Look, Mac, if he's going to nick those diamonds and hide them at Kettle Hill, then the last thing he needs is for someone to connect him with Randall and the mill. But he thinks he's got a fair chance of covering his tracks. Remember, he's got no form. There's nothing on file about him here or in Suffolk. As far as the army's concerned his address is in Ipswich; his next-of-kin – I checked it with Clyde – is his grand-father in Glasgow, and he's more than likely dead. So are his father and mother. The only other relative who can link him with Kettle Hill is his great-aunt at Halesworth, and he's not going to show himself in the town if he knows she's still alive. That'd be too risky. As it is, he knows it'll take some probing to turn up any sign of his connection with the mill. He's in a different county, a good fifty miles away. He must feel he's pretty safe, because he's ready to use his link with the Hall as cover if he happens to be seen.'

'Fine.' McKenzie leaned forward, elbows on the desk. 'He's travelling every day between Harleston and Halesworth, maybe on a bike, and taking a gander at Nettlefield on the way. What comes next?'

'Guesswork,' said Tench. 'Can't be anything else. He's already got some idea of the layout of the Hall, and sets himself to stake it out. He calls there and makes inquiries about a girl, probably the daughter of one of the servants he knew as a child. Does a bit of gossiping down in the servants' hall, and then bides his time till the right moment comes.'

'And that's when gossip tells him that the pendant's going to spend a night in the safe.'

'I'd imagine so, yes. Then somehow he gets into Nettlefield in the small hours, cracks open the safe and makes off with the diamonds. Just how he gets mixed up in this smuggling racket, I wouldn't like to say. The gang was running liquor, so maybe there's a link with the Three Tuns hotel. Perhaps he thinks that the contacts may be useful. The liquor run's from The Hook. It in-volves a Dutch connection, and Amsterdam's the place to market the stones.'

'More than likely,' said McKenzie. 'Maybe that's the link that Maitland's uncovered.'

'It could be, Mac. We don't know.'

'Right, then. He's got the pendant, so what does he do?'

'Well, he's sharp enough to know that if he does a sudden flit, he's likely to make one or two folk a bit suspicious, so he hides the loot somewhere – could be out in the country near Harleston – and stays at his job. When Connors picks him up because someone says they've seen him hanging round Nettlefield, he spins him a tale that's close enough to the truth: says he lived there as a child, and was trying to trace a girl that he knew at that time. The police search his lodgings, then the Three Tuns. And what do they find? Nothing. The staff at the Hall corroborate what he's said, and Connors and his pals are out on a limb. They have to let him go. He hangs around for a spell, then he picks up the stones, takes a few days off and makes for Kettle Hill. There he breaks up the pendant, and while Randall's out delivering, hides the stones around the mill. For safety's sake, he snatches the keys and gets a spare bunch cut; then he's off back to Harleston and his job behind the bar.'

'And a couple of months later he gets himself roped in for this smuggling business, and he's out of commission.'

'He's out for eighteen months. And in the meantime Pashley inherits the mill, pensions off Randall, and sets him up on a smallholding at Binham. When Burns gets out of clink – that's in June this year – what does he find? His stepfather's left the mill, there's a new owner there, and there's no easy way for him to get at his diamonds.'

'Nasty,' said McKenzie. 'So he has to think again.'

'He has to think pretty fast. He's probably dispersed them all over the mill, so he's faced with a problem. How does he get his hands on the stones that he's hidden?'

'Well, we know he's got keys.'

'And that gives us the chance', said Tench, 'to guess a bit more. What's his next step? He hangs around the mill, well out of sight, and waits till he sees Pashley go out in the lorry. Then he uses the keys and lets himself in. Now just how he's hidden the stones we don't know, but he must have stowed them away pretty tightly so that Randall wouldn't find them. That means – and remember, we're still only guessing – that he can't retrieve them all at one go. It takes time, so he has to make more than one visit.'

'But we only know about one.'

'Right. Miss Dixon saw him a month ago. That was early in August. But he'd been at Binham since June, so I reckon that wasn't the first time he'd been there ... When was he released?'

McKenzie checked the file.

'Sixth of June.'

'So when Miss Dixon saw him he'd already had two months to get at the stones, and Pashley must have been out delivering two or three times a week. And he had to buy grain. He had to visit the markets. So if Burns was intent on retrieving the stones, he must have had the chance to make ... how many? Two dozen visits? At least two dozen by the time Miss Dixon saw him. And yet he was still searching. Why should he be doing that?'

'Maybe there were some of the stones he couldn't find.'

'But he must have known where he'd hidden them. Why couldn't he find them?'

'Perhaps he'd forgotten. Eighteen months is quite a time.'

'No.' Tench shook his head. 'He wouldn't just plant them and then forget. He's too canny for that. There's some other reason, Mac.'

McKenzie brooded for a moment.

'You think he killed Pashley?'

'I think there's more than an even chance he did.'

'Then he must have had a reason.'

'Yes, he must, unless he's mad, and I don't think he is.'

'So what's the answer?'

'As far as I can see, there's only one answer. He must have thought that Pashley had rumbled him in some way.'

'Found some of the stones, you mean?'

'It'd give him a motive, wouldn't it?'

'A couple, I'd say. Greed and self-preservation ... So, what's his next move?'

'Well, all I can suggest is this. He goes back to Kettle Hill to root out his stones. He turns up most of them, but something's missing. Perhaps the centre stone, the Star. He knows where he's hidden it, but now it isn't there. So where's it gone? He can only assume that Pashley's found it, and if he has he'll do one of two things: hand it over to the police, or put two and two together and go and see Randall. Either way he knows it's going to mean trouble. He'll find himself back in clink for a good long stretch ... There's only one course to take: he has to get rid of Pashley and make it look like an accident. He knows the mill like the back of his hand, he's got a bunch of keys, and his stepfather has some old sacks lying around in the cottage at Binham. So he does precisely what Lubbock said he did. The mill burns down, there's an opportune stroke of lightning, they find Pashley's charred body, and everyone but Lubbock assumes it's an accident.'

McKenzie stared at the open file. He seemed to be thinking back.

'You know,' he said at last, 'I reckon you could be right.'

'Could be. Might be. Who can really say? But there's one more item, Mac, that may be significant. It seems to fit the pattern.' Tench leaned over and tapped the file. 'That little episode in the army when Burns got ninety days for assaulting a sergeant ... What d'you think he did?'

'Must have clobbered him with a good straight right to the jaw.'

'Well, he didn't. I got Clyde to look up the court martial. Burns didn't use his fists. He used his fingers and thumbs.'

'How d'you mean?' McKenzie frowned.

'He was in the Commandos. Right? Well, one of the things they taught him was how to creep up behind a sentry and chop at a pressure point. Silent killing they called it. Seems there are more than a hundred different points on the human body where pressure can cause unconsciousness or death. Sixty-four of them can be lethal; but that's by the way. They also taught him that if you chose the right point and used fingers and thumbs, you didn't need to kill. You could lay the victim out for five minutes, ten, maybe even twenty. Useful if all you wanted to do was to snatch a bloke and grill him for information. Burns, so Clyde said, was quite an adept at the job. So he did what they'd taught him. Used his fingers and thumbs on an over-zealous sergeant and laid him out for a spell.'

'And you reckon he did the same to young Pashley.'

'Could have done,' said Tench. 'He could have waited behind that door, used his knowledge of pressure points, laid him out silently, and then gagged him and strung him up ... It fits Lubbock's theory, doesn't it, Mac?'

10

'Fits it like a glove, I'd say, apart from one thing. What about Randall? If he's never put a foot wrong in twenty years – and that's what Dodds says – then where does he stand? He's had enough experience of Davie Burns. Don't tell me he knows nothing about what's been going on.'

'No,' Tench admitted. 'He must know something. The question is how much . . . ? Remember Thursday afternoon when I told you I wanted to check Lubbock's ideas, and you said Dodds'd know who the old miller was? Well, after you'd gone I drove out to see him. He put me on to Randall, so I carried on to Binham and looked him up at his cottage.'

'You spoke to him?'

Tench nodded.

'Then what did you make of him?'

'Difficult to tell. He knows his windmills – that goes without saying – but I rather think he tried to put me off the scent.'

'How d'you mean?'

'Well,' said Tench, 'I led him on a bit. Told him right from the start I knew nothing much at all about the way windmills worked, and then asked him what he thought had happened at Kettle Hill.'

'And what did he say?'

'He blamed it all on Pashley's lack of experience. Said he must have tried to ride out the storm, and the brake caught fire. That'd mean the cap was already ablaze when he climbed up the tower to quarter the mill. He seemed to think Pashley was trapped by the flames and couldn't get down when the bell alarm rang.'

'Sounds feasible enough.'

'Oh, it's feasible,' said Tench. 'I told him as much. But what he was saying was the mill was ablaze before the bell rang, and we know that isn't true. Not if we believe Ellison . . . and Miss Dixon.'

'You think he was deliberately covering up for Burns?'

Tench pondered the question.

'No, I wouldn't like to put it as strongly as that, but when I said we thought there might be something suspicious about Pashley's death, he dismissed the idea just a bit too swiftly. Never asked any questions. He was quite blunt about it: we were wasting our time. There couldn't possibly be any suggestion of foul play. Pashley had made mistakes. He was the one who'd burnt down the mill. Nobody else. He hadn't got the nous – that was the word he used – to run a mill on his own.'

'But he'd been running it without a snag for more than twelve months.'

'Yes, he had. I didn't say anything, but it seemed to me that Randall was pressing his point just a wee bit too hard. The lady was protesting a shade too much, Mac.'

197

'Lady? What lady?' McKenzie went blank.

'Shakespeare,' said Tench. 'Dredged up from school.'

'Oh, that's what it was.' McKenzie seemed relieved. 'Well, you've lost me there, Mike. Not my brand of ale. Give me the Crazy Gang any old time ... So you think Randall knows something.'

'I think he knows something. I don't know how much.'

'But if he had his suspicions, wouldn't he have mentioned them to Dodds?'

'No, I don't think he would. Not if all he had to go on was just supposition. He'd need to be certain before he made a move.'

'Did he say anything about Burns?'

'Not a whisper,' said Tench.

'And you didn't see him around?'

'No.'

'You're sure he's still at Binham?'

'According to Dodds, yes.'

'Then let's get the script right. He's been fishing for those diamonds. Where are they now?'

'Guessing time again, Mac.'

'Randall's cottage?'

'Could be. But he could have hidden them anywhere on the coast. There are plenty of hidy-holes: old rotting barns, derelict mills like Blakeney...'

'No.' McKenzie shook his head. 'I'd be willing to put all my money on the cottage. He's nearly lost the stones once, and that means he won't risk it happening again. He'll have them stowed away close, right under his thieving fingers.'

'Where Randall might come across them by chance?'

'Perhaps he already has.'

Tench looked across at him.

'You're painting a pretty scary scenario, Mac. Two men in a cottage. One of them a murderer. The other suspecting him, brooding, resentful ... Who knows what could happen?'

'A hell of a lot,' said McKenzie grimly. 'One wrong word and there could be blood on the floor.'

'You think so?'

'Don't you?'

There was silence for a moment. Tench closed the file and dropped it in a drawer. He was suddenly more serious.

'If you're right, we should take some action.'

'Yes, I think we should ... So what do we do? Call in the Chief Super?'

'Up in London on a conference. Staying overnight. No, we're on our own, Mac, and that means there's only one question to answer. Do we bring them in, both of them? Now? Before there's trouble?'

'Bring 'em in and make 'em talk. That's what I'd say. A bit of pressure on Randall and we may get the truth.'

Tench seemed to hesitate.

'But how can we be sure that we're not simply weaving plots in our minds?'

'We can't. Perhaps we are.'

'We'll be playing a hunch, nothing more than that.'

'So what?' said McKenzie. 'Isn't that what the Chief's been doing all week? Let's pay Mr Randall a friendly visit and see what turns up. Crime prevention, Mike.'

Tench was thoughtful.

'OK, but we're going to need some back-up. If we're right about Burns, he could make a run for it ... Who's on duty?'

'Gregg and Rayner, but they're both out on call.'

'Then get them back,' said Tench. 'We're not moving without them. When we get to that cottage, I want it covered, back and front.'

'Search warrant?'

'No, we haven't enough evidence.'

'What about the Chief?'

'What about him?' said Tench.

'Shouldn't he be in on this?'

'No, Mac, not this time.' Tench was suddenly firm. 'This is our case, mine and yours, and it's up to us to solve it. Lubbock's done his stint. He's too old for the rough stuff, and so is Dodds. Round up Gregg and Rayner. They should be enough. Randall won't be a problem, and if Burns takes on the four of us he'll be asking for trouble. But I want the place sealed off. We can't afford to slip up. If he has got the stones tucked away in that cottage, then we can't let him get away with the loot.'

11

Binham had always seemed to Tench an unremarkable village: a straggle of flint cottages climbing a slope and bounded on the north by its one distinctive feature, the great priory church set among the ruins of its old monastic buildings. He remembered wandering with Kath among the tumbled stones, trying to reconstruct the plan of the priory that the Benedictine monks had built centuries before. They'd pushed open the heavy west door of the church and walked down the steps to the flagstoned floor and the medieval font. He saw it again in his mind's eye, set on its double plinth, its huge octagonal basin carved with figures depicting the Seven Sacraments and the Trinity; and above and beyond it the towering empty vault of the church, rising past its high Norman arches, triforium and clerestory to the dark, timbered roof. It had seemed to him then like some vast, unadorned, abandoned cathedral.

Not that he was likely to see much of Binham on this occasion. It was one of those autumn evenings in the north of Norfolk when the mist from the marshes drifts in to lie like a silver sea across the surface of the fields. There'd been signs of it as far inland as Briston and Melton Constable, and now, as they drew near the coast, the clusters of farm buildings, dotted here and there in the empty landscape, were all but hidden by a thick grey haze that wrapped around them in the darkness.

McKenzie peered through the windscreen.

'How much further?' he said.

'Must be close now.'

'It's bad enough in the swamps when you can see where you are. But on a night like this . . .'

Tench wound down the window. Faintly, through the fog, he glimpsed a flint wall.

'Go steady,' he said. 'I think we've arrived.'

McKenzie gave a growl.

'If we go any steadier, we'll come to a stop . . . Whereabouts is this cottage of Randall's?'

'Down by the river, behind the priory. Stands on its own . . . No,

Mac. Stop the car here. We'll walk the rest of the way. No sense in telling the world we're around.'

McKenzie pulled on to the verge, and the four men got out and walked down the slope. Tench turned off the road, and led them right and then left again, still further down. As they closed on the river, the fog became thicker, and McKenzie, eyes narrowed, stumbled in a rut.

'Where the hell are we?'

Tench pointed ahead. A black shape was taking form in the mist.

'That's it,' he said. 'Flint, pantiled roof.'

They crept closer.

'No lights.' McKenzie crouched down. 'Looks like the place is empty.'

'Then we do the civil thing,' said Tench, 'and knock on the door. After all, as you said, we're just paying a friendly call ... Gregg, round the back. Rayner, you stay here. You come with me, Mac.'

He stepped up to the door and raised his hand to the knocker. The sound echoed through the stillness, but inside the cottage nothing seemed to stir.

He knocked a second time. There was still no response.

'Try the door,' said McKenzie.

Tench turned the knob and felt the door give. He pushed it open. Beyond was darkness.

He flicked on his torch, and the beam cut a swathe through the dingy hallway. He could see the flight of stairs, the hatstand, and down at the far end the door to the parlour.

He pressed the light switch on the wall. Nothing happened.

McKenzie shone his beam upwards. 'No bulb,' he said.

Tench looked up. The socket was empty.

He started to move forward, but McKenzie held him back. He flexed his fingers and thumbs as if gripping someone's throat and pointed to the door.

Tench nodded. He stepped forward silently, lifted the latch and put his foot against the door. It slammed back against the wall.

He played his torch round the room, across the heavy oak furniture: the table, the chairs, the tall Welsh dresser still hung with crockery. There was no sign of life. He trained the beam on the ceiling. Another empty socket.

On the far side was a second door, standing ajar. He slammed it

201

back. A kitchen. Beyond that a scullery. Both empty, both in darkness. Not a light bulb to be seen.

'Upstairs,' he whispered.

They trod stealthily up the staircase. At the top was a landing and three further doors. One was wide open and led to a bathroom. The other two were shut.

They took one each, and at a signal from Tench, kicked both of them open. Tench saw the bed, made up, undisturbed; a set of drawers, a chair and an old wooden chest. Up above, the oak beams running from side to side across the ceiling.

He stood, flashing the torch around. Then he heard McKenzie's voice.

'Mike.'

He turned. McKenzie was standing by the door he'd rammed open, the light from his torch trained down inside the room.

'I rather think', he said, 'that our friend Davie Burns has had a bit of a picnic.'

12

Tench looked down at the crumpled body. Then he knelt and shone his torch on the face, the dead eyes.

'Randall?'

Tench nodded.

'Yes, that's Randall.'

'There's a bruise there.' McKenzie pointed to the neck. 'Looks like someone chopped him with the side of a hand.' He straightened up. 'We're too bloody late, Mike. Far too bloody late. We should have been here this morning, instead of mucking about with those blasted millstones.'

Tench flashed his torch round the room, lighting up the leather bag, the tools scattered beside it.

'What the hell was he doing?'

'Who? Randall?'

'No, Burns. Has to be him, hasn't it?'

McKenzie gave a shrug.

'Looks to me like a spot of woodwork.' He bent down and picked up one of the tools: a long-shanked affair with a corkscrew shaft and a transverse handle. 'Know what this is?' He passed it to Tench.

'Some kind of a drill?'

'It's an auger. Carpenters use them for boring holes in wood. They come in all sizes, augers. This is small compared to some. One with a bit like this would make a hole an inch wide, say, and six inches deep. And he's been using it, too.' He ran his finger round the bit, and held it to the light. 'Look,' he said. 'Sawdust.'

'Then what was he boring into?'

McKenzie swept his torch around.

'Doesn't seem to be the floor.'

Tench flashed his light upwards.

'What about the oak beams?'

McKenzie nodded.

'Worth a look.' He pulled a chair from a corner, climbed up and played his torch on the ceiling. He swept it from end to end of a beam. 'You're right,' he said. 'Holes. At least half a dozen.' He probed one with his finger. 'Quite a cavity. Feels as if it's been plugged with something ... Could be putty.'

Tench peered up at him.

'Auger-holes?'

'Have to be.'

'Auger-holes,' Tench repeated. 'Auger-holes. That's *Macbeth*'.

'Mac what?'

'*Macbeth*. It's Shakespeare again,' said Tench. 'There's a line in *Macbeth* about someone's fate being hid in an auger-hole ... Think, Mac. Think. What would Burns want to hide?'

They stared at one another. McKenzie climbed down.

'It's possible,' he said. 'Cushion the cavity, plug it with putty and stain the whole thing over. It'd be hard to detect.'

'And in a windmill?'

'Easy. Lots of shadow behind the beams.'

Tench seemed to freeze.

'Then he's still around,' he said. 'He's still somewhere in the cottage. Look, Mac, you say that that auger's been used, and it hasn't been cleaned ... I reckon we disturbed him.'

McKenzie gestured towards the body on the floor.

'But if he chopped Randall down, then he'd cut and run from here just as fast as he could.'

'No, he wouldn't.' Tench was whispering. 'Not if he hadn't

planned it. Not if he lost his temper. If he did, then he wouldn't be ready to go. He wouldn't want to leave a fortune locked up in those beams. He'd be in a hell of a panic to get the stones out. Once he'd got them out, he'd run, but not until then ... That's what he was doing when we knocked on the door. If there was a light on in here, at the back of the cottage, we wouldn't have seen it ... He wasn't hiding the loot. He was clearing it out ... He's still here, Mac. We've missed him. Where didn't we search?'

'A cupboard somewhere maybe? Behind that bathroom door?'

They trod slowly, cautiously back towards the bathroom. A floorboard creaked. They stopped and, for a moment, both held their breath ... Nothing moved ... McKenzie edged past the door. He crashed it against the wall and then pulled it back.

'No cupboard,' he said.

Tench peered through the window into the mist.

'There's a row of sheds down there. He could have hopped into one of those before Gregg got round the back.'

'Then let's flush the bugger out.' McKenzie was already out on the landing. 'You stay in the hall in case he's still inside the house.'

He clattered down the stairs, and then turned and darted towards the back of the cottage. Tench followed him down and stood guard by the door. He listened intently, flat against the wall, watching the stairs. He thought he heard McKenzie's voice and the rattle of a door. Then, all of a sudden, echoing through the darkness, came the sound of a shot.

Swearing under his breath, he dashed through the house and out at the back.

Gregg was already running, calling out to Rayner; McKenzie was staggering, leaning against a shed, blood streaming from his nose; and a shadowy figure, limping away at speed, was vanishing in the fog.

'Bloody fool,' said McKenzie. 'Should have been more careful. Slammed me with the door.'

'Did you manage to see the gun?'

'Looked like a six-shooter. Could be army issue. Damn it all, Mike, he came out of that shed like a bat out of hell.'

'You OK?'

'Reckon I'll survive.' McKenzie dabbed at his nose.

'Come on then,' said Tench. He plunged into the fog. 'We don't want Gregg's young wife to end up as a widow.'

13

Later, in the daylight, when he tried to retrace their steps, Tench could never work out just where he and McKenzie had wandered that night before they came to the great west door of the church.

They seemed to stumble through the fog first this way, then that; halting, listening for footsteps, the sound of a voice, anything that would tell them where Gregg and Rayner were. They blundered through hedges, into pigsties, over rutted tracks, once even down to the edge of the river. Then up again through the clinging mist on to what seemed level ground, until Tench tripped over a low wall of stones and pitched forward on his hands. McKenzie crouched down beside him.

'Any idea where we are?'

Tench could see nothing. Close to the ground the mist lay so thick that it almost seemed they were wading through water. He felt around till his fingers touched another line of boulders.

'I think we must be somewhere in the ruins of the priory.'

'Then where the devil's Gregg?'

'God knows,' said Tench.

'That's more than likely.' McKenzie began to inch forward. 'Trouble is we can't ask him.'

They moved ahead again slowly, picking their way over what seemed to be lines of rubble. Then suddenly Tench felt a hand on his arm, and heard McKenzie's voice.

'What on earth's that?'

Rearing up in front of them, climbing through the fog, was what looked like a jagged, irregular tower.

Tench racked his memory.

'Could be one of the old piers of the transept,' he said. 'If it is, then the church is away to the left.'

'But where's Burns?'

As if in reply, there was a shout from a distance, the sound of another shot and someone running towards them.

Tench darted forward, but McKenzie held him back.

'Hold on,' he whispered. 'Don't forget he's got a gun.'

The footsteps slowed and then stopped.

'Get behind the pier.' Tench pulled McKenzie down into cover.

'Davie Burns,' he shouted.

There was silence for a moment, then Rayner approached them out of the mist.

Tench dragged him down.

'Where is he?' he hissed.

'Dodged into the church, sir. Gregg's at the other end.'

'You stay here,' said Tench. 'We'll send him down to join you. And mind, no heroics. This man's armed. He's killed once, maybe twice. He won't hesitate a third time ... If he comes out, keep track of him. Don't try to tackle him. Just give us a yell.'

'Right, sir.'

'How far away's the church?'

'Twenty yards, sir, that's all.'

'OK ... Are you ready, Mac?'

The two of them crept forward till the great black wall showed up in front of them. Hands on the stonework, they followed it round, down the side and round again till they reached the west door. It was standing half open. Gregg was flattened against it, tense.

'Inside, sir,' he whispered, 'but it's pitch black in there. Can't see a thing.'

'Go down to Rayner. Keep watch the other end.'

Gregg nodded and disappeared into the fog.

'What now?' said McKenzie.

Tench gave a shrug.

'Wish I could remember where the lights were inside. Have you ever been in?'

'Ages ago. Can't remember much at all.'

'Then we'll just have to risk it and keep our heads down. Listen, Mac. Inside the door, there's a short flight of steps: five, possibly six; and straight ahead there's a font. If we can get behind that, we'll at least have some cover. Follow me down.'

He squeezed silently past the door and, feeling his way, began to tread down the steps. At the bottom he paused, dropped on all fours and began to crawl towards the font. It seemed an age before he reached it, but at last his fingers touched the base of the plinth, and he dragged himself up the first step, then up the second.

As he did so, a shot echoed up to the rafters, and a bullet struck the stonework just above his head. It whined as it ricocheted away into the gloom, and there was a crack like a whiplash as it struck the wall behind him.

He slid backwards and flattened himself below the plinth, trying to see down the darkened nave of the church. He was vaguely aware that someone was behind him. Then McKenzie's solid bulk dropped down at his side.

'That was close,' he whispered.

'Too bloody close.' Tench peered into the shadows.

'Any way out the other end?'

'Two bricked-up doors, one each side of the altar. May be others. I don't know.'

'Where d'you think he is?'

'Down behind one of the pews at a guess. They're oak, inches thick. Good cover to fire from.'

'Which side?'

'Can't tell.'

'Then we'd better find out. Anything to throw?' McKenzie reached for his pocket. 'Keys,' he whispered softly. 'Watch for the flash.'

He rolled back and lobbed them like a grenade. They fell with a clatter that rang round the church. There was a flash and a crack as another shot glanced off the wall and whined away to the roof.

'On the right, half-way down.' Tench eased himself backwards.

'How can we get at him?'

Tench strained his eyes.

'I think there's a screen at the back of those pews. If we get behind that, we can have another think. What's the best way?'

'Dodge down and sprint for it hell for leather. You wait here. I'll go first.'

'Not a chance,' said Tench. 'If we're going to do it, then we'll do it together ... Count up to three.'

They counted and ran. There was a crack, and another bullet whistled through the darkness. Tench plunged behind the screen, and McKenzie followed.

'Now what?'

'Let's give him a call,' Tench whispered.

He lay flat on the floor and pulled McKenzie down.

'Burns,' he shouted. 'Davie Burns, it's the police. We've got men at the back. Drop that gun and come out.'

The only answer was a volley of shots, a shuffling movement and, after that, silence.

They lay there and listened.

'Burns,' called Tench. 'Be sensible. Throw out the gun.'

This time there was no response.

He raised his head slowly.

There was a faint dragging sound away to the left, and McKenzie gripped his arm.

'He's trying to work round behind us.'

Tench pulled off his shoes.

'When you hear these drop,' he hissed, 'make a dash for the door. I'll try to head him off.'

He tossed them high across the church. They fell clattering on the flags, and he dived towards the font, saw its shadow in front of him and dropped down on the plinth.

There was no shot. No sound.

'Come on, Burns. Come on,' he breathed. 'Where the hell are you?'

He pushed himself up silently, and crouched behind the wide octagonal basin, the cold stone beneath his feet, the deep silence around him. Then, all of a sudden, his legs were whipped from under him, the base of the plinth struck him hard in the chest, and he felt fingers groping for his neck in the darkness. He twisted desperately, clawing with his hands, trying to reach out for the stem of the font, anything to pull himself clear of his attacker. He was dragged back and sideways, and then, as his fingers slid across the plinth, he felt them brush against something heavy that moved at his touch. He clutched at it and gripped it. Twisting again, he wrenched himself over and swung it across his shoulder. There was a hollow resonant sound as it connected with something hard. Then it slipped from his grasp, and a strange metallic clang echoed round the church as it dropped on the flagstones and rattled away.

The grip on his body loosened. He heard a thud as someone fell.

He pushed himself up and ran straight for the door. McKenzie was already at the bottom of the steps.

'Lights, Mac,' he shouted. 'Lights. Find the lights.'

They both groped along the wall, scrabbling with their fingers.

208

Tench found a bank of switches. He pressed them down and swung round.

The pendant lamps on their chains illumined the church. A figure sprawled by the plinth. A couple of yards away was the heavy metal water jug used to fill the font.

14

McKenzie darted forward. He plunged down on the man, dragged his arms behind his back, and clamped a pair of handcuffs on to his wrists.

'The gun,' said Tench breathlessly. 'Where's the gun?'

He ran his hands down Burns' jacket and pulled out the revolver. Snapping it open, he spun the chambers round.

'Empty,' he said. 'It had to be.' He wrapped it in a handkerchief. 'Stones, Mac?'

McKenzie searched through the pockets.

'Not a bloody thing. Must have chucked them away somewhere, and we can't grill the bugger yet. He's out for the count.'

He picked up the water jug and weighed it between his hands.

'Christ,' he said. 'No wonder, if you hit him with this.'

Tench took it from him. He pressed his lips against it almost with reverence and put it back on the plinth.

'There's a place for everything, Mac. Lucky for me it was there.'

'Luck? More like a miracle. Did you offer up a prayer?'

Tench gave a weary grin.

'On my knees in a church? What else was there to do?'

He looked down at Davie Burns. The man stirred and then groaned.

'At least he's still alive, though God knows what for.'

'The end of a rope, for sure.'

'Seems almost a waste of effort, doesn't it?' said Tench.

He picked up his shoes and moved to the door. The fog was thicker than ever.

'Gregg,' he shouted. 'Rayner...'

He turned back inside.

'They can search the place,' he said. 'We've got business with Dodds.'

209

He stood for a moment at the top of the steps.

'We could have saved them, Mac. We could have saved them both – young Pashley as well – if we'd thought fast enough.'

McKenzie was suddenly impatient, dismissive.

'Forget it,' he said curtly.

'If only we'd ...'

'No.'

'But if ...'

'No, Mike. It's not on. There's an order of things. First the crime, then the punishment. In our little game, we always have to lose before we can win. That's why there's still a gallows ... There's no point in looking back. It's a waste of bloody time. Regretting's for others. Our job's to get the killer, and we've got him. End of tale.'

'Death to the sinner? You sound like Lubbock.'

'Maybe I do,' said McKenzie savagely. 'I've worked with him long enough. I know one thing though, Mike. He wouldn't call it punishment. Not in this case. He'd call it retribution.'

He dragged the man up.

'On your feet, Burns,' he said.

EPILOGUE

SUNDAY

'Heap on more wood!'
Scott, *Marmion*

Lubbock leaned on the wall and gazed at the great west front of the church.

'Made a statement, laddie, did he?'

'With a bit of persuasion.'

'Claimed it was all an accident?'

'Self-defence, so he said.'

'I suppose he was being thrashed by a seventy-year-old man.'

'Said Randall came up behind him armed with a chunk of wood.'

'That's a likely tale.'

'Hardly convincing, is it?'

'And Pashley?'

'Said he never meant to kill him. Just to lay him out.'

'So what was he doing there?'

'Searching the place, he said. Did it at night. He'd been there more than once and never had any trouble. Came and went as he pleased. Used a pocket torch.'

'That'd be enough. He knew the mill inside out.'

'Thought he knew Pashley too. Always sound asleep. But this time he wasn't.'

Lubbock paused to light his pipe.

'So what did he say happened?'

'Well,' said Tench, 'seems he'd unlocked the mill and climbed up to the stone floor. Then he heard a noise outside. Said it sounded to him like a door had been slammed. He looked out of a window, and there was Pashley standing by the stables. That set him back a pace. He couldn't understand it.'

'Simple enough,' Lubbock said. 'He must have heard Jacks. The cart was overloaded. It probably creaked when he tried to get it going.'

'Could have been that, yes.' Tench ran his hands across the rubble wall. 'Maybe fancied he'd been dreaming, didn't get up right away and then thought he'd better take a look round to be sure.'

'And by that time Jacks was on the main road.'

'If we believe Burns.'

'And we don't, but go on.'

'Well, he said he saw Pashley making for the mill, so he dodged down the ladder and hid behind the door. When the lad came in, he jumped him. Trouble was, it was dark and Pashley was on his guard. He must have checked the stables and knew that someone had been at his load of burrs. Added to that, the mill door was open. So he came in a bit too warily and spun round too quickly. Made a real fight of it, according to Burns. He grabbed him, but he got away and made for the stone floor. At the top of the ladder he caught him by the legs and tried to pull him back, and in the struggle they fell.'

'Don't tell me,' said Lubbock. 'Pashley went down head first and Burns fell on top of him.'

'Yes, broke his neck.'

Lubbock puffed at his pipe.

'Plausible, but unlikely. Doesn't fit with Ledward's account of his injuries. What about all those fractures? He wouldn't get those just by falling down a ladder. No, he came down feet first, and not from the stone floor either. Higher up than that. But carry on, laddie. Tell me the rest. What did he do when he found the boy was dead?'

'Knew his only chance was to make it look like an accident. The wind was getting up, so he left him where he was at the foot of the ladder, set the mill running and made off down the hill.'

'Doesn't fit,' said Lubbock. 'What about the bell?'

'Mac picked up that point. Thought he'd got him pinned down, but he came up with an answer. No hesitation. Said he was three parts of the way down the track – the one that leads to the kissing-gate – when the bell began to ring. That really rocked him. Said he'd never thought about checking the grain level. Never had a notion that the hopper might be empty. Well, he knew he had to stop the bell, so he turned back up the hill. That was when he saw Ellison.'

'He did what?'

214

'He saw a soldier. That's what he said. Just below the mill. Marching down the track to the Blakeney gate. All he could do was drop flat on the ground and wait until he was out of sight. And all the time the bell was ringing. He said he was sweating buckets in case Ellison came back. It wasn't till he'd scrambled up the hill and put a clamp on the bell that he thought about what'd happen if he left the mill running with an empty hopper. It seemed an answer to all his problems. The stones were already throwing off sparks and the wind was half a gale. So he left the door open, the sails still turning, raced back to his bike and pedalled off to Binham ... Could have happened, sir, couldn't it?'

'It could,' said Lubbock, 'but I'm damned sure it didn't. I still think he did precisely what I said. He had it all planned ... He admitted he stole the diamonds?'

'He could hardly deny it.'

'And he killed Randall, so what does it matter? He'll swing just the same. A strong imagination's going to do him no good with a noose round his neck. Good riddance, I say. The world's better off without types like Davie Burns ... You say you found the diamonds in Randall's cottage?'

'Half a dozen of them there, plugged into the beams. The rest in a linen bag in the font. He must have been pretty desperate. Dodged into the church to hide them and found himself trapped. I think he was trying to get back to the font and then make a dash for it, when we managed to nobble him.'

Lubbock jerked his pipe stem towards the church.

'That's the only door?'

'Yes, the rest are bricked up.'

'Made a bit of a suicidal move then, didn't he?'

'I think he thought he'd lost Gregg and Rayner in the fog, but of course he hadn't.'

'How many are still missing?'

'The stones? Five,' said Tench, 'and that includes the Star.'

'Did he mention the Star?'

'No. Clammed up altogether when we questioned him about it. Could already be over the water in Holland.'

Lubbock shook his head.

'The smaller ones maybe, but not the Star. He wouldn't risk that so early in the game. Too easy to recognize. He'd get rid of the others first.'

'Then it must still be around. The question is where?'

'You couldn't have missed it in Randall's cottage?'

'No, we've had a team on the job. They've even ripped up the floorboards . . . It could be at Kettle Hill. If Maitland thinks there's a chance, no doubt he'll be out there combing the ruins . . . I suppose there is just a faint possibility it could be in Pashley's cottage.'

Lubbock bit hard on the stem of his pipe.

'If it is,' he said, 'then Burns must have hidden it there. And if he did, I'm sure Simon knew nothing about it.'

'But Burns must have thought he knew. He must have thought he'd found it. Otherwise, why kill him?'

'That's a fair assumption, yes,' Lubbock said slowly. 'He must have suspected that Simon had found it. But that doesn't mean that he actually had . . . Look, Mike, I knew him. He wasn't the type to hang around if he found a clutch of diamonds hidden in his mill, let alone a gem like the Star of Nettlefield. He was honest, straight-forward. He'd have been off with them to Dodds or to your lot in Norwich before Burns had got around to planning that murder. No, I'm ready to swear he never laid eyes on a single diamond. But' – he seemed to hesitate a moment – 'there is one other possible explanation.'

'What's that?'

'Well, according to you, Burns did the same thing at Kettle Hill as he did in Randall's cottage. He hid the stones in the beams.'

'It seems likely. Why not?'

'Why not indeed? He probably did. So when the mill changed hands, they were safely stowed away where no one but he was likely to find them. But something could have happened to throw his plans out of gear. You see, Mike, as soon as Simon moved into that mill he replaced some old beams. Had a firm of builders in from Norwich to do the job. He told me about it.'

'You mean one of those beams could have held the Star of Nettlefield?'

'Who knows?' said Lubbock. 'But it could have done, couldn't it?'

There was silence. Tench took a little time to collect his thoughts.

'What happened to them, then: the ones the workmen took out?'

'Simon cut them into blocks with a circular saw and stacked them in the granary. They were there when I first went to pay him a call.'

'And they're still there?'

'No.'

'Then what did he do with them?'

'The usual thing. He sold them for fuel. Oak burns well and it lasts a long time.'

Tench stared at him.

'You mean someone could have burnt that priceless gem in a kitchen stove?'

'They could have done. Very fitting. What are diamonds, after all? They're nothing but carbon.'

'D'you know who bought the wood?'

'Yes, as it happens.'

'Who was it?'

'If you really must know,' said Lubbock, 'it was Walter Bolding. Seems his wife has one of those old kitchen ranges. Takes a lot of heating. Yes, laddie, all the wood went down to the Boldings. I was there when Simon loaded it up on the lorry and took it to Morston Bottom.'

Tench remembered the ancient blackleaded range, the fire roaring up the chimney, the stifling heat.

'Somehow,' he said, 'I don't think I'd dare to tell Maitland that.'

'I wouldn't bother.' Lubbock knocked out his pipe on the wall. 'It's only speculation when all's said and done. Leave the Boldings in peace ... I suppose Hastings was pleased?'

'Seemed to be, yes.'

'Patted you on the back?'

'Metaphorically,' said Tench.

'And so he should, too. He can close all the files on the Kettle Hill case, stack them on a shelf and let them gather dust. There aren't many who can claim they solved their first murder in less than a week. Sit back and enjoy things. You've done a good job.'

'With a little bit of help.'

Lubbock scratched his ear.

'Well, we all need some help. The lone detective's a myth. He's a figment of fiction. It's team-work solves murders. Team-work and luck. Someone tells us one thing, someone else another. We strike out in one direction, think we're on the right track, and then the trail peters out. We have to turn round and start again from scratch. We choose a different trail. Then we turn a corner and reach a brick wall. And it's only on our way back that we happen to

217

notice something underneath our feet, something we've missed: a ticket, a knife blade, a cigarette stub ...'

'Maybe a charm off a bracelet,' said Tench. 'A little gold wind-mill studded with diamonds.'

'Yes.' Lubbock nodded. 'In this particular case that could well fit the bill ... I suppose there are such things.'

'Oh, I think you'll find there are, sir.' Tench straightened up. 'Jewellers here in Norfolk keep quite a stock. A friend of mine bought one not so long ago.'

'Ah, well,' said Lubbock, 'I don't get much call to go shopping for diamonds.' He looked at his watch. 'Wouldn't you say it was time for a cup of tea, laddie?'

'At Umzinto?'

'Where else?'

Tench turned towards the car.

'Why not?' he said.

They drove back slowly through Stiffkey and Morston. Then, beyond the Boldings' farm, they pulled off the road and parked by the desolate tower at Kettle Hill.

They sat for a moment or two in silence, gazing at the empty shell, the waste of charred timbers that littered the heath.

It was Lubbock who spoke.

'It's tragic,' he said, 'when you think what it was like. Throbbing with life, the sails turning in the breeze, young Simon winding the sacks up the mill...'

'Could it possibly be restored?'

'Yes, I suppose it could.' He stared at it wistfully. 'A labour of love. But it'd take far more money than I'm ever likely to see in my life.'

Tench started up the car.

'Perhaps someone'll leave you a legacy,' he said.